I0723713

LADY ARUNDEL AND THE HUNTER OF HAUNTERS

MIRIAM GOMEZ

AUTUMN BIRD PUBLISHING

LADY ARUNDEL AND THE HUNTER OF HAUNTERS

Copyright © 2022 by Miriam Gomez
All rights reserved.
www.MiriamGomez.com

Published by Autumn Bird Publishing, LLC
Autumn Bird Publishing is an imprint of Autumn Bird Publishing, LLC.

Cover designed by MiblArt.

First Edition: September 2022

ISBN: 978-1-959335-00-9

Printed by Autumn Bird Publishing, LLC in the United States of America.

AUTUMN BIRD PUBLISHING

For my Husband
A True Hunter of Haunters

North
town in the mountains
Territory of the Duke of Rowlings
City
Grand House Territory
South

CHAPTER 1

"Don't worry, I'll protect you." The boy whispered and gripped her hand tightly, trying to reassure her and distract her from the danger they were facing.

They had stopped running and were hiding among the old trees next to his house. His heart still raced with fear, and his throat ached.

It was so dark that he could barely see, but his parents had trained him so he could follow the path to the hiding spot even with his eyes closed.

They had said the power inside the ancient trees would protect him from the monsters. Now, he hoped that was true.

The girl looked at him with wide eyes as she tried to catch her breath.

"But your parents..." the girl started, squeezing the necklace with the protection stone he had given her, still held in her hand. "We can't leave them. They need us to help them fight."

Leaves rustled near them.

The Haunter had found them.

Evan shook himself awake from the nightmare.

The darkness inside the shed appeared to consume him as he opened his eyes.

It had been a long time since the memory of the night his parents had died had haunted his dreams. His inability to protect her that day still filled him with guilt; it had caused his parents to sacrifice themselves for them.

The memory would stay in his head all day now.

He rubbed his hand across his face and sat on his makeshift bed, trying to gather warmth from the flimsy blanket covering him.

It was a blessing to have that small shed after spending weeks guarding himself against the wind and snow. Especially when they were so deep in the mountains.

The cracks in the wall didn't offer much protection against the wind, but the heat of the small fire he'd thankfully been able to start was a big comfort.

Awake enough to begin his next round, he mentally checked the energy wards he had created around the shed to protect it while he slept.

The fear he had felt all those years ago had never truly left him.

"Why are you awake?"

Evan startled and turned in the direction of the gruff voice.

"Couldn't sleep," he said, bending down to put his boots on as he remembered the only portion of food he had in the bottom of his bag. He'd need to hunt for more soon. Perhaps in the next hour. "When did you get here?"

"Now."

"Any luck?"

The two of them had been tracking a Haunter for weeks.

It hadn't been easy to spend all that time deep in the icy mountains with a cranky old spirit who claimed himself to be the protector of the North as his only companion, but it had been more than a week since they had lost track of the creature, which was highly unusual.

No Haunter ever escaped them.

"Luck is for mortals," Os replied. "It's gone; it's left the land. My job is done."

"But where did it go?" Evan asked with a frown as he took out the only piece of dry meat he had left in his bag before packing his blanket and reaching for the coat next to the fireplace.

It was dry enough.

"South," Os said. Evan detected a tiny reflection on the black fur as the wolf got closer to the dying embers and laid down next to them. "Something is happening. The energy is shifting far from here, and your destiny is calling you. Our journey ends here."

"Our journey is not done," Evan denied, annoyed at the tone of finality with which the spirit spoke.

He tore the strip of dry meat in half and placed it in front of the wolf. Evan wasn't sure if the spirit needed to eat, but he'd rather not risk it.

It had been frustrating trying to follow his paw prints whenever they'd encountered a blizzard. Os had never slowed down nor waited for him to catch up, and Evan would never forget that, but he knew he needed him and it'd be better not to upset him.

"We haven't found the Haunter yet. The land is not safe, and it won't be until we do."

"You don't understand, mortal. That is not my way. I haven't left these mountains in a thousand years."

"If what you're saying is true—"

"I always speak the truth!" Os's voice rumbled against the walls of the room.

"If what you say is true," Evan continued, unbothered, "and we don't stop it, there might not be a North to protect anymore.

That's part of your duty, isn't it? What if this is your path to freedom?"

Os closed his eyes and kept quiet while Evan waited.

It wasn't until the room began to fill with pale light that the wolf opened his eyes.

"It doesn't matter whether I go or not," Os spoke with a low voice. "You still can't avoid your fate. Your time to act is short."

The thought of seeing Emilie again diminished his resolve. He had known nothing good would come out of having that dream.

"I'll go back," Evan said, bracing himself for the journey ahead. "But you're coming with me."

❧

IT TOOK Evan four days of snow and ice to get to the nearest town.

Before the frost from his beard had had time to melt, he saw Talbot, one of his men, waiting for him at the bar.

"Duke," Talbot said, standing up and rushing to meet him with a relieved expression.

"Talbot, what are you doing here?" Evan asked, failing to control his reaction.

The surprise at finding the agent, who looked as if he had spent nights guarding the entrance of the bar, was too great.

"Duke, your cousin has disappeared," Talbot informed with an exhale. "And your aunt, Lady Hardingham, asks for your immediate return. The city is vulnerable, and we need a leader."

Os's voice thundered in his mind. "*I told you, you couldn't avoid your destiny. It was always supposed to be you.*"

CHAPTER 2

Emilie knew nothing about passionate, secret love affairs.

It came as a great surprise when she found out she'd been having one after she accidentally overheard two young women talking about it in their hostess's library at the most coveted ball of the season.

They talked so passionately about the man that she almost wished it were true.

If Emilie hadn't been on the lookout for the furthest room she could find after spending half an hour with the kind ladies' room attendant who had attempted to fix her ruined dress, she wouldn't have become aware of this exciting rumor on the most important night of her life.

Emilie stayed hidden behind the slightly ajar door so she could overhear their conversation.

"Lady Arundel is so lucky," a woman with a high-pitched voice said. "He was so handsome and tall, and so mysterious, but I've never seen him at any of these balls before."

"Do you think he's...? You know. *That* kind of man?" her companion asked with a timid voice. "I've heard that's the type she usually likes."

"A hired lover? It wouldn't surprise me. He was gorgeous. I

saw him on the street, observing her house from a rented carriage, as if waiting for her. It was obvious he didn't want to be seen, but luckily for me, I caught him right when I was leaving my cousin's house. You never find men of that handsome quality at events like these."

"Don't forget Lord Williamson. He's still the most handsome man of the lot."

"Oh, but he can't compare to her man. It's clear she received a big inheritance if she can afford a lover like that. If I were her, I'd also keep him a secret lest someone else snatched him away."

"You're one to talk. You just made me meet you here to cover for you and Lord Jenner."

"Believe me, Lord Jenner can't compare to Lady Arundel's lover."

The absurdity of it all amused her as Emilie fully opened the door and stepped into the library. The women immediately stopped talking and looked at her with wide eyes.

"Well, he sounds irresistible," Emilie said with a raised brow. "I can't wait to meet him."

The women burst into fits of laughter, glancing at the wine stain in the front of her dress before walking past her and out of the room.

"Wait!"

Emilie couldn't have them spreading rumors and ruining her reputation on the same night that her engagement to Lord Williamson would be announced.

A group of men heading toward the card room blocked her path.

By the time she walked past them, the women had vanished, cloaked in a sea of luxurious, elaborate gowns in different shades of blue, the color of the season.

Nothing was going well for her that night. If only the women knew how unlucky she truly was.

Emilie had noticed the glass of one of Aunt Augustine's friends leaning toward her aunt, and in an attempt to prevent her aunt's dress from being ruined, Emilie had ended up standing between the liquid and her.

The content of the glass had poured all over the front of her cerulean blue dress, specially ordered for this occasion.

The red stain was too big to hide, no matter how much the young ladies' room attendant had tried to fix it with a bowl of salt. Now, Emilie believed the older woman must have never liked her aunt.

The young maid had seemed to be getting rather anxious about the look of the stain, and Emilie had asked her to stop.

According to the maid, the stain had gotten worse, but to Emilie, it had still looked the same.

Before leaving, she had dug a coin from her purse and given it to the young maid for her efforts.

Emilie was glad she had done so when she had heard another attendant scolding the young maid.

After that, Emilie had wanted a quiet place to escape from judging eyes and had thought the library would be a safe spot.

Surely, no one would want to miss the ball outside.

How wrong she had been.

Resigned that there would be no hiding, she walked across the room, surrounded by people she had met a thousand times before and feeling their eyes on her.

It was too late to go home and change her dress. Her cheeks filled with warmth, and she was sure they were turning red. The least she could do was try to maintain her dignity.

It was not the first time she had heard rumors about her having lovers.

The whispering voices liked to say it was too late for her to meet a respectable man, so she must not have any other option but to keep a lover.

Which had amused her.

Emilie hadn't wanted a lover and had given up on the idea of marriage long ago. Instead, she had kept to herself after moving to the city to live with her aunt.

That is, until she had met Lord Williamson.

She glanced around the room, holding her hands in front of her as she looked for her old friend, Anne Marie.

Emilie hadn't seen her in years before tonight, so her sudden appearance at the most anticipated ball of the season had been unexpected. Especially since the majority of high society had so fiercely fought for an invitation.

Emilie saw Aunt Augustine excusing herself from the indiscreet ears of her friends before coming her way.

When she stood next to her, Emilie glanced around them. No one was looking in their direction. She swiftly fixed the unruly hairs on her aunt's hairdo while thinking about how to inform her of the latest rumor she had heard.

"I have news," her aunt said in a rushed whisper as Emilie worked on smoothing the small hairs. "Lady Williamson just told me she would make an announcement tonight. I think you need to prepare yourself!"

Emilie was silenced by her words.

She had already expected the announcement, but hearing it from someone else caused her stomach to twist with anticipation. She had been waiting for so long.

When Lord Williamson's note had arrived that morning, she'd had to reread the words several times before she could accept them.

All those discreet meetings in secluded rooms were finally coming to an end.

"Lady Emilie Claire Williamson. Lady Emilie Claire Williamson..." Emilie whispered to herself in a hushed tone before turning to her aunt. "I told you, didn't I? It's finally happening."

"Of course, my dear! In just a few minutes, you will become the future Lady Williamson."

"I need to look surprised when it happens. I don't want people to start talking; not after what I just heard," Emilie said, resting her hands against her stomach as she tried to control her nerves. "A couple of women were gossiping about me!"

"What do you mean?"

"In the library, two women were talking about my lover. The worst thing is that he sounded nothing like Lord Williamson. If he hears about this, he's going to think I've deceived him, just when he finally wants us to get engaged!" Emilie could feel the panic crawling up her back. "I can't see them anywhere. Now I wonder who else is talking about this. Have you heard anything?"

Aunt Augustine, who Emilie knew was one of the best-informed gossipers in the city, looked at her with astonishment. Her alarm was as great as the number of rumors she knew.

"Are you sure they were talking about you?" Aunt Augustine asked, looking at her with a doubtful expression. "You might have misheard them."

"I clearly heard them say my name."

"The announcement is happening tonight. Just think about that and don't worry about anything else."

Emilie wasn't convinced. She could see that Aunt Augustine was confident that no rumor of that magnitude would have ever escaped her, and because of that, she wasn't taking her seriously.

But she still felt as if someone was watching her, even though Emilie couldn't see anyone looking in her direction.

"Have you seen Anne Marie? She told me she will be leaving town in a few days, and I thought she could bring my news back to the Grand House. She could deliver a letter to Uncle Winston."

"Oh, that girl. I think I saw her leave."

"Was something wrong?"

Emilie was surprised by her departure and felt concerned that someone had been rude to her.

"No, I think she looked rather happy. I'm sure everything is fine," Aunt Augustine dismissed, signaling one of the footmen carrying glasses of champagne. "We had better fetch a drink before my throat becomes sore. Lord Williamson is surely taking his time arriving."

"Yes, we've been here for over an hour. Something must have happened."

Anxiety had been her constant companion since the moment she had received the note. It was difficult not to feel like something was wrong when accidents kept following her that evening.

Lord Williamson's note had said he would be waiting for her at the ball so they could talk. But besides sending his carriage to fetch them, she hadn't heard anything from him all evening.

"Something more important than announcing his engagement? He better have a good reason," Aunt Augustine said, her mouth twisting to the side as she grabbed one of the glasses the footman carried and gave it to Emilie.

"Oh! Can you imagine?" Emilie said with a smile, relaxing at the thought of her imminent future as she held the glass of champagne. "Me, wearing the wedding gown you helped me pick and that we have always wanted. Lord Williamson and I surrounded by white roses in crystal vases while we dance under the chandeliers. He'll look so handsome with that lighting. It'll be so romantic!"

"Settle down, my dear. We have to wait for him to get here first. Lady Williamson will have to get used to sharing her title soon enough."

Emilie sighed dreamily.

She couldn't believe the day she would marry was finally coming. After all these years, it was finally happening.

She was already twenty-seven years old, practically a spinster.

Emilie had received a couple of proposals in the last few years, and even though she should have been married and with children by now, she had turned them down, refusing to consider marriage but secretly hoping that he would arrive: the perfect man for her.

After the announcement of their engagement, the preparations for their wedding would soon start, and so could they also begin planning their trip.

She had always dreamed of traveling and had been excited when Lord Williamson had told her they would go on a journey once they were married.

But most importantly, the whispers of people and their silly rumors would finally stop.

"He's here! Oh, and look. Anne Marie has returned as well," Aunt Augustine pointed out, bringing Emilie back to reality. "Come, dear. The time has come."

Emilie quickly spotted him and hoped he would see her too.

Lord Williamson looked so handsome with his perfectly done blond hair. She loved how it shined whenever he stood under the lights. His slim body in a beautifully tailored suit was a dream come true.

He approached his mother and whispered in her ear.

Emilie and her aunt moved closer to where Lady Williamson and her son stood. People had gathered around them, which made it difficult to approach, but Emilie was satisfied when she could see his face.

"Could I have your attention for a moment?" Lady Williamson asked with a smile. "I want to thank everyone for coming to celebrate my son's thirtieth birthday. I know your father would have been proud of the man you've become and the decisions you've made. Please, join me in congratulating him in this special day."

She waited for the applause to quiet down.

"And now, I would like to make a very important announcement. My son, Lord Williamson, has decided to marry, and his lovely fiancée is here with us tonight."

The room erupted with astonished chatter. Aunt Augustine whispered excitedly next to her, but Emilie's focus was on Lord Williamson.

Everything slowed down.

The surrounding voices became muffled, and to her ears, it was all distant noise. Her eyes followed his every move.

Lord Williamson had the biggest smile she had ever seen on him. His hair shone under the chandelier's light, and the black suit he wore made him look taller than usual. His stroll was confident, and in that moment, it was directed her way.

Her heart beat rapidly, and her body tingled all over, but she felt like she was the happiest woman in the world.

And then, everything stopped when he stood in front of her.

She looked into his eyes, but his gaze didn't meet hers.

She saw his lips moving.

"I've been honored with the hand of the most charming woman I have ever met," he said. "Please allow me to introduce you to the future Lady Williamson, Miss Anne Marie Fotherby."

CHAPTER 3

Emilie heard a gasp next to her.

She had the vague thought it had been her aunt's. But then, right behind her, a familiar voice exclaimed with an excited pitch.

"Oh, Callum!"

Emilie turned and saw Anne Marie standing there with a bright smile on her face. And everything came crashing down on her.

All Emilie could think about was that there was finally a second Lady Williamson, and as it turned out, it wasn't going to be her.

"I can't believe this!" Aunt Augustine whispered angrily in her ear as the crowd surrounding the couple pushed them aside. "How is this possible? And with that girl? When did they even meet?"

Everything became a blur. Emilie stared at them in confusion while her aunt kept murmuring in her ear.

They were supposed to be congratulating her on their engagement!

"Aunt, is it true? Is he marrying her?"

She desperately sought his eyes, but all his attention was on the people in front of him.

Anne Marie glanced her way while laughing and holding the arm of her new fiancé. To Emilie, the action appeared to be rather tasteless.

Emilie quickly stepped away from the crowd. She received curious glances at her hasty departure, but no more than the ones she usually got wherever she went. Lord Williamson and the new Lady-Williamson-to-be took most of the attention of the group.

She could hear her aunt repressing a shout of protest as Emilie kept her head low and headed toward the nearest door, which happened to be the one leading out to the garden.

Emilie had to leave the room before she caused a scene. She couldn't add another layer to the rumors she had heard that evening.

In the past, people had made it their pastime to gossip about her latest rejection, until the suitors had stopped knocking on her door. Afterward, they'd only talked about who she had been seen with and speculated about the men she was meeting in secret, treating her as an interesting diversion.

If anyone found out she was now the one being rejected, they would publicly make her the joke of society.

Emilie was almost out of the room when the hem of her dress got caught up on her heel. It ripped the delicate fabric of her skirt and caused her to bump into an old couple that stood next to the exit.

"Careful, darling," a man said in her ear.

She would have fallen to the ground if not for the quick response of the gentleman behind her, who easily held her in place.

Emilie hadn't realized someone was there. His voice sounded familiar, and she hoped it wasn't one of her past suitors coming to her again.

"Oh, I'm so sorry," Emilie apologized in a hurry as she

straightened herself with the help of the stranger, pulling on her skirt to free it from her heel. That's when she noticed the group of men out in the garden that had gathered for a smoke.

Her face warmed, and she couldn't bring herself to look anyone in the eye.

"You look upset, dear," the older woman Emilie had almost bumped into said. "You should be dancing the night away. You're a beautiful woman, and I'm sure your dance card will be full in no time. You'll see."

Emilie opened her mouth but didn't know what to say. She was sure the embarrassment she felt was displayed on her face for everyone to see.

Fortunately, she didn't have to answer, since the woman had moved her attention to the man behind Emilie.

"Thank you," Emilie mumbled over her shoulder at the man, her eyes never reaching his. She didn't wait for his answer and moved away from them as fast as she could.

The voice of the woman carried outside, and Emilie could hear her asking questions to the stranger.

Better him than her.

With her mind too wrapped up with thoughts of despair and betrayal, the only thing she wanted to do was to remove herself from the unwanted eyes of society before Emilie ended up bursting into tears.

She heard footsteps behind her, but Emilie ignored them as she walked further out, wanting to feel the cold air pushing against her face. The nights were getting colder with winter approaching.

The short sleeves and thin fabric of her gown did little to keep her warm, but Emilie hadn't considered that when she had decided to walk out. The only thing she could do was rub her hands against the goose bumps in her arms.

Even so, Emilie welcomed the sudden shift in temperature and hoped it would give her mind clarity on what had just happened.

Her rapid breathing matched her beating heart, and the tightness in her chest and throat made it difficult to swallow.

Emilie walked without paying attention or caring where she was going. The only thing she knew was that her thoughts made no sense.

Anne Marie with Lord Williamson? She hadn't even known that they knew each other!

Emilie had never thought of Anne Marie as competition, because why would she? Just this morning, she had received his note telling her he would announce their engagement that evening.

Soon, he had promised, they would stop hiding, and everyone would know.

How she wished she had the note with her! Maybe she had missed something. Maybe she had misread it.

Maybe this was nothing but a misunderstanding.

The tears burned in her eyes, but Emilie refused to let them free. The disappointment she felt at his rejection was quickly turning into anger, and Emilie couldn't explain the pain inside of her.

She walked until the tall bushes and darkness surrounded her; until Emilie became aware that she had gone inside the maze that Lady Williamson had recently added to her garden.

Emilie frantically looked around, trying to make out any shapes that could give her any indication of where she was.

There were no lamps in sight, but she could see a faint glow coming from above the wall to her right. If Emilie went in that direction, would it take her further in or back toward the entrance? She wasn't sure.

Her panic was growing by the minute.

Emilie finally decided that she would try to retrace her steps, praying at the same time for the maze to only have one way out.

A small bench to her right caught her attention. It had been specially requested by Lady Williamson a few weeks ago. Emilie could faintly see the roses of their family crest, a symbol she had wanted to carry.

Now, she detested the very sight of it.

That Emilie knew so much about the garden made her even more distraught. A tight knot formed in her throat, and that was all it took. All the tears she hadn't cried in a long, long time came pouring out, forcing her to take a seat on the bench as she cried in despair.

Emilie had been a fool to believe she would finally be happy. There was no doubt now that she was destined to become like Aunt Augustine. She should get used to the idea of spending the rest of her life alone. Maybe she should focus on charity more, or on any of the other things that old maidens were supposed to do.

Emilie didn't care what it was, as long as it made her forget.

She was furious. But if she was honest with herself, in ten years, nothing had truly changed.

That thought only enraged her further. How could Lord Williamson betray her? Emilie should demand an explanation, a reason for his deception.

Before she could gather the courage to confront him, a light tap on her shoulder made her jump in surprise.

Her heart pounded loudly.

"Sorry, darling," an amused male voice said. "I didn't mean to frighten you."

Emilie was mortified.

Had she been crying so loud as to mask the sound of his footsteps? She hadn't expected anyone to be out in the maze with the celebration happening inside. Never mind that none of them had ever seen Anne Marie before.

The most important thing for Emilie at the moment was to prevent anyone from seeing her in her current state.

There wasn't much she could do given the circumstances, but that didn't stop her from attempting to dry her tears and compose herself as best as she could before she turned to face him.

Emilie was sure she had done a terrible job.

Looking up, she saw the figure of a man standing next to her. His back was against the only source of light, which caused his face and eyes to be covered in shadows, but it allowed her to make out the shape of his suit.

She searched his face for any signs that indicated he knew the reason Emilie had been crying, even though she couldn't make out any of his expressions. Emilie felt like she knew him from somewhere, but she wasn't sure from where.

"Are you waiting for your lover?" the stranger asked with amusement. "Do you know that's the only reason anyone comes to a place like this in the middle of the night?"

He had a deep voice, which startled her, yet he sounded vaguely familiar.

"Is that why you're here?" Emilie asked with narrowed eyes. She'd had enough talk about lovers for a lifetime. "You can go pick another spot. I found this one first."

The man laughed, the sound almost rumbling through her chest.

"No," he replied with a hint of amusement. "I just came for a walk."

"Well, I came here to be alone," Emilie remarked with a pointed look, forgetting the man probably couldn't see it.

He took a step back, giving her a chance to study him better.

He seemed young, maybe around her age. His hair was black, and although short, it fell in messy waves around a face she still couldn't see quite clearly.

His voice was deep and low, and Emilie kept having the odd impression of familiarity.

It appeared he was staring at her intently, which made her uncomfortable.

"Keep it, then," she murmured with annoyance as she stood and began to walk away.

"You don't remember me, do you, Emilie?" he asked. His words made her stop and look at him.

Her heart began racing.

His shoulders were broad, but what impressed her the most was his height. She felt small in comparison; an unusual feeling for her since she tended to be taller than most of the men she came across. Even Lord Williamson wasn't that much taller than her.

Emilie only knew of one man as tall as the stranger in front of her.

The man slowly made his way toward her, his steps slow and relaxed.

"It's only been a few years," he started in a low voice. "I'm surprised you already forgot about me. I sure haven't forgotten about you."

"I don't think we have met before," Emilie said while desperately trying to see his face. "From where do you know me?"

His voice was nagging at the back of her mind now, becoming more familiar the more he spoke.

It was like trying to remember something that had happened a long time ago.

Something that she was supposed to remember.

She was busy cursing her memory when the light finally cast over his face as he moved to the side.

"It's me. It's—"

"Evan," Emilie said as she tried to swallow the lump that had formed in her throat.

Oh no.

Her racing heart had known.

CHAPTER 4

Evan had found himself being overwhelmed by the smoke and smell of the city.

After spending all those weeks out in the mountains with Os, the smell of crisp air and snowed-in trees had been very different from the one the ballroom had been full of.

He had delayed his arrival into the ball as much as he could to avoid meeting with the hostess, and not looking forward to having all of his senses attacked by the people gathered in the enclosed space.

That's when he had seen Emilie standing next to her aunt. He had followed her from a distance as she moved from one room to another, curious to see how her life was like these days.

Not long after, and to his delight, everyone's attention had been focused on Lady Williamson's announcement.

The shocked expression on Emilie's face had told him that she hadn't been happy at the news of Williamson's engagement.

He had taken her brisk withdrawal from the crowd as the perfect excuse to follow her outside and away from the intense smell of tobacco, sweat, and strong perfume.

Her pleasant fragrance had called to him as soon as he had gotten closer to her.

It was a fresh, smooth aroma that invited him to relax and forget the harsh scents that he had found everywhere in the city.

Even now, outside and surrounded by bushes, he found it more than pleasant to be standing close to her.

But that must be the only reason he wanted to be close to her.

CHAPTER 5

Emilie's heart sunk to the bottom of her stomach. She couldn't believe her bad luck. After almost ten years without seeing or hearing from him—not even once—there he was.

Right when she was at her lowest.

Oh God, why did it have to be him? This definitely wasn't how she had pictured their reunion at all. In her mind, she would have looked wonderful, with a handsome husband on her arm.

A ripped and stained dress had been far from her imagination.

So much for dreams and fantasies.

Maybe he would still beg for forgiveness so that she could tell him she didn't care about the past anymore. Emilie didn't have a husband to walk away with, but she could improvise.

Her face warmed and she could feel her cheeks burning. Emilie hoped it was too dark for him to notice the red stain on her skirt.

She must look awful! Her eyes felt swollen, and her cheeks were probably full of stains left by her hasty attempt to clean away the tears, not to forget the mess her nose had made. Why did she have to meet him when she looked so messy?

"It's good to know you still haven't forgotten about me, darling," Evan said.

Emilie saw his satisfied smile.

He moved as if he had all the time in the world, walking without a hurry but never taking his eyes away from her.

It was becoming unnerving.

"I helped you back there," he mentioned, stopping in front of her. "When you were about to fall on your lovely rear."

Emilie gasped. Regret pushed against her chest when she realized she hadn't recognized his voice.

"I'm sorry. I...I didn't realize you were here," she said, keeping her hands in front of the stain. "I would have greeted you if I had."

Emilie was annoyed that she had missed the chance to better prepare herself for their encounter, and most of all, that he had found her in such an embarrassing situation.

Now, with him standing so close, Emilie wished she hadn't stopped when she had seen the bench. She might had avoided a meeting with him.

All Emilie could do was look at him, and even though she was trying to mask her expression, she was sure her face was displaying all the uncertainty she felt.

"Is that so?" Evan asked as he lifted his hand to move a loose strand of hair away from her face. "I wonder."

The way he looked at her made her feel like she had nowhere to run to, because the moment she did, he would find her again.

"Of course," she replied, slapping his hand away and reminding herself not to gaze too deeply into his eyes. "It's been a long time since we've seen each other, and I know that Aunt Augustine will be happy to see you. She's always happy to meet with old friends, especially ones she hasn't met in years. I need to go back to her now."

She began to move, more than ready to put as much distance between them before she embarrassed herself any further with her endless chatter, when Evan stepped in front of her, stopping her.

"Here. Take my jacket. I've spent enough time in the cold; this temperature is nothing to me," he said, taking it off and offering it to her.

Emilie stared at it.

It must have been obvious that she couldn't stop shivering, but she didn't want to give him any permission to behave familiarly toward her.

On the other hand, she didn't know how much longer she could stand it before her teeth began clattering.

"Only for a moment."

Emilie could smell a hint of a woodsy, earthy scent on his jacket as he moved it closer to her. The heat of his body still lingered in the jacket as he put it over her shoulders.

Having him stand so close to her made her realize that he was taller than she remembered him.

Emilie glanced at his shoulders and neck before finally settling on his curved lips.

"Don't tell me you are still in love with him?"

"With whom?"

It was a few seconds before she gave any thought to his question.

At first, she was confused by it, but then her body stilled in understanding.

She peered into his eyes to find a clue about his intentions, forgetting all about the full lips that she had been examining.

Had he known about her hopes of becoming engaged to Lord Williamson that night? How could he have? Her face filled with tension as she tried to read his expression.

His only answer was to look at her with raised brows.

Evan couldn't have known about Lord Williamson. Unless he had somehow found out about it now that he was back, which was impossible, since only her aunt had known.

She hoped it wasn't common knowledge. Otherwise, Emilie would become the center of ridicule.

Upset by his words and burning with shame at the thought of him knowing the reason she had been crying, Emilie thought the safest bet was to avoid his question altogether.

It was time for her to go back and join her aunt.

Being surrounded by people who gossiped about her was far better than being out there alone with him where she wouldn't have any other option but to talk to him.

Emilie wanted to return home. She couldn't take any more surprises. The day had already been too exhausting.

She moved around him and started to walk back to her aunt. Evan fell into stride with her.

"You still haven't changed," Emilie said, looking at him sideways. "How long have you been in town? I thought you had left the city for good."

"I got here yesterday," Evan replied, glancing back at her with a smile.

"Yesterday?" she asked, reprimanding herself when her eyes stayed on his face for a second too long. "Where were you before?"

Emilie didn't want to make it obvious, but she was dying to know where he had been all those years.

She had never known the reason for his unexpected departure, and his aunt and cousin had never given her any news about him.

They always avoided talking of him—or to her, for that matter, which was unfortunate, since their families had been close at some point in their youth.

If she hadn't found out that he had actually told other people that he was leaving, including her uncle, Emilie would have had no other option but to believe he had died.

As it turned out, Evan had only chosen not to tell her.

"I've never stayed in one place for long. Most recently, I lived up north for a while," he said, keeping his eyes ahead of them, and Emilie took the chance to look closely at his face. He turned his head in her direction, and their eyes met. "Cold, cold place, with beautiful women to keep you warm."

He slowly smiled with bright, knowing eyes.

Emilie could feel the heat in her cheeks and immediately looked away in anger. He dared talk to her about women!

With cheeks still burning, she discreetly tried to catch a glimpse of his left hand in search of a ring.

Not that she particularly cared, but she had always wondered.

"No wife, darling." She almost choked on her saliva as Emilie averted her eyes in a hurry. She was sure he had caught her looking. He reached out to lift her chin, so Emilie had no option but to look at him. "I'm too much of a free soul to get married. But I'm always willing to have some fun."

His words felt like a slap in the face, and Emilie had to stop herself from slapping him instead as she snatched her chin away from his grasp.

She was sure he was mocking her, and anger was quick to flare inside of her.

The last summer Evan and she had spent together, right before he'd left, had been one of the hardest Emilie had ever had.

She'd found out about her parents' deaths, and Evan had been with her when the news arrived.

Aunt Augustine had moved in to live with her at the Grand House while they awaited the arrival of Uncle Winston, but it had been Evan and his patience that had helped her go through that difficult time. Not for the first time, he had promised her that he would always be with her, and Emilie had believed him.

They had known each other for most of their lives and been best friends just as long.

Her past with Evan was one of those things she had pushed aside and kept locked in a distant place in her memory.

Now, after everything that had happened, they couldn't even

be cordial to each other. He was a mystery to her, and she didn't know what to expect from him.

Emilie stopped walking when she couldn't recognize where they were anymore. The walls of the maze were tall enough that they blocked any light coming from the manor, making it hard to see anything that could point her in the right direction.

"I think we are lost," she said, mostly to herself, feeling defeated and tired as she glanced up at him.

"I'm not," Evan declared with that deep voice, looking undisturbed. "I know perfectly well where we are."

"Oh? Which way should we go, then?"

The hope of being back with her aunt again in no time reignited inside her. She was relieved they wouldn't have to spend the rest of the night walking around in circles.

Emilie wasn't sure she could have found the way if she had been by herself.

Evan simply turned to her with a serious face, and for a few seconds, they gazed at each other. Then a slow smile formed on his lips.

He had that intense look in his eyes again. He had never stared at her in such a way, and it somehow forced her to become aware of just how close she stood to him.

No one had ever watched her so intently; no other man would dare.

Emilie was sure it had to be improper, and she had to control the urge to take a step back, not willing to appear intimidated.

There was definitely something different about him.

Maybe it was the fact that he was older or that he had lived abroad for so many years, but his movements were different.

More precise.

Stalking, even.

It was confusing and intriguing at the same time.

"What are you willing to give me in exchange?"

"Nothing," Emilie answered with narrowed eyes. She didn't like where this was going.

"If I get you out, I must get something in return."

Emilie couldn't believe it.

The nerve of him! She never thought she would have to barter her way out.

Evan stood so close that she could see the shape of his lips clearly, and his scent surrounded her again. She could feel the warmth radiating from his broad shoulders, and Emilie had to stop herself from leaning into him.

She wasn't sure what to say or what to do.

This Evan wasn't the one she used to know.

"What is it going to be?" he asked her, his eyes moving freely across her face.

Emilie could see that he found the situation amusing.

"Stop teasing me," she said in a tone that made it clear she was angry. She tried to step aside, but Evan quickly blocked her way with his arms.

"I have never been more serious," he said while he softly moved a strand of hair that had been sticking to her lashes. "Give me a kiss, and I'll bring you back to your aunt in no time."

Emilie didn't know what to do anymore.

She was beyond enraged.

Not only had she been deceived into believing she was going to become engaged to the latest love of her life, but she had been betrayed by someone who had been close to her once.

And to make matters worse, she was trapped in this infernal place with a man Emilie had thought she was never going to see again!

She screamed in frustration.

With a new strength and surge of determination, she pushed him aside and started marching away, assuring herself that she would find her own way out.

Emilie didn't need him.

She didn't need anyone to rescue her.

She would rescue herself!

"Finally, there you are," Evan said, laughing. Emilie found it even more irritating when her heart almost melted and leaped with joy at the sound. "Em, wait!"

"Don't call me that!"

Emilie was more annoyed than she had been in a long time. Evan had the power to bring out all sorts of emotions inside her, and she hated it.

"But darling, you didn't think I was serious, did you? The Emilie I knew would have kicked me in the chin a long time ago." Evan sauntered next to her, and she could see the smirk and glint in his eyes. "Besides, what's wrong with a kiss? If I remember correctly, you used to enjoy them."

"Please!" Emilie exclaimed, stopping herself short from groaning. She didn't behave in that manner anymore. Emilie was a lady now. "You would have never dared suggest such a thing if we were lost."

"Ah, but I'm not lost. And I would gladly show you the way out."

"No, thank you," she declined, feeling the ten years of etiquette lessons her aunt had given her returning to her. "I can find it myself."

Emilie wouldn't make a fool of herself twice.

"I have all night," Evan said with a casual shrug. "I'm not sure that you do. What would people say if they found us together?"

"I came here by myself." She was determined not to be swayed by anything he said. Emilie wouldn't allow him to push her around. "It's not my fault that you followed me. I know all too well this wasn't a coincidence. You followed me."

"I was taking a walk when I happened to see you." Evan reached out to stop her. "I couldn't call myself a gentleman if I didn't come to your aid, since you appeared to be in such distress."

"How noble of you."

She wouldn't give him the satisfaction of knowing he rattled her. Evan could try all he wanted, but Emilie would never reveal that part of herself.

"Imagine my surprise when I realized that it was none other than Lady Arundel, whom I haven't seen in years. What are old friends for if not to be of assistance?"

"Old friends?" she said, unable to stop herself from asking him in a mocking tone. "An old friend wouldn't expect something in return. Besides, we might as well be strangers! It's not like you ever wrote when you were gone, not even once..."

Emilie stopped herself from saying anything further, and she picked up her pace with a renewed rush of energy.

She didn't want to spend another minute alone with him.

"I can't believe the always busy Lady Arundel had any time to spare on missing me," he said, and Emilie noticed the tension in his face when she looked at him. "If I had known you were going to miss me so much, I would have written you a letter every day."

"What are you talking about? You couldn't even write me one! I know my uncle kept receiving your letters."

His eyes narrowed, turning cold, and the muscles in his jaw tensed as if he was trying to control his anger.

Evan's close presence unsettled her.

He was too tall for her own comfort, and those blue eyes had her fixed to the ground. Emilie thought she saw hurt shine in them for a second before his gaze turned cold and steady.

Emilie knew she had to snap out of it before she got herself into trouble.

"That's all in the past, and right now, I need to get back to my aunt," Emilie said as she glared at him.

For all she knew, he was trying to seduce her at that very moment.

"You're going after him, aren't you?" Evan asked, and the scorn in his voice was hard to miss.

Emilie felt as if her heart was leaping.

"Who are you talking about? Stop playing games and tell me."

Evan must have seen the anguish she had been carrying since

the announcement, because he abruptly stalked past her without saying another word.

He was a few feet away when he looked over his shoulder. "Follow me."

Emilie trailed after him, her mind full of confusing thoughts. Evan led her through the maze without stopping until they reached the entrance.

She paused once she saw the people standing by the doors that led to the garden.

Evan and Emilie were partially covered by the shadows in the maze and wouldn't be easily seen, but she remembered the gossip about the mysterious lover, and uneasiness invaded her.

The last thing she needed was to add more fuel to the fire. Emilie moved closer to him, grabbing his arm in an unconscious attempt to stop him from going any further.

"Don't worry. No one's looking," Evan assured. Emilie kept quiet, trying to decide how to make her way back inside without being seen. "I'll go first. Believe me, that'll be distraction enough."

She turned to look at him, and for a short second, Emilie saw something familiar in his eyes.

As soon as she noticed, it was gone.

Emilie had the feeling that he kept lowering his guard and quickly putting it back on.

"Crying doesn't suit you," Evan said.

Emilie hated having cried in front of him and was doubly embarrassed once she noticed she had been holding onto his arm. Before he could move, Emilie quickly took out his jacket and returned it to him, his warmth and scent lingering on her.

"Evan," Emilie whispered on an impulse. "I'm glad you're back."

As soon as the words were out, she regretted them.

It was clear Emilie was not being herself that night and all she was doing was continuously creating reasons to be embarrassed in front of him.

Evan took the jacket and put it on as he looked at her, his face void of expression. Suddenly, his lips twisted sideways, and his eyes had an extra sparkle.

"I know," he spoke, leaning forward to whisper in her ear.

He turned and walked toward the manor, leaving her with a knot in her throat.

At least one thing hadn't changed.

Evan was still as arrogant as she remembered him.

CHAPTER 6

Emilie was ready to go home as soon as she reentered the room.

Anne Marie was standing close by, surrounded by a group of women. They were a gossipy bunch, every one of them ready to become her new best friend.

It didn't matter they hadn't even noticed Anne Marie before the announcement.

Their praise to her beauty and admiration of the stone in her ring had Anne Marie beaming with satisfaction. It was obvious she was enjoying the attention.

Emilie even heard her ask one of her companions to move because the sound of her voice was giving her a headache.

Emilie was shocked.

She had known Anne Marie to be shy and quiet, but her current behavior was far from how she had acted earlier that night.

When Emilie caught her eyes, Anne Marie slowly raised her hand, and with a triumphant smile, she showed her the finger.

The finger with the giant diamond ring on it.

Had Anne Marie known of her relationship with Lord Williamson? Had Lord Williamson been lying to her the whole time? Emilie tried her best not to react and pretended she hadn't seen her. Instead, Emilie walked further into the room to look for her aunt.

But her luck wasn't cooperating. She had inadvertently walked toward a group of men, with Lord Williamson in the middle of them.

It was too late to turn back, so her body filled with relief when she realized he hadn't seen her.

Emilie took the opportunity to observe him from a distance while she could. His frown and the tension in his mouth were hard to miss.

While the group of men were laughing at something one of them had said, Lord Williamson was distracted looking at something else.

She controlled her impulse to march up to him and demand an explanation, too proud to make a scene in front of everyone. Especially when their meetings had been kept a secret all along. Emilie didn't want to risk uncovering any of that for the benefit of the whispering tongues.

Curious to see what was upsetting him, she followed the direction of his eyes.

There was a crowd gathering around a tall man with black, short, wavy hair. His head was higher than the surrounding masses, making it easy to spot him.

She could only see the tanned back of his neck as he moved, but it was easy to see that the people around him kept attempting to get his attention.

A group of young women moved in front of his path, but he never stopped or slowed down.

Emilie observed the scene as if in a trance.

It wasn't until the man shifted slightly to the side and she saw his strong jaw line that her reverie broke. To her annoyance, it was clear what his destination was.

Aunt Augustine.

Emilie's heart beat intensely as she observed Evan expertly avoid the crowd of people.

Upset with herself for getting mesmerized by him and allowing him to have the advantage, she realized she wouldn't be able to reach her aunt before he did, even if all the guests in his path fell in front of him to block his way.

She threw a last glance at Lord Williamson as she walked past him before almost running to catch up with Evan.

He'd always had a way of charming people into doing whatever he wanted ever since he was a boy, and her aunt was no exception to his charms—in fact, she had been one of his first victims.

"My dear boy!" Emilie heard her aunt's cries of joy as she moved as fast as she could without running. Emilie was only a few steps away from them now. "Are my eyes deceiving me? Is it you?"

"They're not deceiving you," Evan answered with a smile while kissing her hand. "You look as beautiful as ever. If there's ever a time in which I cannot recognize your beauty, it is because I've turned blind."

He looked back at Emilie and smiled when she finally stood at their side.

"Oh, Duke, you're a delight!" Aunt Augustine exclaimed, glowing at his praise while fanning her face. "Emilie, where have you been? I've been looking for you. Look who's here. You remember the Duke? You two were inseparable!"

Aunt Augustine grabbed Emilie by the arm and brought her closer to them. She quickly turned from Emilie to Evan with a beaming expression.

Emilie was sure she knew what her aunt was thinking.

"I can still remember it as if it were yesterday," Aunt Augustine continued, a glint in her eyes as she visited distant memories. "I remember how you two went around creating havoc, and how the poor housekeeper had to deal with your daily messes."

"You're thinking of Lilly," Emilie said with a smile.

"She was quite young to be a housekeeper," Aunt Augustine remembered with a displeased frown. "I know she quit as soon as you came to live in the city with me. Did she ever keep in touch?"

"She never did. I do wonder what happened to her. Oh, and the Duke and I just—"

"Of course. Lady Arundel, it's been a long time."

Emilie was surprised that he was acting as if they hadn't just met out in the garden. She wondered what he was trying to do, and out of curiosity, decided to play along.

"Yes, it's been so long."

Emilie stared at him with a pointed look and hoped that it would transmit her sentiment.

It granted her a polite smile.

"But do tell us, Duke," Aunt Augustine said. "When did you arrive? It's been years since you left, and I think your aunt, Lady Hardingham, mentioned you were travelling a lot. I think you were living in the south at that time. You know, in that forsaken place. I've never been good at remembering the name of those places."

Attention on him, they both waited expectantly for an answer. But Emilie knew her aunt didn't have much patience.

"Have you married, yet?" Aunt Augustine asked him, and Emilie noticed the sideways glance in her direction.

She was certain that her face was turning into different shades of red.

Pushing her lips together to stop a shout of mortification, Emilie desperately looked at Evan's jacket, her aunt's dress, the floor, anything but his eyes.

"I arrived yesterday," Evan replied, and Emilie reprimanded herself for finding his voice so pleasant. "I'm afraid it wasn't something I had planned to do, but urgent matters demanded my immediate return. I'm sure you have heard about our family's situation. I wouldn't have come tonight if business hadn't prompted me. It's a delicate time for us, after all."

Aunt Augustine nodded as if she was aware of what he was referring to, and Emilie knew she had missed something important.

"And I'm going to disappoint you," he continued. "But I haven't gotten married. I've been constantly traveling since I left, not staying in one place for more than a few months."

Emilie's heart beat painfully when he mentioned his departure, and maybe she imagined the dark shadow that fell over his face.

"Oh my, how intriguing!" Aunt Augustine exclaimed, clapping her hands together. Emilie saw the huge smile and the eyes that shined at the news. "You took too long to come back. It saddens me that such an awful event prompted your return, but it's also been awfully boring without you. It's such a nice surprise to see you again. It has more than lifted my spirits after the shock we received tonight."

Aunt Augustine looked over at Emilie, as if expecting her to contribute to the conversation. Emilie widened her eyes at her, warning her aunt not to disclose anything embarrassing.

"Did you hear?" Aunt Augustine continued, turning to Evan while twisting her nose. "Lord Williamson got engaged to none other than that scrawny girl. Do you remember her? Anne Marie was always sneaking after you two, always trying to meddle. But now look at her. I have no idea how she managed to get close to Lord Williamson. Having a religious man as a guardian, she surely doesn't move in the same circles."

"Yes, I remember her," Evan said as he finally turned his attention to Emilie. "Your niece used to be quite close to her."

"Not anymore," Emilie replied with an exhale. Frustration filled her body once more.

Emilie saw the sharp interest in Evan's face before it turned into indifference.

It annoyed her how he kept trying to conceal his real intentions.

"Oh yes, life in the city can be quite busy compared to the

countryside," Aunt Augustine said while glancing around the room. "Your time living at the Grand House all those years ago was too full of freedom, in my opinion. But I'm happy to see you both together once again, both of you completely transformed for the better."

"I should congratulate Williamson on his engagement," Evan noted, glancing behind him at the group of men gathered at the back. "I haven't had a chance to greet him yet. It's only right to say hello to an old friend, after all."

Emilie looked at him with surprise. She didn't know Lord Williamson and Evan knew each other. Where could they have possibly met with Evan being away for so long? Also, Emilie had no doubt he was mocking her.

She thought they were pretending their meeting hadn't happened!

"Yes, of course, Duke," Aunt Augustine agreed distractedly, and then her head snapped back at him. "Make sure to come and have tea with us as soon as you can. We live in Rosewood Street. You know, the old place. I'll be expecting you. It's been so long since we've last had a decent conversation."

Aunt Augustine sighed dreamily and looked at Emilie, who did her best not to run away, mortified.

"You'll see me sooner than you think."

Evan turned to leave, but as he did, he looked down at the skirt of Emilie's dress. Just as quickly, he looked up at her with a wicked smile and a wink before walking away from them.

"Where have you been?" Aunt Augustine asked her in a whisper. "I've been looking everywhere for you. I had to face Lady Williamson and pretend that I was delighted with the news of the engagement. It was almost as if she was teasing me." The words rushed out of her mouth, not allowing for any interference from Emilie. "You were nowhere to be found, and that aroused some suspicion in her. It was a good thing everyone kept distracting her. Otherwise, I would have had to answer some of her compromising questions, which in my opinion she doesn't have a right to ask. Not after her son's behavior."

"I'm sorry. I went out to get some air. I was about to lose my nerves right in front of everyone. I couldn't take it anymore." Emilie closed her eyes, trying to push against the feelings stuck in her throat. A pang of pain in her chest reminded her that she still needed to face what had happened that night. "I feel like a fool. I can't believe Lord Williamson betrayed me like this. I'm still waiting for him to say it's all a mistake and that he meant me and not Anne Marie. But I know this can only mean that he was never serious. He must have thought me stupid."

Emilie's voice started rising in volume as anger rekindled inside of her.

"Don't worry, my dear. Not everything is lost."

Aunt Augustine's eyes shined with excitement, and Emilie followed them to the man who had just left them.

"Aunt, you can't be serious!"

Evan was walking toward the group of men across the room. They were talking excitedly while looking in his direction. Except for one of them, whom Emilie saw seemed annoyed.

"Why not?" Aunt Augustine asked with an intensified sparkle in her eyes. "He's a charming young man, very handsome, splendid family, with an excellent title, and you've known each other since you were children. It couldn't be more perfect. It's a shame he spent all of those years abroad. We could have prevented all of this disappointment and waste of time. But now that he is here, it can be easily fixed."

"There's nothing to fix! It can't be him. Never. There's too much history between us."

"But that's exactly it! Look at him now. He is a young duke, and of course, he's attracting everyone's attention."

Emilie turned to see him surrounded by the men who had been congratulating Lord Williamson and who were now clapping and shaking Evan's hand, welcoming him back.

She also noticed that not far from them, another group was staring at him. This time, all young debutantes.

Some of them had belonged to Anne Marie's group, and they were all giggling and whispering to each other while looking in Evan's direction.

"Now that he's back, Lord Williamson pales in comparison," Aunt Augustine said in a hushed tone. "It's a good thing he came to us first. That gives us an advantage."

"He would need to stay for that to happen, and who knows if staying is in his plans. He could be leaving at any moment."

Emilie knew her aunt's words were correct. She could see that the women would be after him. Some of them were already trying to catch his eye with flirtatious looks.

It wouldn't be long before he found a wife.

That is, if he was looking for one.

On the brief occasions when she had wondered what had happened to him, she had considered the possibility that he might have been married by now, or if not, that he had a mistress somewhere in that mysterious place where he lived.

He could have mistresses in all the places he had traveled to.

All over the world.

"Oh, it's very possible," Aunt Augustine affirmed, and Emilie knew she was about to hear some secret gossip. "Especially with the rumors I've heard tonight."

"What rumors? Is it about me?"

"No, it's about the reason he came back." Aunt Augustine looked at Emilie with a solemn expression. "One of Lady Williamson's friends told me what she's heard. There are rumors that the duke's cousin is dead, but since his body can't be found, some people think he was kidnapped. The shocking thing is that there haven't been any requests for ransom."

Emilie was surprised she hadn't gotten any hints from his behavior earlier that night.

"His disappearance was unexpected. No one saw anything. The matter is unclear, but I was told that the duke had to come back and take charge of all the business his cousin left behind. Since there hasn't been any confirmation of death, Lady Hardingham refuses to proceed with the funeral. And since the duke is the only close relative they have, he couldn't stay away. Oh, but not only that," Aunt Augustine said excitedly, holding Emilie's hand tighter. "Rumors say that he will have to move back because of this."

"Oh no!" Emilie felt the blood drain from her face. After Evan had lost his parents at such a young age, he had become extremely close to his cousin.

The news must have been devastating for him.

"Oh yes!" Aunt Augustine countered happily while clasping her hands together. "Don't worry, my dear. I'll make sure we get you a better husband this time."

"No, please," Emilie said tiredly. It was more than she could handle at the moment. "I don't want to do this anymore. I'm too exhausted. I just want to go home and forget this ever happened."

"Have you talked to Lord Williamson yet?"

"Not yet. I don't feel like doing it anymore. I'm tired; I'd like to leave."

Emilie looked in the direction of the group of men, where Evan and Lord Williamson stood next to each other. The surrounding men were quiet, and some of them looked eager. She turned her face away.

Emilie felt so confused. She didn't understand how the possibility of marrying Lord Williamson had vanished. Most of all, she was angry at herself for not having seen the foretelling signs, or if she had, for refusing to acknowledge them.

Her eyes connected briefly with Lord Williamson's cold glance, and her gaze quickly moved to the person standing next to him. She met eyes that reflected amusement rather than coldness. But they didn't give her the comfort she sought.

On the contrary, she burned with indignation.

"Could we leave?" Emilie asked her aunt on an impulse after

glaring disdainfully at the unwanted, mocking eyes. "I can't bear another minute of being here."

"Yes, I'll tell Lady Williamson I'm not feeling well; that should be enough of an excuse. Go wait outside and find us a carriage. I'll be there in a moment."

Emilie nodded and waited for Aunt Augustine to reunite with her friends before turning to leave the ballroom.

She walked outside. The first thing Emilie saw was an opulent carriage parked in front of the entrance, almost blocking it.

The carriage stood out from the rest in a dark blue color with gold finishes.

The coachman and footman were elegantly dressed in equally dark blue uniforms, but their stoic faces were what caught her attention.

Something was different about them. They seemed ready to ride off at any moment.

One of the footmen on the sidewalk was telling the driver of the ostentatious carriage that they needed to park somewhere else, but the man just ignored him.

Giving up, the footman walked toward her while mumbling to himself.

Emilie stopped him.

"Excuse me, could you please help us get a carriage?"

"Of course, my lady," he agreed, looking relieved as he walked away.

Emilie looked back at the carriage, curious about the seal on the door. The arrival of Aunt Augustine at her side prevented her from taking a closer look.

She was about to ask her if she knew whose family the crest belonged to, when Emilie noticed her aunt wasn't alone.

Lord Williamson stood next to her.

CHAPTER 7

"How dare you!" Emilie whispered, furious at his unexpected presence.

Her heart plunged to the bottom of her stomach.

She didn't know what to do first: scream at him, slap him, or demand an explanation.

All three called for her attention with a similar degree of urgency.

"Good evening, Emilie." Lord Williamson looked around him. "Were you planning to leave without saying goodbye?"

His suit was in a state of disarray, and it gave her a bit of satisfaction to see him looking less than perfect. Especially when her own dress was stained and dirty. The night was bent on being chaotic.

"You lost any right to call me by my name the moment you got engaged to someone else."

Emilie glared at him and raised her chin in defiance.

"You shouldn't be here," Aunt Augustine spoke up, standing between Emilie and Lord Williamson while grabbing Emilie's arm.

Who cared about a stupid stain? All she had left was her

dignity, and Lord Williamson wouldn't take that away from her. He had lost his chance, and there wouldn't be a second one.

Emilie prayed for the footman to return soon, not wanting to be seen together and interacting in a way that wasn't the norm.

"Congratulations on your engagement, Lord Williamson," Emilie said with a mocking smile. She might feel happy for him later, but not tonight. Not after the way he had fooled her. "I wasn't aware that you were planning to stab me in the back or that you knew Anne Marie, but how lovely."

Emilie wondered if he at least felt guilty, but she couldn't find regret reflected in his eyes. His frown told her he was displeased, and that was the only sign she could read from his face.

Lord Williamson ignored her remarks.

"I didn't know you were acquainted with the duke. I saw you talking to him earlier."

"That's what you're here to say? After what you've done tonight, that's the first thing you want to tell me?"

Her disappointment grew, if that was even possible. He wasn't even going to apologize.

Now, Emilie could clearly see the mistake she had made the moment she had decided to accept him.

Lord Williamson tightened his lips, and Emilie felt her body filling with contempt as she stared at the man in front of her.

How could she have ever hoped to marry him?

"Evan," Emilie started loudly and clearly, being careful to imply familiarity when she talked about him. "Came over to greet Aunt Augustine."

Lord Williamson twitched his lips, and Emilie knew she had succeeded in annoying him.

She smiled, satisfied.

"Oh yes," Aunt Augustine said, reanimated by the turn the conversation was taking. "It was delightful to see him again after so long. He's always been such a sweet man. I'm extremely happy to have him close once again. Did you know they used to be inseparable when they were younger? I can't help but wonder what other unexpected, good news we will have very soon."

Lord Williamson kept quiet but his eyes pierced Emilie as if accusing her of betraying him.

The nerve of him!

It was making her uncomfortable to have his full attention when in the past he was always aloof and distracted.

He had never been this interested in her before, but she wouldn't let him intimidate her.

Emilie was upset and hurt, and she wanted him to leave her alone. Her pride was the last thing she had left, and she would defend it at all costs.

"That's not the reason I came to find you. I want to ask you a question," Lord Williamson said, stepping closer as he kept his eyes on her.

Emilie glanced at Aunt Augustine, who stood next to her. At that moment, some of her aunt's acquaintances that were leaving called for her attention.

Aunt Augustine looked back at Emilie with questioning eyes, and Emilie nodded, letting her know that she could go.

"I need to know if what I heard tonight is true."

Lord Williamson moved even closer to her. Emilie could feel the anxiety and apprehension radiating from his words.

She frowned.

Was he talking about the rumor she had overheard? Emilie looked toward her aunt to confirm that her friends were still distracted and weren't looking in their direction. Lord Williamson was standing entirely too closely, and she didn't want any more gossip.

Emilie took a step back.

"I don't care what it is."

Talking about rumors was tiring. Maybe she shouldn't care anymore if he had heard a rumor about her and a lover. If he had, it was too late to talk to her about it, anyway.

Lord Williamson had already made the decision for the two of them.

"The rumor, is it real? Is it him?"

Emilie was about to ask him whom he was referring to when Aunt Augustine came back and interrupted their conversation.

"She's such a lovely girl," Aunt Augustine commented, standing next to Emilie. "If only her husband weren't so old."

"I'm sorry for the delay, my lady," the footman apologized, and Emilie was relieved when she saw him. "Your carriage is ready."

In that moment, Emilie could see over Lord Williamson's shoulder that a carriage had parked right behind the ostentatious one.

She turned to her aunt and tapped her hand lightly before turning back to the footman.

"Thank you. We're ready to leave," Emilie told the man with a smile.

Relieved that she wouldn't have to keep talking to Lord Williamson, she grabbed Aunt Augustine's arm and walked around him in the direction of the vehicle.

"Emilie, we're not done talking. You still haven't answered my question."

"There you are!" a voice exclaimed. "I've been looking for you."

Recognizing the voice, Emilie turned to see Anne Marie walking toward them.

"Lady Williamson wants to speak with us," Anne Marie said, standing next to him. "Oh, Lady Arundel, it's you. But dear, what happened to your dress? What an ugly stain! That's so unfortunate. It was such a beautiful dress. Oh, you haven't congratulated us on our engagement, have you?"

"I already have."

Emilie forced her hands to keep still and not pull at her skirt. Or try to cover the stain.

She loathed having to spend another minute in their presence. Emilie turned to Aunt Augustine, more than ready to leave, when Anne Marie stopped her.

"Oh, you haven't seen the ring yet!" Anne Marie raised her hand and wiggled her fingers in front of Emilie's face. "It's such a beautiful ring, isn't it? I'm so glad I was the one chosen to wear it."

Emilie could see it in Anne Marie's eyes. The mockery. It took all of her effort to restrain herself and not slap the smile out of Anne Marie's face.

Lord Williamson kept quiet, and Emilie hated him for it.

How could he keep quiet when Anne Marie was clearly humiliating her? To think she had been looking forward to their engagement not that long ago! Emilie couldn't believe she would have married a man who wouldn't stand up for her.

"We must go. My apologies, Lord Williamson. Our carriage is here," Aunt Augustine said in a honeyed tone, and Emilie could see that she was forcing herself to stay civil to not raised unwanted attention. "I hope you enjoy the rest of the evening, my lord."

Emilie could barely control herself. Her eyes burned, and she knew the tears would come soon.

Her pride was the only thing stopping them. She didn't want to give Anne Marie—or Lord Williamson—the satisfaction of seeing her cry.

She bowed with a smile and followed her aunt as they walked around them in the direction of their rented carriage.

It would be safe once she was inside of it, and then Emilie wouldn't have to keep her guard up anymore.

They were close to the carriage when Aunt Augustine saw him standing next to the entrance.

There was enough light coming from the candles hanging in the threshold that Emilie thought she could detect amusement in his eyes.

"Oh, Duke!" Aunt Augustine said excitedly as she turned on

her path to approach him. "You found us right on time. We were just saying our farewells to Lord Williamson."

Emilie had had enough meetings with Evan in one night to cover for his absence of the last ten years, and so wasn't eager for any more encounters with him.

"In that case, please allow me to escort you," Evan replied in a deep, pleasant voice as he smiled charmingly at her aunt, then at her. "Two beautiful ladies shouldn't be unaccompanied this late at night."

Emilie saw him glance at the carriage they were about to board.

"We can take my carriage," Evan offered, and Emilie knew from his smile that he was having fun with her predicament. "It'll be more comfortable."

Evan pointed to the carriage next to them, and Emilie flinched.

Of course, the pompous carriage had to be his.

Emilie would have known if she had looked more carefully at the seal on the carriage's door.

The stoic footman quickly opened the door, holding it as he waited for them to board.

"Oh, that would be wonderful!" Aunt Augustine accepted before Emilie could object.

"But aunt," Emilie said, desperately trying to come up with an excuse that would keep them away from his pompous presence. She hated giving him the satisfaction of seeing her struggle. "Our carriage is here already."

"Hush, dear. We don't need it anymore, and we wouldn't have needed to rent one if we had come on our own."

Aunt Augustine pointedly looked at Lord Williamson, who had insisted on sending a carriage for them, and who was now talking to Anne Marie near the entrance.

Emilie's stomach clenched with pain.

She noticed the bitter expression on his face as he listened to Anne Marie talk, and Emilie wondered what she could be telling him.

"I'll take care of it," Evan said.

Emilie realized that he had probably heard her exchange with Aunt Augustine.

Evan walked to the rented carriage and paid the coachman before turning to them with what to Emilie appeared to be a satisfied smile.

Her only hope was riding away, and she couldn't do anything about it.

Returning to their side, Evan's eyes settled on Emilie as he offered his arm to Aunt Augustine.

"Don't despair," he spoke, not removing his eyes from Emilie's. "After all, this is what old friends are for."

Emilie looked at him, hesitating for a moment.

She preferred to go with him than to stay behind with Lord Williamson and Anne Marie. A quick glance in their direction told her that they appeared to be in the middle of an argument.

Emilie secretly hoped they wouldn't stop arguing and was glad to know there was discord between them when they had only just gotten engaged.

"Let's go," she said, turning to Evan and her aunt before walking with them toward the carriage.

"You're such a gentleman," Aunt Augustine gushed.

Emilie was sure Aunt Augustine was beyond thrilled to have Evan escort them where everyone could see, which at the moment mostly consisted of the footmen and a few people still arriving or leaving the ball.

Aunt Augustine must have thought it would be enough to have the rumors spreading, and Emilie needed to give her credit for her expertise in this field.

Before Evan helped them inside the carriage, he approached the driver, and to Aunt Augustine's delight, gave him the directions to their house.

"I can't believe you still remember the Rosewood house!"

Aunt Augustine's voice became high-pitched, and Emilie did

her best not to show how much she wished her aunt hadn't said that so loudly.

"Of course," Evan said, turning to Aunt Augustine with a smile. "It should only be a fifteen-minute ride from here."

Emilie was sure that Aunt Augustine was radiating excitement with her big smile. She pretended not to pay any attention to what they were saying and looked at everything but them. It was hard not to believe that the stoic men were judging her aunt for her outburst.

Nothing worse than to be judged by his staff.

Evan helped them aboard. Emilie waited until Aunt Augustine was settled in her seat before attempting to board with Evan's help. She wished the pretentious footman was the one helping them instead of Evan's warm hand.

Emilie glanced over his shoulder at Lord Williamson, who was watching their departure.

She thought he was glaring at her for getting on Evan's carriage. Once again, satisfaction swelled in her chest, and with a smile, she turned away.

Evan sat across from Aunt Augustine and her, but Emilie wasn't in the mood for conversation.

She had to accept that his pompous carriage was more comfortable than she could have imagined. The soft leather and the silk cushions almost lowered her guard, tempting her to relax and enjoy the ride.

But even if the carriage was more than Emilie had expected, she would never admit it aloud. And most importantly, she would never lower her guard.

"It's so nice of you to take us home." Emilie could hear her aunt's fondness for Evan in her voice. How deceived she was! "I hope we're not ruining the rest of your night."

"Not at all. I'm glad I came at the perfect moment," Evan replied. Emilie could feel him inspecting her face. She hoped she wasn't giving him any clues about how comfortable she found the seats to be. "I hope I didn't interrupt anything important."

"Oh, no," Aunt Augustine dismissed, waving her hand at him. "Emilie was just congratulating Lord Williamson and Anne Marie on their engagement. Weren't you, dear?"

"Yes. Thank you for taking us home."

It was too dark to see his eyes clearly, and that gave her a bit of comfort.

The darkness gave her a chance to gather her thoughts. Emilie couldn't believe she was sitting in front of him, and that he was taking them home.

The events of the night came rushing to her at once, from Lord Williamson's engagement to meeting Evan in the maze to them leaving the ball in his carriage.

It was far from what she had expected the night to be.

With a tinge of embarrassment, Emilie wondered if he had overheard her conversation with Lord Williamson and Anne Marie. Especially with Anne Marie saying those horrible things to her.

Evan's sudden appearance that night gave her so many conflicting feelings that she hadn't felt in a long time.

He had been an important part of her life all those years ago.

They had more than cared for each other.

Or at least, that had been before Evan had run away from her.

CHAPTER 8

E van knew when the carriage turned to their street.
The first thing he had done, once he'd stepped on land, was to ask Talbot for an update on her status.

Evan had been worried that whoever had gone after his cousin might have found out about her as well.

Even though he had known it was unnecessary, Evan had asked the agent to take him from the port directly to her house. He had hoped to catch a glimpse of her for the first time in ten years.

When he had left, Evan had wanted to make sure Emilie would be safe without him being around. One year had turned into ten, and now, he could see the changes that had happened during his absence.

Emilie had changed so much, but Evan could still recognize her dark brown hair as it framed her face, and those brown eyes of hers that shone whenever she smiled.

The sight of her had caused him to dwell on how different things could have been if he had never left. But it was useless to think about the past.

Evan could now see the big houses standing next to each

other outside the window as his carriage brought Emilie and her aunt to their house.

Most of the houses on that street had a strong, imposing facade with tall iron gates separating the properties from the rest. The houses had been designed to intimidate anyone who didn't belong.

In Emilie's case, her city house had been designed with the purpose of protecting her and keeping the Haunters away from her.

The area had served him well for the past ten years. Emilie had lived comfortably and safely, and his agents had become accustomed to the space. They could now detect when something that didn't belong was nearby.

It was a rarity to find creatures in the city what with the wall around it keeping most of them outside, but knowing the Haunter had come in this direction made him feel uneasy.

Once the carriage approached the front of their house, Emilie and her aunt looked up with surprise as if they hadn't expected to arrive yet.

The agent acting as a footman opened the door of the carriage, and Evan got out to help them on their way down.

"I'll wait until you're safely inside," Evan told them as soon as Emilie got out of it. "I shall bid you good night for now."

"Thank you, Duke, for seeing us home," Aunt Augustine said, standing at the side of the gate.

"Good night," Emilie threw over her shoulder without pausing.

"Be sure to come visit us soon," Aunt Augustine finished with a sigh, turning to follow after her niece.

Once they were inside, Evan turned to the agents on the carriage who were waiting for his instructions.

"You can go back. I'll stay behind."

"Yes, Your Grace."

Evan took out the coat he was wearing and exchanged it for the black one the driver was giving him.

He felt more comfortable with his old coat. Wearing party attire wasn't usually needed when his focus was on surviving.

Besides, his priority right now was to hide the clothing underneath, not attract attention to himself.

It'd make it easier for blending in with the shadows.

The horses that pulled the carriage began moving forward with a neigh, and a moment later, Evan couldn't see them anymore.

The night had become foggy, and the chilliness in the air told him the season was changing.

At least he could look forward to winter coming soon. The prospect of the cold air cleaning the fumes of the city was one he hoped for. He would be thankful as long as he didn't have to follow vanishing paw prints in the snow anymore.

Evan walked in the direction where he knew one of his agents would be keeping guard. He wanted to hear his report and confirm that nothing unusual was happening.

Ever since Evan's return, he had tried to reassure his aunt that they would find Robert, his cousin, but the information about his disappearance was extremely limited.

The attempt the men had done to track his cousin and follow the signs left behind had not given them any results.

It was as if whoever had taken him had made sure to cover their tracks, throwing the agents off with fake traces from the start.

For now, Evan had to make sure that the next possible target would be safe.

He had only walked about fifty feet away from the gate of Emilie's house when Evan detected movement in the corner of his eye.

Evan quickly turned in that direction, his senses sharpened by years of experience, and his hunting skills still fresh after his recent stay in the mountains with Os.

But as soon as he noticed the disturbance, the feeling was gone.

Evan surveyed the area carefully, looking for any energy traces that didn't belong.

He knew he could trust himself not to panic, but Evan could feel the change in his body as his senses came into deep focus.

The unnatural often went unnoticed by the untrained eye.

It was important not to miss any of the possible traces. If the Haunter had really come south, according to what Os had said, Evan needed to be extremely careful.

He followed the energy shift further down the block, and that's when Evan saw the agent lying on the ground.

His chest clenched. He hadn't walked far from Emilie's house.

Evan knew the man would be dead. He couldn't detect any life energy coming from him. But the traces left by the Haunter where it would have made contact to absorb the agent's energy were still visible.

Before bending over the body to inspect it closely, Evan looked around him to confirm he was alone.

Not a soul was in sight, and the lack of moonlight provided him with extra cover.

The agent was young, and he had obviously put up a fight, but Evan knew it wouldn't have been enough.

He could see that the energy traces were the same ones that Os and him had been tracking for weeks. Every Haunter had a different energy signature and this one was a dark gray color with a heavy tinge of trouble.

It was the same Haunter.

"You just missed it," a gruff voice said by his side.

Evan turned to Os, who hadn't shown himself on the journey back. Evan had begun to wonder if Os had kept his promise of coming with him to stop the creature.

"*I always keep my promises,*" Os rumbled loudly in Evan's mind. "*I'm not like you, human.*"

"Where were you?" Evan asked, ignoring his remarks as he inspected the body. "You could have saved him."

"It was not my duty to save him," Os replied as the wolf began to sniff around the dead body. "No one could. You couldn't have stopped his fate, just as you couldn't stop yours. The wheels are in motion."

Evan glanced back at the wolf and noticed Os looking over him in the direction of Emilie's house. There was a light on one of the top windows, and he wondered if Emilie slept in that room.

Catching himself, he shook his head to clear the silly thoughts from his mind.

He had something more important to resolve now. The dead body of an agent outside of her house was punishment for his failure to hunt it during those weeks looking for it in the mountain.

Evan inspected the area in the opposite direction, but he couldn't see any energy signs around the body.

A strong, sweet perfume invaded his nose; a citrusy aroma that seemed to come out from the coat of the agent and not from the body itself. Evan noticed that the agent's coat pockets looked as if they'd been searched.

Upon further inspection, he realized that the agent's ring was also missing.

His gaze immediately went back to the sidewalk behind the agent but there were no traces.

Evan punched the stone wall next to him.

Os was right.

He didn't know why the creature was behaving so oddly, but Evan knew that recent events could only mean that they had finally found her.

From now on, he would have no other option but to protect her himself.

CHAPTER 9

A group of about fifteen men gathered in the middle of the street, concealed by the darkest hour of the night, with Evan standing among them. A dozen more were on their way, all of them ready to find the Haunter.

He organized them in different teams in an attempt to track it, but he wasn't confident they would find it.

The city didn't provide the best environment for finding the energy signs that Evan was sure the creature was hiding from them.

Securing the area around the attack would be the first priority, with a special emphasis on reinforcing the safeguards around Emilie's house.

Then, if they couldn't find traces of the Haunter, he hoped the agents would find signs in other areas of the city.

Evan blamed himself for not having gotten there sooner; he could have saved the agent's life. But he also knew the sacrifice of the young man hadn't been for nothing.

It had bought him the time to get Emilie and her aunt safely inside their house.

The thought of having the Haunter meet Emilie on the

street, just steps away from the security the land in her house provided for her, was one that tormented him.

The pain that clutched his chest told him that he wouldn't be able to forgive himself.

He also knew the area was protected by the shields and safeguards that the Organization had set around the area—his cousin Robert had made sure of that.

There hadn't been an attack inside the city in years, which meant there must be a weak spot somewhere for the Haunter to have gotten inside.

Evan didn't want to give too much thought to the other possibility that announced itself in his mind or to the intuition that told him he was right.

None of the men had seen or sensed anything out of the ordinary. They had recently changed shifts, and all had been quiet.

The security teams surrounding the city had been increased after his cousin's disappearance, which had raised alarm. Especially since his cousin, the head of the Organization, was one of the strongest agents among them.

They were the hunters, not the haunted.

As two of the agents wrapped the body, Evan surveyed the residential area around him carefully before turning his attention to the house behind him, where Emilie slept.

Evan methodically reinforced the safeguards around her house, mentally and energetically inspecting the vibration of the shields to confirm that they weren't damaged and adding another layer to the ones the agents had already created.

He wouldn't take any chances. The plot of land was protection enough, but he wouldn't have any regrets regarding her safety.

Some of the men followed him, adding more layers to the new shields he was creating, while the rest swept the surrounding blocks in search of any traces that shouldn't be there.

They would know best, since they knew this area like the back of their hand, and it wasn't a very transited spot; even the slightest form of litter could tell them where to go next.

Three teams had gone forward to try to intercept the Haunter in different spots of the city, but without having anything to follow, the task would be difficult.

It took them almost three hours to fully inspect the area around the house until they were completely sure that they were alone and there were no Haunters near them.

The risk of meeting one was greater at night, but they would still need to be on the lookout during the day so that the smallest shifts in the environment wouldn't go unnoticed.

Evan wouldn't allow any other sacrifices like that of the young agent to happen again.

He wouldn't lose any more people.

He had no other option but to stay close to Emilie. At least until they could stop the creature.

Protecting her had now become a priority, and he couldn't—wouldn't—allow her to get in the way of his mission.

Evan had mentally trained himself for years, and the thought of her didn't affect him anymore. Now, more than ever, he needed to relay on that mental fortitude.

Evan knew he could do it regardless of how uncomfortable she made him feel, even if it meant he had to sleep on the floor of her bedroom in order to keep her safe.

"Your Grace, we are ready to bring his body to his family," one of the agents spoke up. Evan could hear the apprehension in his voice, and knew the death had affected them.

"Thank you, Alcott. Bring someone with you," Evan told the older man while looking around at the agents gathered in front of him. "I want everyone with a partner at all times until we are able to hunt down this bastard."

The men nodded.

Alcott and a younger man walked to the carriage they had

prepared with the body while everyone else waited for Evan's instructions.

He looked up at the sky, noticing there were still a couple of hours left until dawn, when the streets would get busy with people once again.

Evan turned to the expectant faces and realized that he couldn't recognize most of them.

The only familiar ones were Alcott's old face, who in that moment was riding away to deliver the agent's body to his family, and Talbot's, whose reports had become the only constant in his life for the past six years, and with whom Evan had spent the last six days while they made the trip back.

He had been away for too long.

"Everyone, return to your posts. There's nothing else left to do but to continue the search throughout the city. I'm sure the teams inspecting the city would appreciate the support. Sweep the area on your way and look for any traces. You've seen what the Haunter has done to the body, and you know the energy signs to look for. Report any anomalies immediately." Evan turned to the man on his left. "Talbot, stay with me. We are taking his post."

The agents mounted their horses after receiving their instructions, and Evan watched them as they took off.

It was still dark enough that they managed to blend in, even with the clopping hooves of the horses as they rode away.

Evan looked up at where Emilie would likely be sleeping peacefully, unaware of everything that had happened just a few feet away from her house.

Annoyed with himself for allowing such a foolish distraction, he walked away with Talbot following close behind.

The sun couldn't rise soon enough.

CHAPTER 10

It was almost dawn when Evan finally allowed himself to move from the spot where they had been keeping guard.

Talbot and he were waiting for the men who would take the next shift. He had no doubt that the Haunter would be back, and although the probability of it happening during the day was slim, they had to be prepared for when the moment came.

"They're here," Talbot spoke up, interrupting Evan's thoughts as he pointed at the black horses coming in their direction. "If you don't mind, I'll stay with them."

"I'll make the arrangements," Evan said, watching Alcott and the younger man he had left with discreetly making their way toward them.

Evan had hoped to keep his interaction with Emilie to a minimum, but the choice had been taken out of his hands the moment the Haunter had showed up on her street the previous night.

At least it would make things easier for the men, and Evan knew they would appreciate having access to a hot meal now that the weather was turning colder.

Evan only wanted the people he knew would have enough

experience to face this Haunter to be guarding her, and Alcott, Talbot, and himself would be it. Evan also trusted Alcott's decision to bring the younger man with him.

The two men wore the same dark colors, and if common folk saw them, they would be surprised to know who they were.

"Your Grace, this is Harry Reeves," Alcott introduced, pointing at his younger companion who bowed his head in greeting. Reeves was tall and lean and somewhere in his early twenties. His bright orange-red hair almost blended with the sunrise behind him. "How would you like us to proceed?"

"Stay here for now," Evan indicated, glancing between the two of them and the contrast between Alcott's white hair and Reeves' red head. "I expect things to be quiet, but don't let your guard down."

Evan peeked down the street to his left.

"Be on the lookout and report anything out of the ordinary," he said. "Talbot will stay with you. If Lady Arundel leaves the house while I'm gone, don't lose her from sight. I'll be back in an hour."

Evan would be back as soon as he got a message delivered to Mr. Cottrell, his attorney, and gave instructions to his butler. He was sure he could get everything settled in under an hour.

He turned to leave, but Talbot reached out to stop him.

"Someone is coming," Talbot said.

Evan saw a carriage parking in front of Emilie's house. He kept still, taking cover. The carriage's door opened, and the passenger stepped outside.

"Williamson," Evan uttered with a frown on his face.

"What is he doing here?" Talbot asked, looking in the same direction. The other two men moved next to him. "He can't possibly know what happened."

"I don't think he does," Evan replied, feeling annoyed at the unexpected interruption. "He's probably just visiting."

"At this hour?" Talbot asked incredulously. It was clear he

couldn't go against his upbringing. "I don't think anyone is up yet. They usually don't leave the house until noon."

"I just hope he doesn't interfere," Alcott grumbled, shaking his head. "He'd better not fancy a ride through the city with the lady. That would create plenty of inconveniences."

Evan nodded in agreement as they watched Williamson open the iron gate and climb up the stairs toward the house, disappearing from their sight.

"Keep watch of the house for now," Evan ordered, walking toward the horses tied on a tree in a discreet corner next to where they had kept guard. "Reeves, I'm borrowing your horse. I'll be back in half an hour."

"I thought he said he'd be back in an hour." Evan heard the young man say before he mounted the horse.

The anxiety at the bottom of his stomach must be a remanent of the previous night. Evan was certain it had nothing to do with wanting to get Williamson out of her house.

CHAPTER 11

Emilie had been on edge all night, her head filled with constant thoughts and memories going through her mind one after the other.

She couldn't stop thinking about how nice Evan's hand had felt when he'd helped her out of the carriage last night. Her body had instantly recognized his touch, strong and warm.

Emilie hadn't realized how much she had missed it.

The thought of it had her heart clenching with nostalgia.

It'd been the light squeeze he had given to her fingers as their hands parted that had unsettled her, as if he had wanted to keep holding on to her.

Emilie still couldn't believe Evan was finally back.

If anything, that had been the most surreal and unexpected thing that had happened. She'd spent the night wondering if she would wake up in the morning and find out that everything had been a dream.

Instead, Emilie had awoken to a very exhausting nightmare, covered in sweat, and surrounded by darkness, with her heart beating rapidly and the scar on her chest aching.

Her scar would always ache at unusual times. She had given

up trying to find an explanation for it long ago. Emilie couldn't even remember how she had gotten it.

She would have the same nightmares from time to time, but it had been long since she had last dreamed about the night Evan's parents had died. At least, that's what Emilie suspected it was about, having been too young when it happened to remember the details behind their death.

Every time she woke up from it, the feeling that their deaths had been her fault wouldn't go away.

No one had ever explained to her what had happened to them, and over the years, she had felt too ashamed to ask Evan about it. To this day, she wasn't sure if the nightmare was a memory or just a dream.

As soon as the first rays of sunshine leaked through her window, Emilie jumped out of bed.

She still couldn't believe she had met him again, but why had it had to be at that moment? Her luck had somehow gone from bad to worse in just a few hours.

Emilie changed from her nightgown into a simple day dress and twisted her long, dark brown hair on top of her head, looking at her reflection with a sigh.

She might be unmarried, but she was free, and that was more than any of her acquaintances could claim to be.

Her eyes settled on the gown she had left on top of her vanity, and Emilie remembered how much she had loved the dress when she had seen it for the first time. The sight of it had filled her with pleasure at how the fabric would shine with the tiniest reflecting of light.

Now, the gown looked haggard against the vanity chair, as if the sparkle in the fabric had vanished.

The sight of the red stain mocked her, reminding her of what a fool she had been.

Emilie tried to put the thought aside, and even though it was a cool morning, she found it refreshing.

She would spend the morning in the garden tending to the

peonies she loved. For now, the most Emilie dared to do was water the plants, and even then, their gardener often accused her of overwatering them.

Her gardening skills might be lacking, but she was slowly beginning to learn from him.

Even though their gardener wouldn't be happy with her interfering with his precious flowers this morning, and even though Emilie wasn't the most qualified gardener, being in the presence of the flowers would instantly shift her mood.

Emilie had tried her hand at flower arrangement at one point, but the skill seemed to have eluded her as well.

In a last-ditch effort, she had turned to painting them, but her aunt didn't seem to find joy in her art skills and refused to display her creations somewhere other than in the hallway, away from people's eyes.

Sometimes, Emilie wished she could get her hands full of dirt. That was something that immediately made her happy.

Spending time in nature, riding, fishing, and hunting had been her favorite things to do when she lived back in the Grand House.

The gardens had been more than beautiful. The gardeners had grown multiple varieties of roses, along with some exotic breeds that her uncle had brought from his trips, and they had been more lenient with her whenever Emilie had tried to plant something as well.

No doubt, they had to have been constantly undoing all her mistakes and rescuing whatever poor flower she had attempted to plant.

Since moving to the city, the small garden in their backyard was the only source of nature she'd had at her disposal.

Emilie was on her way down the main stairs when she encountered her maid.

"Margaret," Emilie said. "Have you seen Mr. Larson?"

The butler would most certainly be awake. The staff began their day before the sun was out, since he liked sending the footman on supply runs to the market early in the day. The cook, Mrs. Glenda, only liked to work with fresh ingredients, so Mr. Larson would be just about done writing the list for the footman in that moment.

Since it was only her aunt and Emilie in the small house, Mr. Larson refused to have these tasks taken over by a housekeeper, not to mention that Aunt Augustine had insisted that she didn't like the idea of having to hire a stranger and the hassle that came with getting used to someone new.

As it turned out, they really didn't need the extra help.

"My lady," Margaret greeted. She kept twisting her hands in her lap. "Mr. Larson is busy at the moment."

"Busy?" Emilie asked, noticing the nervousness in the maid's voice and how the young woman kept lowering her face and avoiding her eyes. It was as if Emilie were having a conversation with the maid's bonnet. "Is something wrong?"

"No, my lady. Would you like me to bring breakfast to your room?"

Emilie wasn't convinced by the maid's words. After finishing writing the list, Mr. Larson usually liked to have a cup of tea.

Something must be delaying his usual morning routine.

"That won't be necessary. I'll just have a toast in the garden. Could you please let Mrs. Glenda know?"

"My lady, Mr. Larson asked me to make sure you stayed in your room."

"Why would he ask you such a thing?"

"It's because of the gentleman," the maid said reluctantly, keeping her gaze down. The words had barely been a murmur.

"The gentleman?"

Her heartbeat increased at the mention of a man.

"Yes, my lady. Mr. Larson keeps insisting that these are not proper hours, but the man says he must speak with you and refuses to leave."

"Do you know who he is?"

She felt ridiculous for considering the idea that crossed her mind as nerves invaded her body.

"I'm not sure, my lady. I got a glimpse of him, and he's tall and handsome."

"Thank you, Margaret. I'll go find Mr. Larson."

"But, my lady," the maid started, her eyes wide with apprehension. "Mr. Larson will be furious with me for not following his orders."

"Don't worry about that," Emilie said with a smile, trying to ease the young woman's nerves. "I'll take care of it. And now tell me, where's Mr. Larson?"

"He's still at the door. He's preventing the man from coming inside."

Emilie found that odd. Mr. Larson wasn't unfriendly to her guests, even if they were unusually early. She followed the maid down the stairs and across the foyer, where the butler was standing by the closed front door.

"My lady!" the butler let out when he saw her.

"Good morning, Mr. Larson," Emilie greeted calmly as the young maid quickly walked away.

"I'm sorry to bother you this early," Mr. Larson said. He walked toward her, looking eager to distance himself from the door and blocking her path toward it. "A gentleman is looking for you and refuses to leave, but I told him that these are not adequate hours and that he should come back later. He's not in a state to listen to reason. I don't think it's appropriate to meet with him when he's in such a state."

Emilie could tell that Mr. Larson felt flustered, probably having been arguing his point with the man for quite a bit.

She knew he disliked it when people didn't behave properly, especially when it interfered with his morning routine and reign of order.

"I'll take care of it, Mr. Larson," Emilie said with a smile, trying to soothe the old butler whose straight posture looked even stiffer that morning. "I was already awake and on my way downstairs when Margaret found me. Who is he?"

Mr. Larson had been with her family for years, and she knew that his loyalty was unquestionable, which was why he'd followed her from the Grand House when Emilie had moved to the city.

She was curious to see who had caused such a furor in him, and slightly amused at the sight of his gray mustache ruffling every time he spoke. It reminded her of the older blue jays that puffed their feathers whenever they were enjoying a nice moment in the sun.

Except that, in that moment, Mr. Larson was *not* happy.

"Lady Augustine gave us specific instructions last night to not accept any early calls," Mr. Larson said with the conviction of someone who knew they're doing what was expected of them. "I have insisted that you're indisposed and can't see anyone at the moment. He must have left by now."

His perfectly combed hair expressed more authority than what she had seen in the ballroom the previous night.

The old butler was avoiding her question.

Her stomach twisted with anxiety at the thought of who could be behind the door, and one person in particular came to mind.

"Thank you, Mr. Larson. Please open the door. Let's see what's so urgent."

"But, Lady Arundel..."

Emilie could see the old butler couldn't conjure another reason for why he shouldn't comply. She also knew he wouldn't argue with her if she didn't find his reasons satisfactory and would have no other option but to open the door anyhow.

"He might be gone," Mr. Larson said in a whisper, and Emilie thought she heard a hopeful tone in his voice.

Who could be causing this level of commotion in the old man?

She was aware that he didn't agree with such a transgression to the rules, but Emilie needed to know who the visitor was before her nerves got the best of her.

Mr. Larson opened the door, getting out of the way so that she could see the person standing outside.

"Hello, Emilie," he said, standing by the door with an expression full of impatience. "I've been waiting for you."

The man let himself in, not minding the disapproving look that Mr. Larson gave him when he did.

"Lord Williamson," Emilie greeted, shocked at his appearance as the feeling of disappointment filled her body. This wasn't the man she was expecting or wanting to see. "What are you doing here?"

Once the shock started to vanish, Emilie realized that she could count with the fingers of one hand the number of times Lord Williamson had visited her house.

It had always been while accompanying his mother on her visits to Aunt Augustine.

"We didn't finish our conversation last night," Lord Williamson said with a voice full of impatience.

"I thought we had."

"We need to talk in private."

Lord Williamson looked at Mr. Larson with dissatisfaction. Meanwhile, the butler seemed to have grown a foot taller by standing next to him.

Emilie felt annoyed at herself for wavering, but she was curious about what had caused him to behave in such an unexpected way.

"Mr. Larson," Emilie started, turning to the butler. "Could you please bring some tea to the drawing room?"

"Yes, my lady," the butler replied with the unsatisfied expression he usually reserved for when the footman didn't bring something on his list. A look that Emilie didn't usually receive but that still made her feel like a child. "I'll bring it immediately, and I'll call the footman to assist you in a moment."

She watched him rush to the kitchen before Emilie turned to lead Lord Williamson down the hall toward the drawing room.

It'd have been more exciting if the man she had found behind the door had been a different one.

Once they were inside, Emilie sat in one of the chairs by the fireplace and looked at Lord Williamson as he paced around the room.

She was starting to get impatient when he abruptly stopped and looked at her with an intense gaze.

"Emilie, I need to ask you something," he started as he walked a few steps closer to her chair. "I know it's not true. It can't be true. But I need to hear it from you."

"If you already know the answer, then why are you asking me? After what you've put me through, I'm the one who should be demanding answers."

Emilie took a good look at him for the first time that morning. He looked disheveled, unlike his usual groomed self, and he wore the same suit he had worn the previous night.

She had been so distracted coping with her disappointment that she had overlooked what should have stood out to her right away.

No wonder Mr. Larson had been so displeased with him.

It was obvious Lord Williamson hadn't gotten to bed at all, and he smelled like a distillery. There was also a rancid smell that she thought might be smoke.

Emilie hoped he didn't get any closer. She didn't think she could keep the disgusted expression from her face if he did. She also wished she had stayed in bed instead.

Lately, Emilie felt as if she kept being cornered into a wall, with decisions being taken away from her hands no matter what she did.

The feeling of having no control over her life and the constant disappointment told her it was time to take her destiny into her own hands.

Maybe it was time for her to enjoy the freedom that came with not having a husband. Since her last hope of marriage had turned into a fiasco, Emilie would embrace her status as an old spinster and go on the journey she had been dreaming of.

The thought of starting preparations as soon as Lord Williamson left filled her chest with hope and helped her keep her back a bit straighter.

"I need to know if I made a mistake last night," Lord Williamson continued with the same intense and sorrowful eyes. Her stomach twisted with anxiety. "I must know. Was the duke your lover, and are you accepting him as your lover again?"

Emilie definitely wasn't expecting that.

She gasped at his question, utterly stunned and too shocked by his accusation to mutter a word in her defense.

But then, the anger she had been containing exploded.

She was furious at him for daring to even suggest such a thing. After all the time she had spent focused on him, he repaid her by becoming engaged to Anne Marie and demanding answers for ridiculous questions?

Lord Williamson should know better, after all the time they had spent meeting in secret.

And now, not only was there the silly rumor about a lover she had overheard from the young women in the library, but Evan, whom Emilie hadn't seen in ten years, was supposed to be him as well?

"Get out," Emilie hissed with a clenched jaw that barely allowed the sounds out of her mouth.

An unexpected shout from outside the room interfered with her outburst.

Emilie could distinguish Mr. Larson's voice in the background as she waited for Lord Williamson to move while trying to ignore the commotion outside.

Lord Williamson stared at her as if he was still expecting an answer. Emilie was about to repeat herself when she heard footsteps outside of the room.

A moment later, Mr. Larson opened the door and walked inside, followed by the footman carrying a tea tray with him.

"Lady Arundel," the butler said, and Emilie could see the happiness in his eyes and the excitement in the way he moved. "You won't believe who is here!"

CHAPTER 12

M r. Larson looked at him, waiting for Evan to come inside.

When Emilie looked up at him as he walked through the door, Evan saw that she almost jumped out of her seat.

"Good morning, Emilie. I see you have company," he said, stepping into the room.

Evan knew that the familiarity with which he addressed her in front of Williamson would annoy her, and he smiled.

"Good morning, Duke," Emilie greeted, her cheeks tinting with red.

Evan's smile grew when she quickly avoided his eyes.

She sat in a chair by the fireplace while Williamson stood in front of her, glaring at him.

"Rowlings, what are you doing here?" Williamson asked.

Mr. Larson had been right to be worried. Williamson looked as if he had come straight from the ball, his disheveled hair all over the place and wearing the same clothes as the previous night.

He also smelled like he had been drinking.

Combined with the smell from his cologne, which wasn't

fresh anymore, and the tobacco smoke that clung to his clothes, Evan found his presence repulsive.

He didn't know how Emilie could be with Williamson in an enclosed space and still sip her tea.

"Good morning to you, too," Evan replied sarcastically. "I'd like to know what you are doing here."

He was glad he had taken the time to change, although it wouldn't have been hard to look decent next to Williamson in his current state.

Evan took a few steps forward to stand next to Emilie. He raised his eyebrow as he stared down at him.

"I have private matters to discuss with Lady Arundel," Williamson told him, looking at Evan with narrowed eyes. "We are in the middle of a conversation. Nothing to concern yourself with."

"Well, I'll decide that," Evan said, positioning himself in front of Emilie, blocking her from Williamson's view. "I'm afraid she already has a previous appointment with me."

At his words, Williamson tried to look at Emilie while glaring at her.

"Duke, Lord Williamson was about to leave," Emilie finally spoke, standing up and moving to his side, all while keeping her chin up and a straight back.

Just then, Evan saw a maid come inside the room and whisper to Mr. Larson. He had been so focused on Williamson that he had forgotten that the old butler was still in the room.

Mr. Larson turned to Emilie.

"Lady Arundel, Lady Augustine will be with you shortly."

"Thank you, Mr. Larson," Emilie said in a tone that commanded the room. She didn't have to raise her voice to emanate authority. "Lord Williamson, I'm afraid my appointment has arrived, but please, give my best to Lady Williamson."

But Williamson wasn't as ready to finish their conversation. He walked toward her, extending his arm in an attempt to grab her hand before Evan stepped in front of Emilie, not allowing Williamson to touch her or even get close to her.

"I'll walk him out," Evan declared with his back to Emilie, not looking at anyone but Williamson. "I need to talk to him."

Evan knew he had to get him out of the house and over to his men for questioning.

Williamson had some explaining to do about Robert's disappearance, having been the last man who had seen Evan's cousin.

Of course, the satisfaction he felt escorting him out had nothing to do with taking Williamson out of her house, but he couldn't feel more content with the results. Everything had gone better than he had expected.

After taking Williamson to his agents outside, Evan had left the interrogation to Talbot, who he knew would do a good job of sizing up if Williamson had been involved with the disappearance of Evan's cousin.

Returning to Emilie's house, Evan let himself in and was just on his way back to the drawing room when a voice called him.

"My dear boy!" Aunt Augustine exclaimed, and Evan saw her coming down the stairs close to the foyer. Aunt Augustine looked as happy to see him as she had looked the previous night. "I'm so glad to see you again, and so soon!"

"Aunt Augustine—I mean, Lady Augustine," Evan said quickly, and she beamed in response. "Forgive me. Old habits are hard to stop sometimes. I hope I didn't cause you any inconveniences so early in the morning."

"Nonsense. On the contrary, you helped us deal with an uncomfortable situation that we did not see coming at all. It's so odd for Lord Williamson to behave this way; I wonder if something happened to his mother. But I'm so glad you decided to come visit us, and of course you can always call me aunt, at least in private," Aunt Augustine said, laughing and throwing her light brown hair back as she gently covered her mouth with her fingers. Evan could see gray strands of hair mixing in with the rest. "I don't know what we'd have done if it wasn't for you. I can't understand what caused Lord Williamson to behave in such a way, and right after his engagement! Emilie is too sweet to act rudely toward anyone, but he should have known better than to come at inadequate hours."

"I'm happy to be of service. I'm sure Lord Williamson will behave properly in the future," Evan said while smiling softly at her.

She had always been talkative, and he knew he could count on her to keep him up to date with the gossip he had missed in the last ten years.

Evan offered her his arm before they began their walk to the drawing room.

"The reason for my visit was because I was hoping to have a word with you," he continued. "And I thought I could escort you on a walk in the garden. It's a beautiful morning, and I wouldn't like the day to be ruined by Lord Williamson's unpleasant visit. I believe a nice walk could ease your concerns. Lady Arundel is welcome to join us too, of course."

"Oh, dear, there's no need to be so formal when you're among friends," Aunt Augustine said, playfully waving off his concern with her hand. "I'm sure Emilie would love to join us. You practically grew up together! Now, yours is a lovely idea, and I'd like to add to it. I think we should take this opportunity, now that we have reunited, to have breakfast in the garden. It is such a sunny and clear day; a perfect day to be in the company of friends."

Evan smiled at her excitement. Her plan was better than his, and he was grateful that he could count on her to make things less complicated.

"I couldn't agree more."

"Aunt, I see you've met our visitor." Emilie had a surprised expression at finding them together in the hall when she opened the drawing room's door.

He noticed her looking at their linked arms.

"Oh yes, and we will be having breakfast together in the garden," Aunt Augustine informed her with an excited smile.

"Are you? I'll let Mr. Larson know to prepare breakfast for you and the duke then." Emilie's tone was flat while she briefly looked at him before trying to walk around them.

"Oh, I'll do it," Aunt Augustine interrupted, quickly removing her arm from his and moving away from them. "You show Evan the roses that just bloomed. They're beautiful."

Evan watched Emilie's aunt disappear down the hall in the direction they had both come from.

"You don't have to make it so obvious," Evan spoke up as soon as Aunt Augustine was gone. He enjoyed the opportunity to tease her; maybe they could go back to the way things used to be when they were younger.

"What do you mean?" Emilie asked, narrowing her eyes at him.

He knew she found him suspicious, and that only added to his desire to tease her even further.

"It's obvious I make you nervous."

Evan turned to follow Aunt Augustine down the hallway.

"You do not! Perhaps you're the one feeling nervous. Tell me, why did you pretend that we hadn't just met when you greeted Aunt Augustine last night?"

"Don't tell me it upset you?"

He took the time to stop and look at a painting of a flower arrangement that hung on the wall. It looked like a depiction of the flowers at their moment of death.

"No, but I didn't see a need to hide it, either."

"And I didn't see the need to ruin the moment for Aunt Augustine. You should be more considerate."

The sun greeted them when they stepped outside. Evan looked at their surroundings. It was a nice garden with a couple of tall trees at the back of the property and a table with chairs near the back.

He could feel Emilie observing him carefully.

"I brought some rose bushes with me from the Grand House

when I came to the city. Seeing them in the garden reminds me of home."

Evan smiled. Next to the roses, there was a bush full of round, pointy leaves transitioning from a light green to a pale yellow, with clusters of dark berries around the golden leaves.

Behind where the roses were planted, he could see the garden of the house next door.

The fence separating the properties was short, with a small iron gate that had an unusual design on top.

He walked around the flowers and the bushes to take a closer look at it, and he could see the drawings of small birds connected to each other in what looked like a rope.

It must have been left over from when the women were hallowing the ground where Emilie's house was on, and he was sure there would be more imagery around the property in the least expected places.

Apparently, they couldn't trust that their safeguards would be enough to protect her.

As annoyed as the thought made him, he couldn't complain about the measures taken to increase her safety.

Evan tried to open the gate, but it didn't budge.

Lovely.

"The house has been empty for years. All we've heard is rumors, and now we think the houses might have been part of the same property in the past. The outside of the houses look too similar, but the whole situation is odd." She looked at him with a smile. Evan knew Emilie had always liked a mystery. "People show up to clean the house every few months. I've never seen anyone taking care of the garden, though, so I usually climb over the fence to take care of the roses there. The house is completely locked, and even though I've tried to open the back door and windows, I've never gotten inside."

Evan raised an eyebrow at her confession, finding himself amused at the idea of seeing her climb over the fence and trying to break into the house.

Just like the old days.

It'd be entertaining to see her try with the long skirt she was wearing at the moment. Long gone were the days in which they would be running around in their riding gear.

"Do you know who the owner is?"

"Well, it's always been a bit of a mystery. No one seems to know," Emilie said in a low voice, leaning toward him as if the empty house could overhear her. "My aunt told me she heard a rumor that the houses used to belong to the same family, but then the properties were separated, and the fence was added later on. My aunt hasn't been able to find out who the owner is."

"And the house has been empty since then?"

"Yes. It's been nice not having to worry about having neighbors with a house that close to us."

Emilie moved away from the gate and walked toward the table and the chairs Evan had noticed earlier. It had to be their designated breakfast spot.

"Would you like to have me as your neighbor, darling?"

Emilie scoffed.

"We'd have to build a bigger fence for that."

CHAPTER 13

Emilie knew Evan was only trying to tease her. She didn't feel like entertaining him, but her hosting skills were so ingrained in her that she could rely on them to get her through any situation.

Almost forgetting it was Evan she was talking to, she had let her guard down. It was as if they had gone back in time, and they were walking through the gardens at the Grand House.

She had always believed their relationship was different from others.

They used to talk all the time, and Emilie had once believed there were no secrets between them. Or that there wasn't anyone who knew him as well as her.

She had clearly been mistaken.

Emilie wondered what was happening that morning. Everyone kept showing up so unexpectedly, and her door had never been so popular.

To think that after all the time she had wasted on Lord Williamson, he had dared to come up to her with accusations.

How could he have thought of Evan and her being lovers? Evan had just returned! When could she have possibly had the time for that? She felt anxious as she remembered what those foolish women had been talking about in the library the previous night.

"Wonderful! It's so nice to see you two together. Just like old times."

Emilie saw her aunt standing at the door with Mr. Larson, the footman, and the maid. They were carrying trays, jars, and teacups.

"Oh, aunt." Emilie waved her hand as she sat down. "We are not children anymore."

Evan waited for Aunt Augustine to help her take her seat.

"Oh, but I'm counting on that," Aunt Augustine whispered as she winked at her.

Emilie was sure she looked as bright as her favorite roses behind her. She knew Evan had heard her aunt's comment, if his attempt to suppress his laughter was any indication.

Emilie just knew that he would have a smug face all the way through breakfast.

It'd be better if Aunt Augustine prepared herself for the letdown and didn't get her hopes up when it came to Evan.

He was good at making promises, but in the end, Evan always disappointed.

"I hope you like what our cook, Mrs. Glenda, has prepared," Aunt Augustine said.

Emilie hadn't seen her aunt display so much cheerfulness with anyone else. Not even when she'd believed Lord Williamson and Emilie would be getting engaged.

Aunt Augustine seemed more than eager to please Evan.

"I'm sure I will. I have missed the food from home," Evan said with a smile, and Emilie saw him quickly glancing in her direction before turning to face her aunt.

"Oh, dear. I can have Mrs. Glenda prepare anything you'd like. There must be plenty of dishes you've been wanting to eat."

"There's no need. This looks delicious," Evan complimented, grabbing his fork and knife. "After all, the most important part of a meal is the company."

"You speak nothing but the truth. Don't you agree, Emilie?"

"I do," she said.

But Emilie was frowning at his attempts of charming her aunt, which were succeeding. It was a fine day with scarcely a cloud in the sky, and she couldn't wait for him to leave.

After Lord Williamson's visit and now with her aunt succumbing to Evan's charms once again, the idea of traveling the world as she pleased seemed more and more appealing.

She would take advantage of her status as an old spinster. The possibility of turning her ideas into a plan cheered her. It wouldn't be long before she could get away from the misfortune which seemed to follow her.

"Dear, what did Lord Williamson want?"

Emilie almost choked on the tea she had just sipped.

"Oh, nothing in particular."

"I still don't know what we'd have done if you hadn't shown up." Aunt Augustine was looking at Evan while holding her hands close to her chest. "I was worried that something had happened to Lady Williamson for him to show up so early in the morning. It surprises me coming from him."

"I think he just wanted to confirm we had arrived home without a problem," Emilie said with a weak voice.

She had never been good at giving excuses under pressure, but she didn't want to answer her questions with Evan at the table. Hopefully, her aunt would get the hint to not push for more.

They were halfway done with breakfast when an unexpected noise on the other side of the fence caught their attention.

Emilie could see that people had arrived at the house next to them. They were opening windows and doors, and seemed busy with cleaning. Through one of the windows, she saw a maid shaking off a white cloth, which could only mean they were dusting the furniture.

"It looks like it's that time again," Aunt Augustine commented, returning her focus to the plate in front of her.

"This soon?" Emilie asked with a frown. "I think I saw them last week."

"Sometimes they show up twice a month, but it's useless to ask them anything." Aunt Augustine leaned to her right, toward where Evan sat at their small, round table. They could barely fit their plates and goblets onto the white surface, let alone offer much privacy from the other occupants. "They've never said a word about who sends them, no matter how many questions you ask."

At that moment, a couple of young maids walked out of the house next to them and into the garden. They were chatting animatedly and seemed excited. The maids turned toward her house, and Emilie saw them trying to peek over the fence.

Their efforts stopped when they noticed her looking in their direction. Before Emilie could greet them, the young maids practically ran inside with their eyes cast to the ground.

"They weren't expecting us, were they?" Aunt Augustine said with a hearty laugh. "Poor girls; they didn't need to look so frightened. We're only having breakfast."

"Do you ladies have any plans for today?"

"Oh, I'm not sure I have the energy to be out in public." Aunt Augustine rested the back of her hand on her forehead. "I'm afraid I'm not as young as I used to be. These days, I can't spend a night out without paying for the consequences the next day."

"But aunt," Evan said in a comforting tone, and Emilie knew he was well aware that her aunt beamed every time he called her that. "You haven't aged a day since the time we were children."

Emilie narrowed her eyes at his words.

He was up to something.

Aunt Augustine laughed happily, touching her cheeks as her face turned a soft shade of pink.

"You are as charming as ever," Aunt Augustine playfully scolded him. "I'm sure Emilie must have something planned for this evening. As you are reintroducing yourself to society, it might be a good idea for you to join her. Emilie knows everyone, and she's never without an invitation to the best events."

"Oh, I'm sorry," Emilie said. "I'm planning to spend a quiet day at home, but perhaps another time."

She felt satisfied at the opportunity of declining him and not having to act as his hostess once again. Her voice might have sounded too cheerful, but she couldn't help it.

"Another day would be perfect," Evan agreed with a smile, and Emilie didn't like his relieved expression. "I'm afraid today I have a busy schedule. Now, I must go."

"So soon? But you've just arrived," Aunt Augustine said.

"The duke is a busy man, aunt."

Emilie was pleased that he was leaving and was ready to stop her aunt from inventing any excuses which would tempt him to stay.

"Thank you for receiving me so early. I didn't know when I would have another opportunity. It was a lovely breakfast."

"You have to make sure to come again soon," Aunt Augustine requested. "We can have another early breakfast if it's easier for you. You're like family to us, and you're always welcome here."

"Thank you, you're very kind," Evan replied as he stood up. Emilie and her aunt imitated him. "It was my pleasure to spend a lovely morning in your company."

Emilie had gotten a better look at him now that it was broad daylight. He looked more handsome than she remembered him to be. The way he walked appeared relaxed, but it didn't fool her.

Something in his movements made him look different, and he was bigger and more muscular. His expression wasn't as open as it used to be, and even if he behaved as if he was happy, Emilie could tell that he wasn't the same Evan she used to know.

That fake sense of familiarity saddened her.

Evan didn't have any idea how much it had devastated her when he'd left without letting her know.

Apparently, Lord Williamson and Evan had both moved on, and both times she had been the only one left behind.

Evan had traveled all over the world, surely meeting dozens of women, only to come back after ten years and find her still in the same place with no one at her side.

Emilie knew she should have left a long time ago. Gone on an adventure of her own and away from all the gossip and betrayals.

But if she was being honest with herself, a small part of her had held on to the hope that Evan would return one day.

Or that at least, she would find happiness with someone else.

A useless hope.

With the inheritance her parents had left her, it'd be possible for her to go somewhere—anywhere—as long as it was far from this place.

And it was something she would do by herself.

She couldn't ask Aunt Augustine to come with her, but she could use her freedom and travel with Margaret, her lady's maid.

A plan began solidifying in her mind.

Now that her dream of going on an adventure with Lord Williamson wasn't a possibility anymore, she would plan it for herself.

Aunt Augustine would be shocked, but she had been telling Emilie that she needed to go out more. At least, it would be appealing to her aunt if she were to become a more worldly woman.

And besides, Emilie couldn't stay in town anymore.

She couldn't allow herself to be left behind, full of resentment, once again.

Not anymore.

Emilie would not stay to collect the disappointments that men always gave her.

Going to see her lawyer, Mr. Cottrell, that morning would be the first thing she would do. Mr. Cottrell had always asked her if she had any grand plans for the dividends of her investments, or if she had decided how else to use some of the money besides reinvesting it. It kept growing without being used.

Well, now Emilie had a plan, and it'd be a grand one for her.

She could feel the excitement running down her back. As soon as Evan left, she would talk to Margaret about going on a trip.

If it were up to Emilie, she would be leaving in that very moment.

With or without her luggage.

CHAPTER 14

"The reason I came so early today is that I wanted to make sure you're careful when you go outside," Evan said. He had been debating with himself which would be the best way to handle the situation. "I've been informed by the authorities that there might be a group in the city committing attacks. It'd be best to avoid leaving the house unless it's completely necessary."

It was partially true.

The authorities would be informed about the attack the previous night, but they wouldn't be allowed to see the young agent's body now that it was in possession of his family.

"Dear Lord!" Aunt Augustine exclaimed. "Is it related to your cousin's disappearance?"

"The matter is not clear yet," Evan replied quietly, avoiding Emilie's eyes and focusing on her aunt. "But I'm afraid it could be."

"Oh, what are we to do? We're but two women living by ourselves. I know we'll be seen as an easy target!" Aunt Augustine asked, her voice full of anguish.

They now stood in the foyer, facing the dark, carved wooden door. Upon closer inspection, Evan could see the same symbols as in the iron gate in the garden that separated the two properties.

"I'm sure it'll be fine," Emilie spoke with a flat voice and a neutral expression. "Our neighborhood is one of the safest in the city."

Evan stared at her in silence, trying to decide how to proceed with his plans.

"Is anything the matter?" Emilie asked, and he realized he had been staring at her for too long.

"I didn't want to alarm you," he started with a sigh as he turned to Aunt Augustine. "But I think it might be best, for your safety, to advise you of the circumstances. I've been informed that an attack happened last night. Just next door."

Aunt Augustine gasped in shock, and Evan had enough time to hold her at the first sign of weakness and prevent her from hitting the floor. Aunt Augustine looked at Evan with wide eyes and a pale face.

"Aunt! Let's have her take a seat," Emilie said, pointing toward the hallway as the butler, followed by the maid and the footman, ran to them. "Mr. Larson, please bring us the smelling salts and some strong tea."

Evan held Aunt Augustine in search of the nearest chair. The maid quickly helped him arrange one, and while Evan helped the woman sit, the butler gave Emilie the salts.

Emilie quickly moved them under Aunt Augustine's nose while Evan stepped to the side and waited.

It took several tries before the color returned to both their cheeks.

When the footman arrived with the tray of tea, Emilie quickly grabbed it.

"Aunt, drink this. You gave us quite a scare," Emilie said, holding the cup of tea for her.

Emilie also looked as if she needed a chair, and Evan stood close to her in case he needed to catch her.

"I'm sorry to have disturbed you like this," Evan apologized, struggling to come up with the right words. He had spent too much time away from decent society, but his upbringing always came back to him in his moments of need. "It wasn't my intention to distress you."

"No, no, it's not your fault," Aunt Augustine said, waving her hand at him with a smile. The color on her face was better than a few minutes ago, and Evan felt her energy slowly increasing. "It just surprised me, that's all. It's been such a quiet neighborhood for years, and now this is happening. Thank goodness you brought us back last night. I don't want to imagine what could have happened if we had arrived in the middle of the attack."

He thought it best not to cause them any further alarm, especially when Aunt Augustine was on the verge of fainting.

Evan just wanted them to be aware so they wouldn't expose themselves to the Haunter now that it appeared to have found Emilie.

It would make his life easier if there wasn't another incident.

"We will have to wait for the authorities to give us more information."

"Oh!" Aunt Augustine exclaimed. Evan could see droplets of sweat forming on the edge of her forehead. "I've always thought the empty house next door would become a magnet for ruffians. We haven't been able to get a hold of the owner for years, and now this happens!"

"Please, Aunt, calm down," Emilie said, refilling the cup of tea on her aunt's hands, even though there wasn't much to refill. "I'm sure that has nothing to do with it. I'll write to Uncle Winston immediately and ask him to send some of his men to add extra protection to the house."

"That won't be necessary. I find it my duty to make sure no harm comes to you."

Emilie looked at him, her face showing surprise.

"Your duty? What do you mean?" The teapot and the salts in her hands were long forgotten.

"I'll assign some of my men to keep guard around your property." Evan's tone of voice had sounded more commanding than he'd wanted to make it. Clearing his throat, he tried to sound more reassuring. "Nothing will be able to get to you."

"Wonderful!" Aunt Augustine exclaimed, clapping her hands in excitement. "Oh, Evan, I feel so relieved to have you here!"

"What's your reason for doing this?"

The distrust in her gaze was more than evident to anyone in the room.

Evan knew Emilie wouldn't like the idea of having his men on the front of her house, but his main goal was to keep her safe at all costs, even if the arrangement caused her to hate him.

Which she seemed to already do, though he didn't know the reason why. He had been gone for too long to have caused any of her distrust.

"Reason? I have two, actually," Evan said, strengthening the confidence in his voice when talking to her. "The first one is that I owe it to your parents. I promised them that I would always take care of you."

He saw the shock on Emilie's face.

"As for the second reason," Evan continued, feeling satisfied with the logical way he was presenting his argument. Oh, because he knew an argument would come after he made his announcement. "I find it my responsibility, as the owner of the magnet of ruffians, to make sure that no harm comes to my neighbors."

CHAPTER 15

Evan saw Emilie glancing at the smelling salts she held in her hand.

It had gone better than he had expected, and the best part of telling them his news was that he wouldn't have to give them the whole truth. This way, they would be more willing to reduce their outings and social interactions.

It would also allow his men to have full access to their property.

"What are you talking about?" Emilie demanded. Her face changed to a furious, angry blush, and Evan found it charming. "You can't own the house. I'm sure you're confused and there must be a mistake. We're talking about the house next to us."

"That's the one I own."

Evan was amused by her protest and happy that he had followed his instincts that morning and had the house prepared for his upcoming arrival.

"But it's been empty for years!"

"I've owned it for years. Would you like to see the deed?"

"Oh, dear Evan! That's such good news!" Aunt Augustine said, clapping her hands.

Evan could see the color returning to her face, her eyes bright with expectation.

Emilie had a disapproving frown on hers, but her aunt seemed to have forgotten how upset she had been at the owner of the house for having neglected it for so long.

"Why have you been keeping it a secret? Are you preparing it to move in?" Aunt Augustine prodded. "I'd have arranged the cleaning of the house for your return if you had only let me know."

"But Aunt, it doesn't make any sense," Emilie interrupted, trying to hold her. "Didn't my parents tell you something about this?"

"Hush, hush," Aunt Augustine said, moving Emilie's hand away and standing up from the chair. "The most important thing is that now we won't be at the mercy of some criminal. Dear, when are you expecting to move in?"

"Everything should be ready by this evening."

He didn't want to risk spending another moment away from Emilie, especially when the Haunter had found her.

"This evening?!" Emilie and her aunt exclaimed at the same time, although with different degrees of excitement.

"Yes, and sooner, if possible. The staff can finish settling in over the next few days if necessary. I didn't want to risk leaving you unprotected any longer. But don't worry. I'll take care of everything."

"There's no need for that," Emilie dismissed with a firm tone, raising her chin in a defying manner. "I'll write to Uncle Winston. I'm sure he'll send us some of his men. Or we can hire someone else. There's no need for you to worry about us."

"In that case, I'll write to him and reassure him that I'll be taking care of your safety. I'll have it sent today."

Evan could feel his amusement fading at her stubbornness, and he had trouble controlling the authoritative tone he wasn't planning to use.

"In that case," Emilie countered in the same tone of voice as his. "I'll write to him and tell him I think it's a bad idea."

She took a step forward and stood directly in front of him with her fists on her waist and a defiant look on her face.

"He can send his men, but I know he'll instruct them to follow my orders," Evan said.

He couldn't lose control of the situation, not when it was important to have their cooperation. Evan tried to relax his posture and keep his demeanor soft.

A snicker in the back of his mind told him Os had to be close by, observing their interaction. That annoyed him even more.

"No, he won't! You have no right to demand anything!"

Emilie stood so close to him that she was almost stepping on his toes. Her jaw was clenched, and her eyes seemed to be screaming at him about how much she hated him. But somehow, he could still smell the scent of flowers on her.

"That's enough!" Aunt Augustine declared, looking from Evan to Emilie with a disapproving look on her face. "I'll write to him, and I'll inform him that our dear Evan is back, and he has offered to aid us in our time of need. We're happy to have a friend under these awful circumstances." She looked pointedly at Emilie, and Evan smiled. "I'm sure he will send more men if he deems it necessary. Whatever it takes to make sure we won't have vandals at our door."

Evan nodded in agreement when Aunt Augustine's eyes moved to him.

"If you write your letter now, I'll send it together with mine," Evan offered in a tranquil voice.

It was a tense couple of minutes while Aunt Augustine finished her letter on top of a side table.

Mr. Larson and the staff stood to the side, waiting for instructions after having delivered the paper and writing instruments for their letters.

"Emilie, walk him to the door," Aunt Augustine ordered, standing straight and handing him the envelope with her letter.

"Let us know if you need any help in settling in. It can't be easy for a young man to take care of domestic matters. Especially when you have just arrived."

"Thank you, but my butler is taking care of everything at the moment."

"Oh, I'm sure it can't compare to a lady's touch," Aunt Augustine said, looking in Emilie's direction. Evan could see the color in Emilie's face changing, just as it had been doing all morning. The sight of it brought him a smile. "Emilie can go over there and supervise that everything is as it should be."

"I'm sure they have everything under control," Emilie spoke, raising her head higher as she narrowed her eyes in his direction. "I'll walk you to the door."

Evan bade goodbye to Aunt Augustine and followed Emilie, who was already opening the entrance door.

"I see you still try to charm my aunt into doing whatever you want," Emilie said.

"I'm not trying. It's just who I am."

"You're so arrogant, but you don't fool me. I want an explanation, and I want to know the truth."

"The truth about what?" Evan asked. He didn't want her digging too much into what was happening.

"Was there really an attack last night?" Emilie challenged while looking at him with narrowed eyes. "Or is it just an excuse for you to do whatever you want, as you usually do."

"Are you calling me a liar?"

Emilie raised her chin in defiance.

"I'm asking you to tell me the truth. You show up after years of not hearing a word from you, making all these changes and trying to take control of our lives. Do you expect me to just go along with it?"

"I don't expect you to follow my warnings, but I hope for your sake that you do. I have to go now. My men will be here at noon; they'll be discreet. You don't have to worry about anyone seeing them in front of your house."

"You still haven't answered my question. You make it sound as if you're certain that we are in danger when you don't even know what happened, do you?"

"I'll make sure you're not in danger. I'll come by this evening."

"There's no need. I'm sure you're busy. Don't bother sending your men, either; I'll just send them back. I'll write to Uncle Winston myself today and make sure he understands there's no need to involve you."

"Well, let's wait for his reply then. In the meantime, I'll send my men over." Evan stepped outside and turned back to her. A light breeze was picking up, and that helped him soothe his temper. Doing something he hadn't planned to do, he leaned closer as if to tell her a secret. "You still owe me a kiss for taking you out of the maze."

Emilie looked at him with wide eyes and mouth half opened.

After a moment, she narrowed them at him, ready to argue, but Evan didn't give her a chance.

He smiled and winked at her before beginning his descent down the few steps.

"You know I never agreed to anything like that!" Evan could hear the indignation in her cries. "And you better not send anyone!"

His only response was to wave back at her without bothering to look in her direction.

Evan waited for the sound of the door closing behind him. He couldn't resist the impulse to tease her.

An impulse he was already regretting, since it was making him do things that had nothing to do with his job.

The way Emilie reacted was devilishly satisfying.

Evan knew they could have some fun together if she was willing, but he wouldn't be a fool once again and allow himself to believe there could be something more than that.

He wasn't the same naive boy he used to be. Her safety and the safety of the city were now his responsibility.

Closing the main gate behind him and walking the remaining distance to the house next door, he met with Talbot and the other two men.

"I assume everything went well," Talbot said.

"More or less. What happened to Williamson?" Evan asked.

"We had to let Lord Williamson go," the man answered, shaking his head. "He didn't tell us anything new compared to when we interrogated him after your cousin, Lord Hardingham, disappeared. Lord Williamson still insists he didn't know about your cousin's plan to leave the city when he saw him the day before he left."

Evan wasn't expecting him to share anything new, but he still found Williamson to be unreliable.

"I'll be living here until we have everything under control," he said, pointing at the house behind them. "That way, we won't arouse any suspicions."

"It'll be nice to get a hot drink when it's freezing cold."

"That's not all," Evan continued. "I need you to be at the ladies' place at noon."

"At their house? Can we do that?" Talbot asked with a frown.

"I told them what happened last night. Not the whole truth," Evan assured them when he saw their astonished faces. "But enough for them to be willing to agree to my plan."

"If we don't have to avoid getting noticed by them," the older man, Alcott, said. "I daresay it will be an improvement over how we've been doing it these past ten years."

"You will have access to the property, but be as discreet as you can. We don't want anyone to know we're there."

Evan started heading inside. He wanted to confirm with his butler that they would be prepared to receive him that afternoon.

"If you don't mind me asking," Talbot spoke up, glancing briefly at the other two men. "Lord Williamson wasn't happy when we interrogated him. He insisted he needed to talk to Lady Arundel. It seemed to be the only reason behind his visit, but he didn't seem happy to have found us here. Do we need to be on the lookout for him as well?"

Evan thought for a moment about what role Williamson could have had in his cousin leaving so suddenly and wondered if there was something the man was hiding from them.

"Yes. Until we clarify his role in all of this and can confirm his claims of innocence, it's better if he doesn't come near Lady Arundel. I don't trust him. I've never understood why my cousin does."

Evan noticed Talbot and Alcott exchanging glances.

"I know Robert's alive. We just have to find him."

Evan went inside the house to look for Mr. Gidley, his butler, to ask him how the preparations for their move were going before he left to make his rounds of the day.

He knew his ring would have alerted him if the agents had spotted the Haunter, but Evan wanted to confirm that there hadn't been any complications.

The creature must have found an unprotected spot to enter the city, and he needed to know where it was.

Evan needed a plan to bring the Haunter out of its hiding spot. Hunting it would be easier now that he didn't have to face the freezing weather of the unwelcoming mountains.

His only hope was to have enough time to save everyone.

CHAPTER 16

Evan spent most of his morning patrolling the area and visiting the different posts on the outskirts of the city. No one had seen anything out of the ordinary, but he was sure it would be something hard to detect.

Little by little, with the help of the agents, they had carefully swept the city, looking for residual energy traces.

Anywhere where it could have snuck its way in through the safeguard surrounding the city.

Before leaving the house, he had received a letter from Mr. Cottrell, his lawyer, confirming that he had notified the authorities of the young agent's death.

Evan would try his best to prevent any other casualties and wouldn't stop until he caught the bastard.

He was riding to the next post when he felt something shift in the air around him, his horse getting restless. Evan patted his neck, trying to soothe the horse under him.

The animal was clearly detecting something. Evan looked around the busy street with the mixed smells and the loud noises.

Instincts alerted and focus sharpened, he became aware of every movement around him.

Evan thought he had seen an energy trace from the Haunter, but upon closer inspection, he realized he couldn't follow it with all the people walking on the sidewalks carrying bags and boxes next to the busy shops.

Evan was sure he had felt the change and that the creature had taken advantage of the traffic on the street.

Jumping off the horse, he tried to follow the trace by foot, but he didn't walk more than twenty feet before he had to stop. He waited a few minutes to see if he could find it again, moving slowly as he inspected the surrounding area, but Evan couldn't find it anymore.

Mounting once again, he continued his ride to the next post where two agents would be waiting for him.

"Your Grace," one of the guards greeted him while Evan descended from the horse. "I'm glad you're here. I'm afraid I don't have good news."

"What happened?" Evan asked, his senses still on high alert. He could feel their tension.

"We found something," the agent replied. "We almost missed it while we were doing our usual rounds. It's barely visible, but there seems to be a fissure in the wall. We don't know how it could have been done. There's always been someone present at all times."

"Show me what you found," Evan said, walking toward the safeguard that acted as a wall. "I thought you might have noticed something earlier. I just felt the Haunter's presence on my way here."

"We didn't feel anything. Nothing but that." The other agent pointed at the wall in the distance.

Evan followed the men as they lead the way toward a desolate area about two hundred feet from where the post stood.

With no people or carriages going around, and no buildings to stand in the way, they had a clear view of either side of the safeguard.

The sun was already at the highest point, which lessened the odds of encountering the Haunter. There wasn't much shade where it could take cover, so even if it was lurking around, it would be easily detected.

Evan wasn't worried about an ambush, but his hunter instincts had taken over him since detecting the traces of energy, and now, he couldn't stop being on the lookout.

The agents looked baffled by the fissure they had found, and when they stopped, it was in front of an empty lot with land that extended about a mile on either side, until reaching the next post.

"There it is," one of the men said, pointing at a spot in the safeguard.

Evan looked at the energy wall in front of them. It wasn't visible to those who didn't have the ability to see it. A glimmer in the air was what it usually gave it away to him, and as he stepped closer, he carefully read the safeguard, inspecting it.

At first, it all appeared unaltered, with everything having the same uniformity and flow of energy. But after a moment, it was clear that there had been a change in the cluster.

It could be easily missed if not for the slight shift of energy that threaded the safeguard together.

Something had found a way to modify one spot, leaving it standing as if it were part of the wall.

It seemed to be slowly spreading and infecting it.

"I've never seen this before," Evan said, his hands close to the wall while he read it.

He quickly created his strongest energy shield and surrounded the fissure, isolating it.

"Do you think that will work?" the agent asked, standing behind Evan as he set up the shield.

"For now. It might not be the only place where there's a fissure."

Evan wished Os would show himself and tell him what was happening. He was supposed to help him find the Haunter, not leave him with all the work. The wolf wasn't keeping his promise.

The fissure on the wall was unnoticeable at first glance.

With this new information, Evan needed to find out what the fissure was as soon as possible.

He didn't know if the shield he had created around it would be able to hold it in and prevent it from spreading into the rest of the wall.

Or if it would infect the shield as well.

"We have to make sure it's the only one," Evan said. "It might be happening all over."

The two agents nodded and began to scan, one on each side, with Evan going back and forth between them.

The rest of the agents would have to be notified of their new discovery.

If the Haunter had been able to interfere with the wall, and if their defenses had been weakened without them being aware of it, it would be like an invitation for all the creatures in the surroundings to come into the city.

The Haunter was close, and the proof was right there, mocking him.

CHAPTER 17

Emilie had been trying to talk to Margaret, her maid, and propose her plan of leaving ever since Evan had left, but Aunt Augustine wouldn't leave her side and insisted that they sat together to talk about what had happened that morning.

Or at least, that was what Emilie thought Aunt Augustine was interested in talking about.

That Evan's men would be close to her aunt reassured her, especially if he was planning to move into the house next to them.

It gave her the courage to do what she had never dared to do: go on an adventure of her own.

"Oh, dear. I can't understand you sometimes," Aunt Augustine sighed, taking a sip of the teacup she had on her hand, a displeased look on her face. "Dear Evan has the most obvious interest in you, and you can't pretend you haven't noticed."

"Of course I have," Emilie replied as she closed the book on her lap, giving her aunt her full attention. "But that doesn't mean I'm willing to receive him with open arms. There are things about our past that you don't know, and I don't want to bother you with them."

"Well, tell me. You have always refused to speak about him, and I know there's something you've been keeping from me."

Aunt Augustine set the cup on the side table and leaned forward on her dark blue chair.

"Yes, but it's not as easy for me to talk about, and I don't want you to get upset. You've just regained your strength after the scare of this morning."

"Anything involving men is always easy," Aunt Augustine said with a scoff, as if that had been the silliest remark she had heard in a long time. "You're just making it more difficult than it is."

Emilie kept quiet, but her calm exterior couldn't compare to the commotion on her chest, and she wondered if her aunt could hear the rapid beating of her heart as well as she did or if the torture had only been reserved for her.

She didn't want to talk about the past. It had been a long time since Emilie had talked about the reason behind Evan's sudden departure, but maybe this would prevent Aunt Augustine from wanting to involve him in their lives.

"The Duke of Rowlings proposed to me the last summer we spent together, after my parents died."

"Oh, my dear Lord!" Aunt Augustine exclaimed, bringing her hands to her chest and standing up from her chair before sitting down again. "And you refused him?"

"I didn't." This was the part Emilie didn't want to talk about. It always left her feeling confused and angry. "I never gave him an answer."

"Why didn't you give him an answer?" Aunt Augustine asked as she jumped out of her seat once again, and this time, began to pace back and forth in front of Emilie, ruining her attempts to not upset her. "Even back then I could tell the boy was smitten with you, and I didn't even know he had proposed."

"He left before I could give him one."

"Why would he do that?" Aunt Augustine asked, stopping for a moment to look at her. Surprise was evident in the way she raised her eyebrows. "Does anyone else know about this?"

Emilie was about to shake her head when she remembered there had been one other person aware of what had happened.

"Anne Marie."

"That girl? Why does she always have to be involved?"

Emilie had forgotten about how she had confided in her.

His proposal had brought forth a torrent of emotions that had overwhelmed her, but she'd mostly been sad that her parents wouldn't be around to share that special moment with her.

If Anne Marie had told her anything comforting, she couldn't remember anymore.

"Anne Marie was there after he proposed. He told me he would give me time to think about it," Emilie said to her aunt. She could still remember the moment as if it had happened yesterday. "My parents had just died, and I needed someone I could confide in. After all, she used to be my friend."

"Well, I wouldn't be surprised, after what happened yesterday, if she'd had anything to do with Evan leaving in the first place."

"I don't see how," Emilie replied, getting tired of the conversation. Talking about it was more draining than she had expected. "I think she was busy with her own problems that day, and besides, she also disappeared after that."

Thinking back made her realize how many people had suddenly disappeared from her life. Was that the way it was always going to be?

"Oh, I don't think it impossible," Aunt Augustine said, sitting next to Emilie on the divan while holding the book she had discarded. "That girl has always been more than she lets on. Otherwise, she wouldn't have been capable of snatching Lord Williamson from right under our noses."

"Perhaps you're right," Emilie admitted, bowing her head while fidgeting with the light pink fabric of her dress. "I never gave much thought to Anne Marie's behavior before. Maybe if I had seen it, she wouldn't have had a chance to get engaged to

Lord Williamson. Maybe I would have noticed that something was wrong. But it's too late now."

"That's right," her aunt spoke, putting her hand on top of Emilie's. "What matters is that Evan is here now, and this is the perfect opportunity to secure his affections. First of all, you have to tell him you were going to accept his proposal. He has come to us twice in one day, and he even moved in next to us! If he didn't have any interest, he wouldn't have gone as far as he has right after his arrival. Bless his soul, he's a man of action."

"What I want you to understand," Emilie started, ignoring her words, "is that you can't trust what he says. He will use his charm to get whatever he wants, but only that. The reason Evan left without even telling me was probably because he regretted asking me to marry him."

"My dear girl," Aunt Augustine said, and Emilie could hear the pity in her voice. "We don't know what happened, and until you find out, you should let him prove himself through his actions. So far, I can tell he's trying."

"Yes, but trying to do what? That is what I'm cautious about."

Emilie stood up and walked out of the room, determined to proceed with her plans of leaving.

CHAPTER 18

Emilie opened the door to her room, where she knew Margaret would be doing her usual tidying routine, which would give her the perfect opportunity to talk to her without anyone overhearing them.

She hurriedly entered the room, not knowing what to do with her hands. The uneasiness in her chest was probably the result of attempting to do something Emilie had never done before.

The authorities would resolve the mysterious murder on her neighborhood soon enough, and when that happened, she would be able to leave without having to worry about her aunt being left on a dangerous situation.

Although Emilie knew if it ever came to that, Evan would look after her. Not that she wanted him to.

She still had a letter to write to her uncle asking him to send his men. Just because Evan made promises, it didn't mean he would keep them.

"Margaret," Emilie called out, standing by the door and quickly glancing around the room.

"Over here, my lady," the maid replied, coming out of the dressing room.

"I've been looking for you." She grabbed the young woman's hands, excitement filling her. "I have something to tell you."

"How can I help you?"

"Oh, it's nothing to worry about," Emilie said, patting the maid's shoulder to reassure her. "I'm planning a trip, and I want to ask if you want to come with me."

"A trip, my lady? Can I do that?"

"Yes. You're my lady's maid, and I wouldn't take anyone else. Would you join me?"

"Of course, my lady," the maid answered with a smile. "I'll have to let my brother Julian know that I'll be gone. When are we leaving?"

"As soon as possible. But don't tell your brother or anyone else until I make the arrangements. I'll take care of all the details today."

Emilie looked around the room. She wasn't sure what she would be bringing, but she would make do.

Her aunt had always insisted that she should go out more, and as Emilie had become older, Aunt Augustine had mentioned Emilie should go on a trip somewhere exotic. Well, now she wanted to go on one. It wasn't her fault that her aunt's previous wish now interfered with the marriage plans she had for her.

"Of course, my lady. I should start fixing your bag immediately," Margaret said, glancing at the dressing room behind her. "How long are we going to be gone for, and should I bring the big chest?"

"Oh, at least for a few months. I want us to visit all the big cities, which means we can make do as we go. We should probably bring a few belongings, and since the days are becoming colder, a couple of coats. I'll buy what we need when we arrive in the first city."

Emilie smiled. This was the beginning of her adventure.

Even though she wouldn't be traveling with Lord Williamson as she had intended to do after their marriage, she would still do what she had dreamed of and visit those places Emilie had talked to him about.

She was sure her aunt would understand her need to go on a trip after her disappointment, and even if it took longer to plan than she was hoping for, Emilie knew she would do it.

All she had to do was go see her lawyer, Mr. Cottrell, and inform him of her travel plans.

The lawyer could help her with the details of her itinerary and to secure tickets for a departing ship as soon as it became possible.

Emilie no longer cared about the destination as long as it was far from here. After she returned from seeing Mr. Cottrell, she would talk to Aunt Augustine about her plans. Or maybe she'd just write her a letter informing her about them.

She immediately discarded that idea. Emilie didn't want to disappoint her, but she also felt that she needed to take this step on her own, and hoped her aunt would understand.

The determination she felt to move forward with her plan filled her with excitement. She was making progress, and things were now in motion.

Emilie didn't think Evan would try to stop her.

By the time he realized she was gone, she would be far away from the betrayal and the mockery. And for once, Emilie would be living up to the expectation of the gossiping tongues.

CHAPTER 19

Emilie had written a letter to her uncle in the privacy of her room before going to see her lawyer, who would send it for her.

She had left as soon as her aunt had gone into the study, only informing Mr. Larson of where she was heading. Nothing suspicious about that, since her monthly visit to her lawyer was usually at the end of the month.

With promises that she wouldn't be taking long, Emilie had left before Evan's men had arrived.

Mr. Cottrell had told her he would buy the tickets as soon as she informed him she wanted to proceed. After that, he would send her a message with the time and date for the next available ship. He'd also write some credit letters for her to use on her journey and prepare letters to his contacts in case she needed them.

Emilie had preferred not to dwell on the failure of her engagement to Lord Williamson or on the feelings of disappointment over unfulfilled dreams from when she thought her future would be next to him.

It also didn't help that she had been feeling strange and confused over the last few weeks. Emilie felt different.

The bitter feeling, she could easily recognize.

Especially with Evan showing up and suddenly having an interest in her life.

His appearance had not only reminded her of her failed hopes, but his obnoxious declaration had also brought her parents to mind.

A knock on the door almost caused her to drop the book she had on her lap. Emilie straightened herself on the divan, her favorite spot in the drawing room, before Mr. Larson and Margaret entered it.

"Lady Arundel, a boy just delivered a message," the butler informed.

"Thank you, Mr. Larson."

She was excited; the message from the lawyer's office had arrived sooner than she had expected.

Mr. Larson handed her the note, but when he did, Emilie frowned. It couldn't be from Mr. Cottrell, since it was not his usual stationery.

She looked at the folded paper in her hand. There wasn't anything written on the front; nothing about who had sent it or who it was addressed to.

It was just a note.

"Did the boy say who sent it?" Emilie asked, confused to receive such simple correspondence.

"The boy didn't know," Mr. Larson said with a shake of his head. "He said that a woman paid him a coin to deliver it to Lady Arundel."

Emilie unfolded the note. When she opened it, all she could do was stare at it in confusion.

A pain in her chest bothered her, but the same spot had been bothering her for a few weeks now. It might be the seasonal change affecting her old scar.

The note was short, with just a word in elaborated calligraphy. It read, *Hello*.

She didn't know what to make of the message; the boy must

have made a mistake. Emilie had never been the victim of a prank before.

What the boy had told Mr. Larson didn't shed any light on the cryptic message, and she didn't understand who the woman could be.

There weren't many women among her acquaintances, and most of them weren't in town at the moment. Even if they were, they would never send her such a message. Anne Marie had already stolen Lord Williamson from her, so Emilie doubted she would have anything to do with it, either.

The handwriting wasn't familiar. It was more elaborate than was the fashion.

As she read and reread the word, something in the emptiness of the note made her nervous.

Emilie wasn't easily scared, but after what Evan had told them had happened the previous night, she felt uneasy about receiving such a message. The only reason anyone would send her something like that would be to scare her.

Deciding that it was most likely a prank, Emilie turned to the butler.

"Mr. Larson, could you ask the men the duke sent to come see me? I have something to tell them."

Emilie had hoped she could pretend they weren't there, but she wasn't a fool to keep something like this to herself. Especially when it appeared to be a delicate time in uncommon circumstances.

If there was anything to worry about, Emilie didn't want to worry about it alone.

"Of course, my lady."

Mr. Larson looked surprised by her request, but he left the room with the maid following close behind.

She couldn't relax until the men told her their thoughts about the note. Even if it irritated her that Evan had been right.

The message could be nothing but a threat.

At least, that was the only way she could interpret the lonesome word. As if whoever had sent it was watching her and didn't have any qualms in letting her know that. In teasing her.

The note had to be nothing but nonsense.

"Hello," she read aloud, trying to feel the meaning behind the words.

A shiver ran through her body.

Mr. Larson returned with a man a few years older than her and a younger man next to him.

"This is Mr. Talbot and Mr. Reeves, my lady," Mr. Larson introduced, and the two men bowed.

"It's a pleasure to meet you, Lady Arundel," the older of the two, Mr. Talbot, said. His brown hair was short, but she could still see the waves of curls on top of his head. "Mr. Larson has informed us that you wish to talk to us."

He looked at her attentively, waiting for her reply, while the younger man shuffled next to him.

"Thank you, Mr. Larson, please give us a moment." Emilie turned to the men. "Please, sit down," she said with a smile as she waited for the butler to exit the room. Emilie vaguely recognized them from somewhere. Their names, as well as their faces, tugged at her memory. "Not too long ago you must have seen a boy deliver a note. I wanted to ask you if you had noticed anything out of the ordinary, and if maybe there was anyone waiting for him."

The two men looked at each other for a moment before turning back to her, but Emilie couldn't detect anything from their silent exchange.

"There wasn't anything uncommon about the boy," Mr. Talbot spoke. "No one was with him. Is there anything we should be aware of?"

Emilie found his answer odd; she could feel the intensity of their focus on her as they waited for the reply to his question. She took a moment to assess the situation and observe them carefully before finally deciding to show them the note.

"It's the message the boy delivered. Please, read it."

Emilie waited for Mr. Talbot to unfold it. Once he did, the expression on his face changed slightly before turning impassive. The man briefly showed the message to his companion.

"Is there anyone with whom you've had a recent dispute?" Mr. Talbot asked. "Anyone who could be angry at you?"

Emilie paused for a moment, thinking again about Anne Marie, but the woman had already gotten what she wanted. It was ridiculous to even consider the idea that Anne Marie would be upset about something.

If anything, Emilie should be the one sending her threatening notes!

"I can't think of anyone," she replied, trying to prevent her frustration from showing in her voice. "I'm just telling you about it because of what the duke told us happened yesterday. I don't know if it could be related to that situation, but since the duke is determined to have you keeping guard on our front yard, I think you should at least be aware of what happened."

She was annoyed at Evan, but she also knew these men were only following his orders. Emilie would ask Mr. Larson to send them something to drink after this.

"Would it be fine with you if we keep this note for further examination?" Mr. Talbot asked her.

"I don't know what else you can find out of a word, but if anything calls your attention, please let me know."

"Don't worry, Lady Arundel. We'll be outside at all times, so please, let us know if you need anything else."

He stood up and put the note in the pocket of his jacket.

"Before you leave, is there anything you need to make your stay more comfortable?" Emilie inquired.

"No, my lady. We have everything we need."

"Please make sure to let Mr. Larson know if that ever changes."

The men walked out of the drawing room, and Emilie relaxed against her seat. She hadn't realized how tense her body was until they left.

Her aunt couldn't know about the message she had received. It would make her more nervous and give her another excuse to want Evan around all the time.

Whoever wanted to scare Emilie would have to face Aunt Augustine's wrath for daring to interfere with her marriage plans.

CHAPTER 20

Evan felt exhausted.

The sun had set not too long ago, but it was dark when his horse stopped in front of his new residence.

Evan wondered if Emilie had been waiting for him. He hadn't expected to be away for so long when he told her he would be back.

Staying on his horse for a moment, he examined her house. Even if he felt tired, Evan still had a long way to go that night.

After finding the fissure in the wall, he had ridden to every post around the perimeters of the city to notify his men. Every time, they had found more fissures—more than should be possible—with no explanation for how they had happened.

Evan had gone to his cousin's residence to collect the books Robert had, hoping to find any information, any clue which could bring light to what they were facing.

His aunt had met with him and shown him to the library where his cousin, as head of the Organization, had kept the three books of their ancestors under lock and key.

Evan dismounted his horse and walked toward the gate.

"Rowlings."

Evan saw Talbot hiding in the shadows and walked toward him.

"Talbot, I hope there weren't any problems today. Did you receive my message?"

"We did," Talbot confirmed, Reeves at his side. "I'm afraid we have another problem."

The agent on Evan's property, Alcott, approached them.

"There is some news concerning the lady," Talbot said.

Evan's eyes immediately focused on him, wondering if Williamson had appeared again, since he hadn't had time to go see him like Evan had planned.

"What happened?"

"She received a note."

Talbot took it out of his pocket and gave it to him.

His body tensed at the sight of it, the energy traces of the Haunter were there. When he read what it had written inside, his body burned with fury at the mocking words.

"When did it arrive?"

"This afternoon," Talbot said. "A boy delivered the note. The butler told us he said a woman paid him to do it. There wasn't anything out of the ordinary with the boy. No one was following him, either."

"How did you get the note?"

"Lady Arundel gave it to us," Reeves spoke up, looking at Talbot.

"I think she believes it to be a prank," Talbot continued. "Lady Arundel said she couldn't think of anyone who could have sent it, but was letting us know in case it was important."

Evan's anger subsided at hearing his words. Emilie had willingly told them. At least, she had trusted him enough not to keep it from the men.

"It knows we are guarding her," Evan said, clearing his throat. "The bastard is playing with us. We need to find it soon. Os warned me we wouldn't have much time to stop it. For now, the Haunter can't go past the gate, since the land was shielded by the women, but we need to find out how it realized it couldn't go inside the property. This wasn't a message for her; it was a warning to us."

The urge to dig deep into the old books he had in his bag took a stronger hold of him.

Evan looked at them, evaluating the situation. He had to immerse himself in reading the old texts. Talbot was one of his best hunters, and he knew he could trust his judgement.

"We need to be on constant guard," Evan spoke. "The creature seems to be a step ahead of us. I need to read the books, and we have little time. Has Os shown up yet?"

"Not yet."

"Let me know if he does," Evan said. "Take turns coming inside. Mr. Gidley must have dinner ready."

The men nodded, and Evan saw them disperse further into the shadows before he turned toward his house, anxiety settling in his chest.

CHAPTER 21

"There was a story in today's paper about Lord Williamson's birthday celebration," Aunt Augustine told her as they finished dinner. "Lady Williamson must have arranged it ahead of time because there wasn't any mention of his engagement. Or perhaps they're already changing their minds."

Emilie sipped her tea, aware of what her aunt was curious about, but refusing to think about him.

"You still haven't told me what he wanted this morning," Aunt Augustine said with her eyebrows raised. "I can't forgive him for what he did to us, but don't tell me he's actually regretting his engagement to Anne Marie?"

"Not exactly," Emilie finally spoke. "I think it has something to do with the rumor I heard last night. The one you didn't take seriously."

"The one about you having a lover? What did he tell you?"

"He asked me if Evan was my lover."

The silence extended for several seconds.

"Oh, my dear God! Isn't that wonderful?" Aunt Augustine clapped her hands.

Emilie knew Aunt Augustine wouldn't be angry. That Lord

Williamson had used such a specific accusation went beyond Emilie's comprehension, but apparently, it wasn't something that worried her aunt.

"You don't need to look so happy; I was utterly angry at him," Emilie continued. "After what he did to me last night, Lord Williamson thinks he can show up and make accusations? I refused to answer him. I refused to talk to him at all. It didn't help that the duke arrived at that moment."

"Of course! Dear Evan came to the rescue. Was that the reason Lord Williamson wanted to talk to you before we left the ball?"

"Probably, but I don't care."

"And we also left in the company of sweet Evan," Aunt Augustine noted. "How delightful! It couldn't be more perfect."

Emilie was sure her aunt would have pleasant dreams that night, something she wasn't sure would happen to her.

She was worried about the note and had been half waiting for Evan to make an appearance that evening. It hadn't happened, and it had reminded her not to give too much value to his words.

A slight fear had begun to creep up on her, settling in her stomach. The constant pain on the scar in her chest was also making her restless. Emilie wanted to talk to someone about it; someone who could tell her if she was making a bigger deal out of it than it was.

"I need some air," Emilie said, standing up. "I'll be out in the garden."

"Of course, dear. I'll have my tea in the drawing room."

Emilie welcomed the slight breeze on her cheeks when she stepped outside. She had always felt better when surrounded by nature. It reminded her of her younger days.

When she'd lived at the Grand House, Emilie would ride, fish, and hunt with the best of them. It had been a thrill to feel the wind on her face as she raced down the field.

But Emilie had lost the joy of those things when she'd moved to the city, where her new life had begun, and where she couldn't do any of those things anymore.

In her old life, she hadn't cared about dresses, about marriage, about any of the things that were now a daily part of her life. Emilie wondered if she would ever get a chance to do those things again.

Wandering on the soft grass aimlessly, she found herself close to the small gate that separated the two properties.

She discreetly tried to get a view of the house next door. Everything appeared to be quiet, and Emilie couldn't see anyone outside.

She turned away, disappointed.

"Em," a deep voice said.

"Don't do that!" Emilie jumped, her hand on her chest.

She turned to look at him, but the only thing she could see was a big black wolf staring at her across the gate. Emilie involuntarily stepped back, and this time, she couldn't stop herself from squealing in surprise.

Evan moved away from the shadows, laughing at her reaction.

He stood next to the wolf, who hadn't moved and was still sitting in the same straight up position. Its eyes never moved away from her.

Emilie could see that Evan looked tired. His hair was disheveled, and his clothes weren't as neat as that morning. Oh, and he had a big wolf with him.

She pretended not to be embarrassed. In her defense, she wasn't used to having neighbors.

"Do you always feel the need to appear out of nowhere?" Emilie asked, glaring at him.

"Not always," Evan said with a smirk. "But it was worth it, seeing you make that face."

Emilie glanced at the animal, who wouldn't stop staring at her. She even thought it had somehow moved closer to her.

"Who is this?" Emilie asked with a frown.

Evan walked toward the fence, leaning on it, while the wolf stayed in the same spot. She noticed that the small fence was barely an obstacle for him.

"This is a friend," Evan replied. "He's an old spirit. I call him Os."

"That's a weird name for a...wolf... spirit?"

"Don't worry. He won't bite you."

The wolf glanced at Evan, and Emilie was sure it hadn't liked what he had told her. With a last look at her, it turned and disappeared into the shadows.

"He comes and goes as he pleases," Evan said, watching him go.

Emilie wasn't sure how good of an idea it was to have a beast like that living in the city, and most importantly, living next to her.

She knew it would cause panic among the staff, but for the moment, she was glad to see it go.

"Did you just return?" Emilie asked him as she got closer to the fence.

"Yes. I still have work to do, but I saw you walking outside, and you know I couldn't resist."

She wondered if he had seen her peeking over the fence.

"You couldn't resist from scaring me, you mean."

Emilie could still feel the rush of adrenaline going through her body.

"Talbot told me about the note."

Evan jumped over the fence as if it was the easiest thing to do and stood in front of her. Emilie ignored his attempt to show off. Some things never changed.

"I don't scare easily, but I can't think of anyone who would send me a note like that," she said and narrowed her eyes at his arrogant expression. "At first, I thought it had to be a prank; it was such a weird note. I don't know if Mr. Talbot showed it to you, but there's something disturbing about it."

Emilie moved away from him, heading down the path to the rest of the garden without waiting to see if he followed her.

"I saw the note. Don't worry, it's probably someone trying to prank you. From what I've heard, you've always been the talk of society." Evan reached for her hand, but she avoided him. "Until we know for sure, my men will be here day and night. You only have to call them when you need them."

Even though she still hated the idea of having his men so close, it calmed her to hear him say that. It would be good to have them around for her aunt.

"Aren't you happy I didn't listen to you?" He asked, a smirk clearly on his face.

Emilie immediately regretted the momentary peace she had felt.

"No, this is nothing to be happy about," she said with narrowed eyes. "I'm sure my uncle will send his men as soon as he receives my letter. I haven't told my aunt because I don't want to worry her, so you better not tell her anything about the note."

"Not a word," he promised, crossing his heart as they resumed their walk. "I missed talking to you."

"What?" she asked, stopping and looking at him in shock.

Evan grabbed her chin and lifted her face, giving her no option but to look at him. Emilie was sure she couldn't hide what she was feeling from his eyes. She tried to say something, but no sound came out of her lips.

He softly and carefully caressed her cheek, watchful of her reaction. Emilie momentarily leaned on his hand, and he must have taken that as permission to continue.

Bringing her body toward him and moving her hand around his waist while still holding her face, he leaned forward, getting closer.

All logical thought gone from her mind, Emilie could only focus on the color of his eyes, so dark and blue. They stared at her with intensity, as blue as the paintings she had seen of the ocean. She moved her hand, feeling the muscles in his lower back tightening in response.

It was that small change—and the feelings it awakened in her—which brought her back to reality. Emilie became aware of what was happening and of what he was doing, and she didn't like it one bit. On the contrary, she was rather angry.

She kicked him hard on the shin and pushed her hands against his chest and against his charm and untangled her dignity from his arms.

"Duke, you're getting rusty," Emilie said with a mocking smile. "Your charm is not what it used to be. That might have worked with the poor women abroad, but not with me."

Just like that, Evan had tried to trap her in a daze to make her forget and fall once again as a victim of his charm.

This time, he wouldn't succeed. She wasn't the same naive girl she used to be. His tricks wouldn't work anymore.

Emilie had allowed him too many liberties that he didn't deserve because she had longed for the comfort of his company. But it was for the side of Evan that used to be her friend, not the charmer.

He let her get away from his reach, distracted by the pain in his leg.

"You might not look it," Evan said with a smile. "But you still know how to kick. It's fun getting these glimpses of the past."

Emilie wasn't pleased with his attempts to kiss her, and she pressed her lips together.

"That's where you're staying," she told him, marching toward the back door of her house. "In the past."

"Did Williamson bother you this morning?"

Emilie heard the bitterness in his voice as her body completely tensed up at his question. She wasn't willing to uncover what Lord Williamson had wanted to know, especially since it involved him.

"Nothing of your concern," she answered, looking over her shoulder.

"I know you weren't telling your aunt the truth this morning. Was it something you didn't want me to hear?"

She couldn't stop herself from glaring at him and at his arrogant assumption, which wasn't, in fact, far from the truth.

He always seemed to know more than he should. More than Emilie wanted him to know.

"Well, well, isn't that interesting?" Evan smirked, and she felt herself blush in anger.

Emilie wanted to wipe that arrogant smile from his face. First he had tried to kiss her, and now he was mocking her! She could play dirty, too.

She softened her expression, going from a frown to a smile as Emilie stepped closer to him, her pace slow and steady.

Evan smiled with raised brows, but she didn't stop until her body was almost touching his.

And then, her face was only a few inches away from his, their lips almost touching.

"He wanted me to tell him about my lover," she whispered.

Evan frowned, narrowing his eyes at her, and Emilie smiled, completely unaffected. She felt like she had the upper hand, for once.

"You don't have a lover," he declared, his voice full of arrogance.

It was her turn to raise her brows at him in amusement.

"You obviously haven't heard the rumors," Emilie said, and with a smile, she turned to go back inside the house.

"If you want a lover, I'll be your lover."

Emilie almost stopped at his words, but she quickly composed herself and glanced at him over her shoulder with a flirtatious smile Aunt Augustine would have been proud of.

"But darling, I already have one. I'll let you know if I need another."

She quickly walked away without giving him a chance to reply, leaving him in the middle of the garden with what Emilie could have sworn was a rough laughter echoing as his only companion.

CHAPTER 22

Evan returned to the house in a sour mood. He knew Emilie had been bluffing and she didn't actually have a lover—his men had only reported back about her involvement with Williamson, nothing about her meeting with another man.

She had to be pretending.

But he would have believed her if Evan didn't know any better.

What fool would refuse having her in his bed if the possibility was ever presented to him? Evan knew he wasn't a fool, and most importantly, he would make sure no one ever was presented with that opportunity.

If she wanted a lover so much, she would have to satisfy herself with him. Emilie would never have to look anywhere else.

Evan went back to his study, mumbling and fumbling in annoyance, with Os following after him.

"Where have you been? Have you felt it?" Evan asked as he dragged from under his desk an old chest that his parents had left him after their death.

He looked over his shoulder, seeing that the wolf had chosen to lie down in front of the fireplace with the clear intention of ignoring him.

Evan pressed his ring against the lock in the chest, the ruby fitting perfectly. It unlocked.

Pulling the lid open, he looked down at the books piled inside. Thirteen books to be exact—sixteen with the ones he had brought from his cousin's house.

It would take him all night to go through a few of them.

Evan sat down, taking out the three books from his bag and placing them on top of the desk.

From the corner of his eye, he noticed Os watching him as Evan opened the oldest one and started flipping through the pages. It was written in the old language.

There were a mix of stories, mostly recounts about the Haunter attack which had created the group who now acted as hunters—his ancestors.

In one of the most recent books, there were also retellings of creatures which had been captured, and of others which had gotten away. In it, there was a description of a Haunter capable of traveling from one body to another.

This Haunter could easily suck the soul out of whoever got in its way. Besides the occasional body left behind, it was extremely difficult to find.

Evan had always thought of it as a myth; a description that had been twisted over the years. Nothing but the ultimate hunter myth.

That was until three months ago, when he had encountered the remnants of something he had never seen before.

Evan and some of the other hunters had been tracking a different creature for a few weeks when they'd come across the body of a man, but it looked as if the insides had been sucked out from within, leaving nothing but an empty shell.

When Evan had seen it, it'd reminded him of the story his father had told him when he was a child. Although the particulars were different, he'd followed his instinct and ended up in the North by himself, where he had met this cranky old spirit.

Os had been right.

The Haunter had come south.

Evan hoped his cousin hadn't had the same fate as the young hunter he'd found on the street. The annoyance at all those unsuccessful weeks going after the creature was getting to him.

When he'd left the mountains, Evan had hoped his cousin's disappearance wouldn't be related to the Haunter, but he hadn't expected Emilie to be the one in danger.

With that thought in mind, he began the night in his study, flipping through the pages of the books in his stack.

One candle burned after another. The only sounds came from the wood in the fireplace and the slow, steady breaths from the black wolf lying in front of it.

Evan was getting frustrated.

He grabbed the last book he had brought from his cousin's place. Evan was more than halfway through it when he came across a piece of folded paper tucked between the pages.

Evan unfolded it and stared at the words written on it.

You must return or—

It was his cousin's handwriting. The note looked as if it had been ripped at the start of another word. He carefully read the pages where the paper had been hidden in search of a clue, but he couldn't make any sense of the words.

Why would his cousin leave a note inside a book that no one but him would look at? Unless he had expected Evan, the only other person who could get access to them, to go through the books at some point.

If Evan's suspicions were right someone had taken the rest of it.

But the most important question was, how did his cousin know that Evan would look through the books?

It was possible that Robert had encountered something—

that would explain the unfinished message and his disappearance.

"Do you think this note has something to do—" Evan started as he looked up from the book.

The space before the fireplace was empty.

The wolf had left.

CHAPTER 23

Two days had gone by since that night in the garden. Emilie still couldn't believe she had told Evan she had a lover.

It had been an irresistible impulse; a dramatic attempt to stop him from trying to intimidate her.

She'd wanted to show him she was in control of herself and that he couldn't just come back and act as if nothing had happened.

Perhaps it wasn't a bad idea that Evan believed she had someone. He had almost shaken her determination when he had offered himself as one.

Emilie remembered his remarks about the beautiful women he had met and wondered if Evan was in the habit of taking lovers.

He might have left someone behind; a paramour, or worse.

The thought solidified her resolve of not falling for his charms and following through with her plans.

"It's been so long since we saw Evan," Aunt Augustine lamented as they drank their afternoon tea. "Maybe we should call on him."

"I'm sure he's busy."

Emilie had been hearing Aunt Augustine lamenting his absence for the past two days. Even though she enjoyed being with her aunt, Emilie wished she wouldn't talk about Evan so much.

"I'm surprised Lord Williamson hasn't shown up today," Aunt Augustine continued.

For the past two days, he had been coming over at different hours, and every time, Emilie had avoided him with the help of Mr. Larson and Evan's men.

Finding the men at her house seemed to annoy Lord Williamson the most.

"Have you received a letter from Uncle Winston, yet?" Emilie changed the subject. "It's taking him longer than I expected."

"Not yet. I hope nothing is wrong."

Emilie kept quiet and hoped her uncle would be sending replies to both their letters. There had been too many changes in a short period of time, and she was longing to see her uncle's familiar handwriting.

She wanted to know if he had decided to send them some of his men. It would be better than having the guards Evan had provided at the front of her house.

Emilie had been surprised the first time she'd wanted to go outside on a small jewelry errand. The men had insisted on one of them going with her, and they'd only wanted her to go at noon.

It had to be Evan's doing.

"I think I'll go to the dinner hosted by Lady Lawrence tonight."

Going would give her a break from his sudden intrusion and take her back to the days before his return.

"Lady Lawrence?" Aunt Augustine asked with raised brows. "But you can barely stand her."

"I can barely stand being here. I'm tired of being followed wherever I go; at least they can't follow me there."

"You know it's for your own safety. Besides, you need to be

careful. People can't find out you were meeting with Lord Williamson in the past."

"I feel like I'm being watched all the time. I can't even spend time in the garden anymore with that awful dog staring at me all the time."

"What dog?"

"The duke's dog," Emilie said. "Haven't you seen him? He's huge, black, fluffy, and looks like a wolf. It always shows up as soon as I go outside and all he does is stare. I can't believe you haven't seen it. It's hard to miss."

"No one has mentioned it."

"Well, it doesn't matter. Either way, I'm going out tonight," Emilie declared as she stood up. "I'll be in the library."

She crossed the foyer full of determination before her heart almost leaped out of her chest at the rapid knocks on the front door.

Emilie scampered away in a hurry, looking for a room where she could wait while Mr. Larson answered it. She was only doing it as a precaution after receiving that weird note.

Going into the first room she could reach, Emilie listened to the steps of the old butler as he walked past her door.

Emilie quieted her heart so the loud beating in her ears didn't get in the way of her snooping to hear who was at the door.

A voice full of sweetness reached her ears. "I came to see Lady Arundel."

She was violently overcome with the intense urge of slapping the sound right back into the mouth it had left from.

Emilie couldn't believe Anne Marie had dared to come see her.

The idea of sneaking out of the house was appealing. Perhaps through the gardens so she wouldn't have to meet her.

Another set of steps approached them.

"What do you want?"

Aunt Augustine had arrived.

Emilie wondered if Anne Marie was aware that her fiancé had been seeking her since their engagement.

With renewed confidence, Emilie resolved to meet the woman she'd never thought she would come to despise, and urged herself not to feel intimidated.

Emilie had only taken a few steps out of her hiding spot when she felt someone behind her.

In a second, there was an arm pulling her backward, and her scream of surprise was muffled by a hand over her mouth.

In that moment, Emilie remembered the note she had received, and panic bubbled inside of her.

She was quickly turned around to face the one holding her, who signaled for her to stay quiet.

Emilie was pulled once again until she was running through the hall and out into the garden with an exhilarating feeling rushing through her that could only be happiness.

CHAPTER 24

Emilie tried to catch her breath as soon as they slowed down. The run had filled her with a sense of adventure she hadn't felt in a long time.

Quickly letting go of the hand she was holding, she silenced the feeling of happiness inside of her while fixing the strands of hair that had become loose.

"Duke," Emilie started, out of breath. "What are you doing dragging me around like a little girl?"

"I'm obviously saving you from an unpleasant encounter," Evan replied with a devious smile.

"Saving me? I don't need anyone to save me. Did you sneak through the fence? Remind me to put a guard in there, once my uncle's men arrive."

"It's more convenient this way."

Emilie could feel his intense stare focused on her face.

"Where's your dog? I'm surprised he's not outside already," Emilie said. "He's a weird dog; all he does is stare."

"I think he likes you."

"I think he's planning to eat me. I tried to give him food the other day and he ignored it. All he did was sit in front of the gate, staring at me as stiff as a statue."

Evan smiled and strolled further into the garden.

"Since you're hiding from your visitor, do you want to go with me instead?"

"I'm not hiding. And go where?" Emilie frowned. "Never mind. Besides, I already have plans. Which reminds me, I don't need your men following me everywhere. Tell them to stop."

"Oh? Where are you going?"

"It's none of your concern; just tell them off," Emilie demanded. "Why are you lurking around my property like a thief?"

"I wanted to see you, isn't it obvious? You say it as if you aren't happy to see me."

"I'm going back inside," she said, ignoring him as she turned toward the house.

"I wanted to know if you had considered my proposition."

"I already told you. I'm not interested."

Evan always did as he pleased. Emilie was tired of being on her guard all the time.

"I'll go with you." He walked to her side. "I'm sure Anne Marie won't mind."

Emilie fixed her eyes on his face, trying to decipher how much he knew about her failed engagement to Lord Williamson, and the reason behind it.

Once they entered the house, she saw Mr. Larson coming down the hall toward them.

"Lady Arundel," the butler spoke. "I'm sorry to disturb you, but Miss Fotherby is in the drawing room with Lady Augustine."

"Thank you, Mr. Larson. The duke is here to see my aunt," Emilie said, turning to Evan. "While I talk to Anne Marie, you can take my aunt for a walk; she will be so happy."

Emilie didn't want him to hear what Anne Marie had to say; she didn't want to be embarrassed in front of him.

"I'm sure she will," Evan replied with a frown.

They followed Mr. Larson back to the drawing room, where the butler opened the door and announced them.

Right before Emilie walked inside, Evan gently held her hand and squeezed it. She almost slapped it away, but instead, looked at him with annoyance. He winked at her before letting go of it.

Emilie stepped into the room with Evan following after her.

Inside the room, Aunt Augustine and Anne Marie sat in front of each other; it was obvious they had been arguing.

"Look who is here," Emilie told her aunt, ignoring Anne Marie.

"Evan," Anne Marie said with the biggest smile Emilie had ever seen on her, implying a familiarity that she knew they had never had. "I was hoping we'd meet again."

Aunt Augustine scoffed as Evan inclined his head. Emilie thought she saw him smile for a second.

"Duke, dear," Aunt Augustine called, looking at Evan with a smile. "I'm so glad you're here."

"I thought I'd have to wait all day to see you," Anne Marie said, almost talking over Aunt Augustine.

"I can't believe how inconsiderate you are!" Aunt Augustine scolded. Emilie moved next to her, putting a hand on her aunt's shoulder. She hoped she didn't get too upset.

"Anne Marie, what a surprise!" Emilie interjected with her best hostess voice. "I hadn't seen you in years, yet these days I keep seeing you very often."

"I have an important announcement to share. Since you're the only person I know in town, I want to make sure you're aware of it." Anne Marie glanced at Evan. "I broke off my engagement to Lord Williamson."

Emilie kept quiet. Even Aunt Augustine seemed speechless, but she noticed Evan looked rather amused.

"I've been thinking about how shocking his proposal must have been for you," Anne Marie continued with a smile. "I know how much you like him and how disappointed you must have felt when he announced our engagement. You've always been so nice to me, and that's why I've decided to step aside."

Emilie had never thought she would ever find herself in such a ridiculous situation. She didn't know whether to cry in outrage or laugh at how absurd the whole experience was.

"I'm not sure what you're talking about," Emilie said, feigning confusion. "Lord Williamson and I are only acquaintances. I'm sure you must be disappointed, but you shouldn't have worried about me. You've always been too kind. I hope you didn't go out of your way to make the trip here. Are you leaving town soon?"

Emilie saw Anne Marie pressing her lips and her eyes shifting toward Evan.

"It's been so long since the last time we met." Anne Marie kept her eyes on Evan while talking to her. "I'd love for us to get reacquainted. We have so much to talk about."

"Oh, I know," Emilie said with a smile. "These days I'm extremely busy, though. But I'd love for us to meet some other time."

"Mr. Larson, please make sure you prepare an umbrella for Miss Fotherby on her way out. I think it's going to rain soon," Aunt Augustine spoke.

Emilie knew that Anne Marie would have no other option but to leave.

The woman stood from her seat with a straight back and a dissatisfied expression on her face, finally moving her eyes away from Evan and setting them on her.

"There's no need," Anne Marie said. "The sun always shines on me."

Mr. Larson held the door open, and Anne Marie had no other option but to walk out of the room, with the butler following after her.

CHAPTER 25

"What a shameless woman," Aunt Augustine muttered, standing from her seat. "I'm going to my room; this has left me too disturbed. Dear Duke, stay for as long as you want."

Aunt Augustine didn't give them a chance to reply, moving too fast for Emilie to stop her from leaving them alone.

Unchaperoned.

Emilie was sure her aunt was hoping for an engagement before the day was over.

Once Aunt Augustine was gone, Emilie sat down, thinking about what had just happened. She couldn't believe Anne Marie had broken the engagement and wondered if Lord Williamson's mother had found out about her past.

"What you told Anne Marie," Evan started. "Does it mean you're not in love with Williamson anymore? I know he's been coming to see you these past few days. The best way to show him you don't care about him anymore is if you become my lover."

Emilie gaped at him as she felt warmth rising from her neck to her cheeks. She almost stuttered while searching her brain for an answer.

"Don't bother. Like I told you, I already have one. In fact," Emilie said in a desperate attempt to maintain the upper hand. "Lord Williamson has been trying to find out who he is."

She tried to keep an impassive face.

"Is that so? I'm surprised you told him about it. Weren't you planning to marry him?"

"Not that it's any of your concern, but *he* wanted to marry *me*. And how do you know all of this? For someone who has just returned, you seem to be well informed." It was then that an outrageous idea occurred to her. "Have you been spying on me? Is that the reason you have your men out front?"

"This lover of yours," Evan said, avoiding her eyes. "When was the last time you saw him?"

Emilie scoffed. "There's no need for you to worry about that."

She could see that he wasn't bothered at all. Evan was so sure of himself; it made her insides burn with resentment. What a waste of a heartbreak he had been!

Emilie relaxed against her chair and did something she never thought she would do again.

She smiled at him.

"Well, darling," he spoke, looking distracted. "Like I said, let me know if you get bored. I'd be happy to be of assistance."

"How kind, but I always have my lover close." Emilie touched her chest.

The pain on her scar was stronger than usual, but she ignored it. She wanted to erase the arrogant expression from his face at all costs.

His smile vanished.

Emilie saw his eyes go to the hand on her chest.

She had unconsciously been playing with the golden chain of her ruby necklace. The one, she vaguely remembered, he had given her when they were kids. She couldn't remember the reason for the gift, but she immediately let it go and hoped that he wouldn't recognize it.

"Have you found out anything about the note?" Emilie asked, settling her hands on her lap.

She had tried not to think about it, but the worry had joined the unknown feeling she had been carrying around for the past few months.

"Nothing yet," Evan replied. His face turned serious, and his gaze averted from hers. "But don't worry; my men haven't seen anything suspicious."

"What about my uncle? Have you received any letters from him yet? It's taking longer than I expected."

Emilie was sure she saw a flicker of tension in his face.

"Not yet. There seems to be a delay in the road," he answered, still not meeting her eyes. "I'll bring your uncle's response as soon as I receive it."

"I'm sure my aunt will be pleased to have you as her personal messenger," Emilie teased with an amused smile. Evan's eyes returned to her. "Not everyone can say they have the great Duke of Rowlings at their beck and call."

"But darling," Evan rumbled with a deep voice. "You always do."

He winked at her.

Her reaction must have said a great deal because Evan burst out laughing.

She was startled by how pleasant the sound was. It made her chest fill with want and longing, and Emilie immediately crushed those feelings.

More than ready to finish their conversation, she stood up when there was a knock on the door. It was Mr. Larson.

"I'm sorry, my lady," the butler said. "Mr. Talbot is requesting to see His Grace at the door."

"Thank you, Mr. Larson. The duke was on his way out."

CHAPTER 26

Talbot was waiting by the front door when Evan stepped outside. He wasn't alone; there was a boy standing impatiently next to him.

"Duke," Talbot said with relief. "There's a message for Lady Arundel."

Evan saw the warning in the man's eyes.

"Who sends it?"

"I don't know," the boy spoke with impatience in his voice. "I work as a messenger for the King Hotel on Cedar Street. Here's the message."

Now that he had mentioned it, Evan could see the boy was wearing a uniform.

"Were you the one who received it?"

"No, I only get paid to deliver them, and I'm already late," the kid said, waving the letter.

Evan took it and watched the boy run out the gate.

This time, the message was inside an envelope, but he'd still felt the energy as soon as he'd touched it. The words "Lady Arundel" were scribbled in elaborated handwriting at the front, mocking him.

He broke the wax seal keeping the envelope closed and took out the single sheet of paper.

His blood boiled with anger.

"Son of a bitch!"

Evan moved away from the door and descended the steps, Talbot following after him. He didn't want anyone in the house to overhear them.

"What's the matter?" Reeves asked while Alcott moved next to him.

Evan handed the note to Talbot, who read it then with a grim expression passed it to the other men until Evan had it in his hands again.

Evan reread the words.

Are you ready, my love?

He turned to Talbot.

"Do you still have the first note? Let's compare the handwriting."

"The previous note didn't come in an envelope with a seal," Reeves pointed out. "It wasn't the same boy, either."

"I have it hidden here," Talbot said, walking a few steps away from them. "I buried it as a precaution, in case it happened again."

Talbot bent over a spot on the ground next to the fence. After a moment, he stood up, shaking the dirt off the piece of paper, and gave it to him.

The men gathered around Evan while he compared the writing. Even though the words were different, they were written in the same style.

"It's the same," Evan said, crumbling the notes in his hand and giving them to Talbot. "Burn them. We don't need them anymore."

"How is it writing these notes?" Reeves asked, looking at Alcott. "I didn't know Haunters could write. They don't have bodies."

"They can't," Evan said. "At least, not the common type. But this one...this one might have been around for a while."

"What do you want us to do?" Alcott asked. "Should we go to the hotel? It's not far from here."

"No, I'm sure we won't find it there anymore."

He looked at the men and then at the street. The sky was beginning to turn dark.

"It thinks we're too stupid to go after the first clue it gives us," Evan spoke. "The sun is setting. The bastard is just taunting us. With all the shields we have set in this area, this is the most it can do."

Evan had hoped for a couple of hours without an incident. He had spent the last two days going through most of the books he had without finding anything useful.

Without making sense of the note his cousin had left.

His senses were heightened, and his instinct told him they needed to stay where they were.

"No one leaves," Evan ordered. "I have a feeling it's expecting us to act. Don't let anyone out of the house, either."

"I hope the lady doesn't need to go anywhere tonight," Talbot said. "Otherwise, she won't be happy about it."

"If Lady Arundel gets difficult, tell her it's an order from me and drag her back inside. I'm sure the bastard is waiting for the right moment to catch her, and I won't risk it. It's now only a matter of time. Remember, no one leaves. I'll be in my study; I know there's something I'm missing in one of those books."

Evan waited until Reeves and Alcott scattered to their posts. He saw Talbot crouching over the spot where he had unburied the message. Since Emilie didn't want him back, he might as well continue reading for the rest of the night.

He turned and began walking down the service hall toward the garden, a feeling of unease staying with him.

Soon, the smell of smoke filled the air.

CHAPTER 27

Emilie changed as soon as she went into her room. She wanted to arrive early to Lady Lawrence's dinner to spend as much time as she could away from Evan and his men.

"Mr. Larson," Emilie called as soon as she went downstairs. "Could you please get the carriage ready for me? I'm going to Lady Lawrence's."

"Will Lady Augustine be joining you?"

"No, it'll just be me tonight."

She waited in the foyer for a few minutes.

"My lady, I'm afraid I wasn't able to prepare the carriage," Mr. Larson said when he returned. "The men have instructions to not allow anyone to leave the house tonight."

"And who gave these instructions? Let me guess, the Duke of Rowlings."

"I was told they received news related to Lord Hardingham's disappearance. The authorities reported a sighting from the attackers in the area."

"Who's outside?"

"Mr. Talbot, my lady."

"Tell him I need to speak with him," Emilie indicated. "Please bring him to the drawing room."

When she saw the butler walk through the front door, an idea began forming in her mind.

Emilie immediately ran toward the kitchen where she knew she would find the footman. She wanted to use the absence of the men out front to have the young footman find a carriage for her.

He could use the service exit to leave without them noticing, especially while Mr. Talbot was waiting in the drawing room.

She hoped Mr. Talbot would bring the younger man with him as he had done the last time she had called him.

As soon as Emilie entered the kitchen, she started her plan.

"Julian, I need you to please go to the corner and stop a carriage for me."

The young footman quickly stood from his seat at the table and nodded his head vigorously.

"I thought we're not allowed to leave after the sun sets," he said.

Emilie felt guilty. She didn't want to incriminate the young man for something she wanted him to do.

"Don't worry," she told him. "It'd be better if you stay here. If Mr. Larson asks you, tell him I ordered you not to go find him."

"I can't do that, my lady," the footman denied. "I'll go find the carriage for you. Please wait here."

He quickly ran out through the kitchen door, which was also used as a service entrance, and Emilie followed after him.

Emilie walked toward the front gate, careful to keep to the shadows; she couldn't see the young footman anymore. She knew the men had to be close, but Emilie wasn't sure how many of them would be keeping guard. There had always been at least two in the previous days.

Her goal was to walk past Evan's house to the nearest corner, where she knew the footman would be heading to hail a carriage.

Reaching the iron gate, she hesitated for a moment remembering Evan's warnings. That is, if they were true at all. Emilie walked through the gate.

She had only taken a few steps away when suddenly, all of the lights went out. Emilie couldn't even see any glimmer coming from the surrounding houses, nor could she see the footman ahead of her.

The street was too dark, but luckily, she had walked down this path plenty of times.

Emilie hurried her pace. They must already be looking for her, but the darkness would make it easier to stay hidden. She slowed down as she approached the gates on Evan's house, but the front yard was empty and quiet.

Extremely quiet.

She had just walked past his house and picked up her pace when Emilie saw a figure walking down the street toward her.

It was too dark to see it clearly, but she thought it might be the footman who had already hailed a carriage for her.

Emilie didn't want to bring any attention to herself in case it was one of Evan's men, but as they got closer, she wasn't sure of what she was seeing.

It was darkness.

It was shadows.

It was the shape of a man, but it was nothing.

And it had stopped right in front of her.

CHAPTER 28

The figure lifted its arm as if to touch her, moving forward.

Emilie stopped abruptly and stumbled back, not knowing what to do. The shadow kept advancing. She could see it more clearly now, though she couldn't believe it was possible.

Hurriedly, she tried to get away from its reach, but no matter how slowly it seemed to be moving, she couldn't get away fast enough.

The darkness was always in front of her.

"Get away from me!" Emilie yelled, but all she heard was laughter in her mind.

She tried to turn and run, but her body was heavy, and her legs weren't responding fast enough.

"Weren't you expecting me?" a voice said aloud. "I asked you if you were ready. I thought you were and that you'd like my letters."

Her heart sank, and she became desperate when she couldn't move. That's when Emilie noticed something crawling up her legs: extensions of the shadow in front of her. They felt cold, as if they were made of ice.

She tried to shake her legs free, but it didn't stop them; instead, they kept climbing toward her torso.

A cold feeling spread through her chest, pressing against it.

Her breaths became shallow.

All the warmth in her body was gone.

The familiar, dull pain in her chest became her sole focus. Emilie knew the pain in that spot had to be her scar.

But this time, the pain was agonizing.

She screamed like she had never screamed in her life, but to her ears, it sounded like a faint whimper.

A growl behind her was the only indication that someone had heard her.

Suddenly, warmth surrounded her body, stopping the pain in her chest. The darkness snapped away from her, and Emilie fell hard against the ground.

Everything afterward happened so fast.

Os leaped in front of her with its fangs bared at the shadow. From the ground, he looked even bigger.

Emilie tried to speak, but no sound came out; her insides had turned cold and numb but seeing Os had sparked something inside of her.

The wolf pushed her further back, forcing more distance between her and whatever was in front of them, and all she could do was drag herself across the dirt.

She heard a laugh, then another.

The figure shifted, and suddenly, the darkness expanded, surrounding them. Os jumped toward it as if he could stop it.

"Os!" Emilie called him, her voice strangled and rough.

But Os didn't stop. Something had changed; it was as if light was coming from him, and his brightness was stopping the figure from surrounding them.

Emilie didn't know what to do. She noticed she wasn't far from the fence in Evan's house and tried to crawl toward it.

Mr. Talbot and Mr. Larson would already be looking for her, but where were the rest of Evan's men?

She leaned against the wall to support herself, trying to stand. Her legs felt weak, and her knees felt like they would give out.

Emilie noticed Os from the corner of her eye, but she could barely see him. The light was too bright.

The shadows retreated until the shape of a man became defined once again, but she still couldn't see a face. Emilie could still see through it.

In the time it took her to blink, Os and the shadow disappeared. All she could see was a bundle of light and darkness revolving around each other, suspended where they had been.

"Help!" she tried to scream, hoping someone would hear her.

Her voice wouldn't rise above her whimpers of pain, and silence was the only answer.

One moment, Emilie was looking at the vision in front of her, and the next, she was bending over with her hands pressing against the scar on her chest, trying to make the pain stop as excruciating pain blurred her vision.

She couldn't focus on what was happening in front of her anymore. Emilie had to close her eyes against the brightness and the pain she felt.

"Help!" She yelled, trying to push her voice out.

The light against her eyelids became less bright.

Emilie opened her eyes and saw the darkness dispersing, along with the pain in her scar. The lamp in the corner of the street lit up once again, along with the light from the surrounding houses.

Os sat across from her in his usual straight pose, staring at her.

"Os," Emilie said, reaching toward him. The wolf moved closer without much effort.

"Where is it?" She asked him as she rubbed her hand against the scar on her chest and placed one arm around Os. "What happened?"

All he did was stare at her.

Emilie pushed against the wall with Os next to her for support and lifted herself to a standing position. Os was surprisingly obliging.

"Do you think it's gone?"

Her legs were shaking, but she was able to straighten herself.

She closed and opened her hands to bring warmth back to them before she started trudging toward her house with one hand holding onto the wolf at her side.

Emilie had only given a few tentative steps when the sound of running caught her attention.

She could see Evan and his men coming toward her.

"Em!" Evan exclaimed as he stopped in front of her, holding her by the arms. "Are you alright? I couldn't find you."

Mr. Talbot stopped next to Os while the other men stood in a circle around them, looking out toward the street.

"I'm fine," Emilie replied. She looked into Evan's eyes, hesitating on whether or not to tell him what she had seen. "I...I don't know what happened."

Evan glanced down at Os, who hadn't moved from Emilie's side and whom she was still holding on to.

"Let's go back inside," Evan indicated, holding her free arm.

Emilie allowed herself to receive his help when he put his arm around her back, finally letting go of her hold on Os as they started moving toward her house.

"You shouldn't have left," he said.

Emilie could tell Evan was angry.

He didn't show it, but she knew. She could feel the shift from worry to anger, but Emilie was angry, too.

Evan should have talked to her before making decisions that concerned her and her house.

Emilie couldn't pretend that what she had seen hadn't happened. It had been too real, but her only witness was the wolf following after them.

She had known there was something odd about that dog.

Emilie peeked over her shoulder at Os, but all the wolf did was stare back at her.

CHAPTER 29

Evan went back to his house and straight to his study, Os and the men following after him.

He had tried to ask her questions, but she had kept quiet the whole time, shock clear in her face.

Evan had waited for Mr. Larson to bring her a strong cup of tea before insisting that she went to bed. He had left after making sure the butler would see to it that she did.

Adrenaline and fear were rushing through his body, making it impossible for him to sit down, and so the men watched him pace in front of his desk.

"Tell me what happened," Evan demanded, looking at the wolf.

"It's my fault," Talbot spoke up. "I had just sent Reeves to ask Alcott for his daily update when Mr. Larson showed up and asked me inside. I should have asked Reeves and Alcott to guard the front before I went; I didn't think she would try to leave. I take full responsibility. When I felt the shift is when I met the footman outside of the house. He confessed what had happened, but it was too late."

"I didn't feel it coming," Alcott added, looking at Reeves, who shook his head. "I only felt the shift."

"If it got this far, the safeguards around must be down or compromised," Evan said, his hands going through his hair. "I knew the bastard was close! I felt it, but I was too late."

Evan had run from his study as soon as he'd felt the Haunter's presence, but by the time he'd left his house, Emilie had already vanished.

He had tried to fight the shift, tried to reverse it, but the creature had been out of his reach. It had hidden Emilie and brought her to where it was, and Evan couldn't do anything about it.

That had scared him. If it wasn't for Os, he would have lost her, truly lost her.

"He'll be back," a rough voice rumbled through the room, startling them. The words bounced between the walls instead of in their heads. "He couldn't finish what he came to do."

Evan and the men looked at Os.

"He talked to her," Os grumbled, and Evan could feel the power coming from him. He knew his men weren't used to having Os around like he was, and they were probably uncomfortable. "He already had her trapped and was halfway done with her by the time I arrived."

"Are you sure?" Evan asked with teeth clenched.

"You still question me!" Os growled, and the loud echoes of his voice resonated in the room, causing the lights to flicker and the crystal glasses and liquor bottles to vibrate. Evan saw Reeves covering his ears, wincing in pain. Os turned around and walked toward the fireplace. "It did something to her. She's changed, and I can't interfere anymore. I told you; you don't have time."

Evan watched as the wolf lay in front of the fireplace, and with a big yawn, it went to sleep.

CHAPTER 30

"I think I've been going around in circles." Evan pushed away the latest book he'd been reading.

A small pile of them rested on his desk.

He and Talbot were sitting across from each other. It was early dawn, and the sun hadn't come out yet.

Evan had spent the night reading through the rest of the books he had—Os's warning constantly running through his mind—before carefully selecting, out of the sixteen books, the ones he thought could be closer to what Evan was looking for.

"Have you found anything useful yet?" Talbot asked.

"Not yet," Evan said with a sigh. "It's like having a map that doesn't take you anywhere. So far, I still don't have anything that could tell me exactly what we're dealing with." In truth, he had nothing but a story, and at the moment, it wasn't of any use. "Have they found something?"

Evan had assigned overnight a team of hunters to find out how the Haunter had gotten to the area once again.

"They haven't detected any presence. It looks like it's gone," Talbot replied. "They've set up more safeguards and are currently inspecting the others."

"If the shields are still up, it shouldn't have been able to go through them," Evan said, his hand combing through his hair.

"There's a problem, though. There are signs of tampering in a few of them. It seems to be the same thing that's been happening at the wall."

A knock at the door interrupted them.

Evan had to contain his impatience, but was relieved when he saw Jones, one of the agents at the wall, walk inside. After what had happened, Evan had alerted them to be on guard; the agents had been constantly monitoring the wall around the city since.

"Your Grace," the agent started. "Things are not looking good."

"I was afraid you were going to say that," Evan sighed as he stood up and walked around the desk. "What is it?"

"The wall is getting more fissures; I've confirmed it with all the posts in the city. Little dots above the ones we found before, higher up on it. We've put shields around them for now."

"The same is happening to the safeguards around here," Evan said, starting to feel the weight of the night upon him. "It's the creature's doing. We're running out of time."

"But how is it doing it?" Talbot asked, standing next to Evan. "Never in the history of the Organization have the Haunters been able to go past the wall or interfere with it."

"That's what we have to find out," Evan said.

"Have you considered...?" Talbot trailed off.

"I have," Evan answered with a sigh. He knew that only hunters had the ability to create safeguards. It was in their blood; it couldn't be easily tampered with. "Keep monitoring them for now. Signal me as soon as you notice any changes and be aware of any strangers approaching the posts. Don't let them out of your sight."

"I'll let the men know," Jones said.

"Please, ask Alcott and Reeves to inspect the safeguards

around the house," Evan told Talbot. "Make sure they know what to look for."

"Leave that to me," Jones said. "I'll show them what to do with them."

The agent was turning to leave with Talbot when Evan's butler entered the room in a hurry. Evan was surprised to see him so unsettled.

"Forgive me, Your Grace. The messenger has just returned from the Grand House, and he has news."

"Bring him in. There's no need to make him wait."

"He's injured, Your Grace. Mr. Alcott and Mr. Reeves are moving him into the yellow room."

"Do you know what happened?" Evan asked him as they ran out of the study.

"I think he was attacked on the way here," the butler replied.

Evan was the first to walk into the room where Alcott and Reeves had laid the man on the bed and were looking over his wounds.

"What happened?" Evan asked for the second time.

"Your Grace," Argyle, the injured agent, began. "I'm sorry it took me so long to come back. The village next to the Grand House was attacked."

"When?"

"On my way there. I was riding through the road next to the village when I felt them. A group of Haunters. I'd never seen them together."

"They were in a group?" Alcott asked. "But they don't do that."

"The whole village was unprotected and under attack," the lying agent continued. "I rode as fast as I could to notify Lord Arundel, and we immediately went back to the village. It was chaos. People couldn't understand what was happening. It took some time to kill the Haunters, but we got rid of them. The problem is that the safeguards surrounding the village have disappeared, and Lord Arundel doesn't know how it happened or where the creatures came from."

"That territory had been free of pests for over a decade now," Evan said, frowning.

"How did you get injured?" Talbot asked. Evan saw him looking at the messenger's exposed leg, where the skin was burned and scarred from the knee to his ankle.

"I got caught in a fire while trying to kill one of them," Argyle said. "I had to push my way out, but other than that, no one died."

"It's rare to find the Haunters in a group," Evan noted. "Why were they gathering?"

"Lord Arundel has given me letters for you." The agent dug through the pocket in his coat. "He's sending a team to inspect the neighboring villages, and he'll send word on what they find. It's so disgusting to see what the Haunters can do, especially when no one else can see them."

He took out the letters and gave them to Evan.

"I've seen it before," Jones spoke. "The village I grew up in was attacked when I was a boy. No one but us could see them, but the people could feel that something wasn't right. You know how it is; they come with that eerie feeling that gives them away. The healthiest boy in the village fell unexpectedly sick, and not long after that, so did everyone else. Only a few of them survived, but I could see what was happening. It was frustrating. No one understood."

"That'd have happened if I hadn't been riding through that road," Argyle said with a wince of pain as he adjusted his position. "There wasn't much damage yet; I think they had just gotten there."

"We need to find out if it's happening in other regions as well," Evan said as he flipped through the letters. "Before I went up to the mountains, we had been seeing an increase of activity in the north in the last three months, but I just knew it had to be related to this Haunter."

Evan opened the letter addressed to him; the other one was for Aunt Augustine.

He had written in his letter that he would take care of protecting Emilie and her aunt, and that Lord Arundel didn't have to send any extra men. But with the attacks on his territory, the option had been taken out of their hands.

Lord Arundel asked him to look after his niece, and he would send some of his men as soon as they had the situation under control.

In the meantime, they would be working on creating safeguards around the towns close to the Grand House, and Lord Arundel would be sending Evan a letter in a week.

If he didn't receive one, it meant something had gone wrong, in which case he wanted Evan to stay in the city.

Evan held the letter in his hand, squeezing the paper around the edges.

"He wants us to stay here, whatever happens. Mr. Gidley, please have this letter delivered to Lady Augustine." It was still dark outside, but the old butler next door would be up by now.

Evan refused to think about Emilie and her meeting with the Haunter when that should have never happened.

He couldn't lose focus.

"What should we do?" Talbot asked.

Evan saw the tension in the men's faces as they shifted nervously while waiting for his instructions.

"We have no other option," Evan started, already thinking of the letter he had to write. "We will have to bring the Legion into this."

CHAPTER 31

Emilie kept thinking about what had happened the previous night.

The freezing pain in her body where the shadow had surrounded her, the intense pain on the scar in her chest, her legs refusing to move.

Nothing made sense.

And the lights...

She remembered how the lights had gone out and how they had come back when Evan had found her.

Emilie tried to remember the details she had dismissed in her hurry to leave the house, and it scared her: everything had been the same as usual, until it hadn't. The only difference had been that unexpected figure and Os.

The wolf had been able to see it, he had fought it, and Emilie had seen him become something else.

Evan had said he couldn't find her, but she had been outside of his house the whole time.

That dog had found her.

At least now Emilie knew he wasn't going to eat her.

She left her room. Everything was dark and quiet when

Emilie descended the stairs and made her way through the hall toward the library.

Going inside, she grabbed the nearest book Emilie could find before sitting in her favorite armchair. Next thing she knew, a knock on the door woke her up.

"Good morning, my lady," Margaret greeted. "We're about to serve breakfast."

"Is my aunt awake yet?"

"Yes, my lady. She's in the parlor."

"Thank you, Margaret. I'll be there in a moment."

Emilie placed the book aside and went to meet with her aunt.

"Good morning, dear," Aunt Augustine said. A stack of letters was at her side on the table. "Are you catching something? You don't look too well. I'm glad you didn't go to Lady Lawrence's dinner last night."

"I'm fine. I just didn't sleep too well," she explained, taking a seat next to her.

"Oh, I see. You better make sure to sleep early today," Aunt Augustine replied distractedly. "What a gloomy day! Looks like it's going to rain."

"I hadn't noticed. Are those Uncle Winston's letters?"

"Oh, Mr. Larson just gave them to me. Apparently, a messenger arrived last night."

Emilie watched her flip through the envelopes. Aunt Augustine picked one and left the rest on the table, giving her a chance to reach for the stack.

"There's none for you, dear," Aunt Augustine stopped her as she was opening her letter.

"Are you sure? I sent mine the same day. Did anything happen?" Emilie asked when she noticed Aunt Augustine's face began to lose color.

"No, no, your uncle sends his greetings," Aunt Augustine said, folding the paper and putting it back inside the envelope.

"Will he be sending any of his men?"

"Not yet. He'll send them later. In the meantime, he has asked the duke to help us, so there's nothing to worry about."

"I wonder why Uncle Winston didn't write to me."

"He was probably busy. One letter is enough."

"Can I see it?"

"No, I haven't finished reading it." Aunt Augustine clutched the envelope tightly in her hand. "I'll let you know what else he says when I read it. It's probably just the usual things. Finish your breakfast, dear; it's getting cold."

Aunt Augustine put the envelope back on the table and grabbed her cup of tea.

Thunder rumbled through the room.

"That was loud," Emilie said. "You were right; a storm has started."

Aunt Augustine smiled and put down her teacup, but Emilie noticed it was rattling against the saucer.

CHAPTER 32

Before leaving the town in the mountain, Evan had sent a letter to his contact in the northern territories to let him know he had to leave. If something had gone awry, his contact would be aware.

If they were facing an uprising of Haunters, Evan wanted to be prepared.

He would make a decision based on his contact's reply, but it would take some time to receive an answer.

Evan loathed the Legion. They tended to deal with the unnatural in a drastic manner, without concern for those unaware of the Haunters' existence.

The Legion didn't care about the consequences or the damage they caused, and they killed anything and anyone unfortunate enough to get in their way.

They were for when things got desperate, and once you contacted them, there would be no going back.

Evan was getting close to desperate.

He had gotten a few hours of sleep that morning and had just come back from inspecting the safeguards around the house. No damage had been done to them, which had given him some reassurance. A storm had fallen while they were out, and it had given them extra coverage from people's eyes.

Evan had noticed the men acting as if there was something they wanted to say. As he dried himself, he finally spoke.

"Out with it."

Thunder filled the silence.

"It's about Miss Fotherby," Talbot said. "She said something strange when she left yesterday."

"We meant to tell you sooner," Reeves added before Evan could reply. "But with the note and the attack on Lady Arundel..."

"What did she say?"

"She was angry at Lady Arundel for the way she'd treated her," Talbot said. "She was murmuring something about her plan not working."

Evan's interest perked up.

"What plan?"

He saw Talbot glancing at his young companion, who looked uncomfortable and kept avoiding his eyes.

"Miss Fotherby was so upset that she didn't notice us," Reeves finally said. "But she was talking to herself about how she would see you again."

"Did she say anything else?"

It was as if Evan had asked him to do an unbearable task. Reeves hesitated and looked at Talbot, as if asking for help, but the older agent shook his head and shrugged.

He had been declared to be on his own.

"She said you'd be falling in love with her soon."

Annoyance was all Evan felt at the revelation while the young agent's face turned red.

Anne Marie had always been a source of annoyance growing up.

She would always try to put them both in awkward situations, more so as they got older. Evan had always found a way to untangle himself from the mess she created, and it quickly became his habit to avoid her whenever they met at the Grand House.

He had never liked her, but Emilie could never understand why. She hadn't known what Anne Marie had put him through.

Evan had hoped he wouldn't have to deal with her anymore, now that both women weren't on good terms.

But Anne Marie was the least of his concerns. All Evan knew was that he didn't want her near Emilie again, since she was very likely to start messing with both their heads.

He couldn't afford to take any more risks, no matter who it was.

"Remember to keep the gates locked," Evan instructed, turning to Talbot. "Don't let any visitors in. Staff errands should be kept to a minimum, between sunrise and no later than noon. Everyone must stay inside until further notice."

"Yes, Duke."

"I hope you're talking about your own house," an unexpected voice said.

Lightning and thunder filled the room as Evan turned toward the door where Emilie stood dripping wet, a puddle of water had formed at her feet.

CHAPTER 33

"What are you doing here?" Evan asked her.

Emilie slowly walked toward them. Her hair was wet from the rain, and her clothes were almost fully soaked. He handed her a towel.

She had felt uneasy at the unusually somber way in which her aunt had behaved. Aunt Augustine had been so immersed in her thoughts that she hadn't noticed when Emilie had walked out of the room.

Emilie couldn't talk to anyone at home about what had happened the previous night. Evan and his men were the only ones whom she could talk to; at least, Emilie had thought she could.

It was clear they knew something she didn't.

Emilie had remembered what Evan had done the previous day and entered his house through the backyard. She didn't feel like she would be going outside anytime soon; not until they resolved his cousin situation.

An odd sight had been waiting for her at the garden. More crows than Emilie had ever seen in her life had stood on the small gate dividing the two properties.

She'd had to scare them away to go through it. It was a good thing Emilie wasn't that afraid of birds.

Some of the crows had followed her as she crossed Evan's backyard, and she'd had to cover her head to make sure they wouldn't pull at her hair as she ran inside.

Crows. Emilie hated crows.

She had hoped none of his staff would be out in the hallway; Emilie didn't want to be seen by any of them in case they told him, or worse, gossiped about her.

The thought that she would be sneaking into a man's house at her age had never occurred to her, but there she was.

Emilie was angry at him and angry at what she had heard. After what she had gone through the previous day, the stabs to her heart hadn't stopped. Every time she thought about it, her chest clenched in pain.

"I came to find you," she said with narrowed eyes, ignoring the towel he gave her. "What is this about closing the gates without our permission? You're treating us like prisoners in our own home."

"You're not a prisoner," Evan placated. "It's for your own safety. I thought that'd be clear to you by now."

Emilie stood in front of the desk while the men stood at her side in silence.

"I had my suspicions, but now I know something is wrong. You need to explain yourself; I won't leave until you do. I'm tired of you and my aunt avoiding my questions."

"Aunt Augustine is avoiding your questions?"

Emilie glared at him in response.

"I won't tell you anything until you explain to me what is truly happening. I know what I saw last night was real, and you also know what it was." She looked over at the fireplace where Os slept. "And where exactly did you get that dog?"

Emilie walked toward the sleeping figure and took a napkin out of her purse. Inside, there was a piece of cooked sausage. She bent over and patted Os in the head, leaving the sausage in front of him.

"Thank you. I don't know how you did it, but you helped me." Emilie caressed his head. "Good boy."

Os opened his eyes slightly and allowed her to pet him as he took the offering between his fangs and chewed with gusto.

Emilie felt the men tensing behind her while she petted his head. For a second, she thought she had seen a smug expression on the wolf's face.

CHAPTER 34

Receiving that second note and what had happened to Emilie under his own nose immediately after had scared Evan.

It had brought forward his ruthless self. His priority was to keep her alive, even if she didn't like it.

He turned to his men, who were looking at everything but at the interaction between Emilie and Os.

Evan could see that the wolf was enjoying having her hand on his head, looking like a puffed-up dog instead of the fierce wolf that enjoyed scaring his men.

"Talbot, please inform Mr. Larson that Lady Arundel is with me at the moment, and that she will be back shortly," Evan said. Looking back at Emilie, he added, "And keep those gates closed."

Emilie gasped and stood up abruptly.

Os growled at him, and Evan wanted to laugh at the hypocritical wolf.

As much as the spirit pretended otherwise, it was more than obvious that he liked Emilie. Maybe even liked her too much.

CHAPTER 35

Emilie clenched her teeth in fury at his obvious challenge and dismissal of her authority. At the same time, she felt inexplicably nervous about being left alone with Evan. There was something different about him. A different look in his eyes that made her feel unsettled.

This wasn't the same Evan whom she had met the previous day, but Emilie wouldn't let him intimidate her.

She raised her chin in defiance.

"The gates stay open until you explain yourself."

His body appeared calm, but Emilie sensed it was a forced calmness. Evan's eyes wouldn't leave her, giving her the feeling of being intensively observed and stalked, as if the slightest movement from her part would provoke a reaction out of him.

A reaction she wouldn't like.

Emilie watched the men silently leaving the room while Os settled next to the fireplace, going back to sleep.

She removed another sausage from her purse and placed it in front of him. The wolf shook his tail when he saw it.

Moving toward the chair in front of Evan's desk, Emilie cleaned her fingers with the napkin and reached for the towel he had offered her before.

"Well?" Emilie asked as she dried her hair and then dropped the towel around her back. "Are you going to explain what is happening?"

Evan sat down with a displeased look on his face.

"Do you have any more food in any of those pockets?" He asked instead. "Apparently, Os likes sausages."

Emilie hadn't noticed how full his desk was. Papers and books covered it completely. Her eyes scanned the pile in front of her with curiosity.

"I have seen this book before," she said while pointing at the one on top. "But I can't remember where."

When Emilie reached for it, Evan moved the pile away from her. She was startled by his reaction.

"What is it you want to know exactly?"

He spoke with a bored expression, as if he were already tired of the conversation that hadn't even started yet.

His attitude annoyed her more than she cared to reveal.

Emilie knew she had to tread carefully in view of his peculiar mood. She frowned in thought, going through the questions that were springing through her mind while trying to decide which one was the most pressing one.

Her first thought was to ask him about Anne Marie and his lack of reaction to what Mr. Reeves had told him, but Emilie didn't want to reveal how much she had heard, or how much she cared.

"Why do you want to keep the gates closed?" She finally asked, her eyes set on him, waiting for his answer.

Evan just kept staring at her, not saying a word. At his silence, Emilie sighed in exasperation and abruptly stood up, marching straight to the collection of bottles on the shelf. After a few seconds of close inspection, she glanced at him over her shoulder.

"Gin or whiskey?"

"That's hardly a question you should be asking."

"Double whiskey it is," Emilie said, looking at him with a

raised brow. "You can pretend all you want, but I still remember the times we were caught sneaking into the house's cellar."

She poured the liquor into two small glasses and carried them back to the desk, placing the glass in front of him.

"Now that I've procured us a drink, let us have an honest discussion."

Emilie sat down, leaving her glass untouched on top of the desk, while looking at him expectantly. Evan leaned forward and picked up his, turning it slowly in his hand.

"I don't have time to drink," he said, putting it down. "I have things to do."

"Fine." She waved him off. "You weren't so skittish in the past. Whatever happened to your rebellious reputation? You used to be the staff's worst nightmare back home."

"Was I the only one who grew up? I wasn't expecting you to go through my collection of bottles with so much freedom."

Emilie finally saw a glimpse of the Evan she used to know and relaxed her back against the chair.

"I know there's something you're hiding," she started. "Are we in danger?"

"Yes."

Emilie felt a small tremble run through her body.

"Does it have anything to do with the note I received? I mean, related to what happened last night?"

Evan slowly nodded.

"There was another note yesterday," he said. "Right before it happened."

"Letters," Emilie whispered with a faint voice. She felt herself sink against the chair. "That's what the shadow meant."

"What? What did it tell you? You need to tell me exactly what happened."

"What did the note say?" Emilie asked instead. "Did it ask if I was ready for a meeting?"

Evan pressed his lips, but his silence was enough of an answer for her. A cold feeling of dread settled down her spine.

"I saw a man last night. Or rather, I thought it was a man, but it wasn't. It was only a shadow, but it was moving by itself. The lights had gone out, but I could still see it, and then it talked to me. It sounded like a man. It asked me if I had liked the letters. It acted as if I should know who it is."

Evan looked at her with a tense expression, and Emilie hesitated. She didn't know how to explain what had happened next.

"The shadow grabbed my legs and crawled up my chest," Emilie said, her eyes settled on the wall behind him. "I couldn't move. It was as if it was made of ice. I was freezing, and then, I don't know what happened, but I felt a sharp pain in my chest. It hurt so much. I didn't know I could feel so much pain. Then Os appeared, and I stopped feeling cold and could move again. The shadow let me go. I think Os made it stop; he made the shadow go away. Os...he wasn't like that for a while. He became something else. Os fought the shadow and he made it go away. That's when you arrived." She looked over to where the spirit lay next to the fireplace. "From now on, Os can have as many sausages as he wants."

The wolf's ears perked at her words.

"Look at me," Evan said. "Do you trust me? I promise you, if you listen to me and stay in the house, it won't happen again."

His voice was full of conviction, and Emilie almost believed him. She wasn't sure she could trust him with matters of the heart, but Emilie had a feeling she could trust him about this.

She nodded.

"Is the shadow coming again?" Emilie asked, glancing at the fireplace. Os was looking at her at that moment. Should she stay close to him?

"*Yes,*" a deep, rough voice rumbled in her head.

Emilie looked around the room, wondering if someone else had come inside, and turned to look at Evan, confused.

"Yes to both questions," the loud, rough voice repeated. This time, the sound resonated across the walls of the room.

Emilie turned to look at Os and just as quickly turned to look at Evan, desperate to confirm he had heard it too.

Evan cursed under his breath, and she felt the blood quickly draining from her face.

"Oh," Emilie let out, looking back at the wolf. "Thank you."

"For God's sake, Emilie," Evan spoke. "Must you always need to know everything? Take a sip of the whiskey; you're going to need it after all."

"That's what I prepared it for. Yesterday was weird enough. I just wasn't expecting this part."

She saw Evan frown as she quickly grabbed the glass and flipped it into her mouth, letting the liquid burn down her throat. With a shaking hand, Emilie put the empty glass down again.

"We haven't been properly introduced," she said to Os. "But I must thank you for your help yesterday. I...even though I'm not sure what happened exactly. And you"—Emilie faced Evan—"Mr. Talbot told Mr. Larson that you were keeping the gates closed because of something related to your cousin. Do you think... could his disappearance have been something related to what happened to me?"

"None of this is your fault," Evan assured her. "If anything, it's my fault. There's something else I haven't told you. I'm the one who discovered the body outside of the house, the night the man died. The killer had run when I got there."

Her back shivered.

Too close. The tragedies were getting too close.

Emilie saw pain flash through his face, and something within tugged at her. She realized Evan felt guilty. A part of her, deeply buried, yearned to come out and soothe his pain.

Another sip of the whisky might have helped her ignore what she saw, but the glass was empty.

"You haven't told me how it's related to your cousin."

Emilie reached across the desk and grabbed Evan's untouched glass, taking a big gulp.

"I think we should stop for now," Evan said. "You need to change your clothes or you're going to catch a cold. I'll walk you home."

"No. Stop ignoring my questions and stop treating me like a delicate flower."

"But darling, you're a delicate flower."

His crooked smile was met with an unladylike scoff from her.

"You've lost your touch. I'd be surprised if that has gotten you anywhere."

"It's taken me places."

She frowned, and his expression turned serious.

Evan moved his hands on top of the desk, as if he was about to tell her a secret. Emilie couldn't read anything from his expression, but the impulse to lean closer invaded her.

"There are things I can't explain to you; things that can't be easily explained to anyone. You're going to have to accept that," Evan said, his eyes focused on her. "I've been looking for a clue about what happened to my cousin, about what's threatening you. It all seems to be connected. Because of Os, I can still keep you safe."

"But why you? Shouldn't we inform the authorities about this?"

"It's my duty. Your uncle already knows about the threat against you. He trusts that I will keep you safe. There are disturbances near the Grand House, and he can't part with any of his men at the moment."

"What kind of problem? My aunt didn't say anything about that."

"It's probably nothing. Something to do with his crops this year."

"I didn't tell Aunt Augustine about the note, and I haven't mentioned what happened last night. She thinks I decided not to go to the ball. I don't know what you told Mr. Larson," Emilie said. "But do you think Uncle Winston told her something about the note in his letter? She's been acting weird since she received it."

"I don't know. It's possible he might have mentioned it."

Emilie felt something wasn't right, but she couldn't put her finger on it.

She didn't have much time to wonder. A commotion outside caused Evan to look up. In a few seconds, he had crossed the room to the door.

"Wait here," he ordered, walking out of the study.

But Emilie wasn't going to stay behind.

As soon as he was out of the room, she removed the towel from around her shoulders and quickly followed him.

On her way to the door, Emilie noticed that the spot before the fireplace was empty.

The wolf was gone.

CHAPTER 36

Emilie carefully walked toward the half-opened door and leaned against it, trying to make out what the voices said. She could discern three or four different ones, but she didn't dare to look out in case they saw her.

There was one in particular that was louder than the rest, almost yelling. It sounded oddly familiar, and Emilie tried to focus on what it was saying, but it was hard to follow.

She recognized Evan's voice, which seemed to cut through the noise, clear and steady. "What are you doing here?"

At his question, the voices stopped, except for the loud and angry one.

"That's what I came here to ask you," it said.

Emilie gasped in recognition.

She couldn't stop herself from peeking out the door. Her view was partially blocked—Evan was so tall that he obstructed most of it—but the voice was unmistakable. It was none other than Lord Williamson.

Emilie could see him trying to free himself from the men that held him back, and in his struggle, he ended up in her line of vision.

He was soaking wet. His usually immaculate hair looked

messy, and his shiny boots splashed against the tile when he moved. Lord Williamson's face was contorted with anger and his furious eyes set on Evan.

She attempted to sneak back into the room before being seen.

"Emilie?"

Realizing that she couldn't hide anymore, Emilie reluctantly stepped into the hallway and became self-conscious.

Emilie knew she must look flushed from the whiskey she'd been drinking, and her hair was a wet mess from all the times she'd touched it. Without the towel around her back covering her chest, Emilie was sure she looked as if she'd been behaving indecently.

"You bastard!" Lord Williamson yelled as he tried to hold Evan by the collar. Mr. Talbot and Mr. Reeves came forward to restrain him. "How dare you? How dare you do that to her?"

She was startled by his outburst against Evan, but his indignant cry brought her back to her senses and made her remember that *Lord Williamson believed Evan was her lover!*

Emilie didn't want him to disclose that in front of Evan, so she quickly made her way toward them in an attempt to stop him from saying anything else.

"Is anything the matter?" She asked with as much serenity as she could, standing next to Evan. "I could hear screaming all the way to the study."

"Yes!" Lord Williamson exclaimed, adjusting his jacket and looking with disgust at the men surrounding him. "You shouldn't be here with him. I just found out that he moved in next to you. You shouldn't allow him such liberties."

"Lord Williamson, it's your behavior that I find improper," Emilie chided.

"I'll escort you back to your aunt. You shouldn't be here by yourself."

"I assure you, I couldn't be safer anywhere else," she said.

"Now, if you'll excuse us, the duke and I have private matters to discuss."

Before Emilie could go back to the study, Lord Williamson lifted his arm as if to grab her, but Evan stepped in front of her so quickly that it forced Lord Williamson to stumble back.

"Emilie, wait! I've been visiting your house all week. I have something to tell you. I broke my engagement to Anne Marie," Lord Williamson announced, trying to push Evan aside. "We're not getting married anymore. I know it was a mistake. Please, forgive me."

She didn't know what to feel. Emilie suspected the whiskey was starting to have an effect on her because her mind wasn't working as fast as usual.

"Lord Williamson," she started, moving away from Evan's shadow so she could see him clearly. "I don't care whether you marry her or not."

"Talbot, please escort Lord Williamson outside," Evan instructed.

"I'm not done yet. Emilie, we need to talk, I'll come again soon," Lord Williamson said, narrowing his eyes.

"Please don't. I don't have anything else to say to you."

Evan turned to her and put his hand on her back.

"Don't worry. You can go back to the study for now," he told her. "I'll send a tray of food and some strong tea." His voice was gentle, a whisper meant only for her.

"Thank you, Duke."

Emilie headed back to the study, wanting to put as much distance away from them as she could. She wanted to be faster than the tears threatening to fall down her face.

The last thing Emilie heard before she walked into the study was Lord Williamson calling her name, shouting the words that Emilie had hoped she could hear one day.

CHAPTER 37

Evan was furious. He wanted to punch Williamson in the face.

"Don't embarrass yourself," Evan said, forcing himself to hide his anger.

Williamson looked at him with fire in his eyes.

"This is between Emilie and me, Rowlings. Stay out of it."

"According to Emilie, there's nothing between you and her. The note I sent you said to meet me this afternoon. It wasn't an invitation for you to barge in whenever you wanted."

"I don't care about your note. I won't let you take advantage of her like this."

"No," Evan said with an amused smile. "It's me that'll stop you from taking advantage of her."

When Evan had sent the note to his lawyer to schedule an appointment with Williamson for that afternoon, he had wanted to ask Williamson about any documents his cousin might have left behind. Anything that would give him a clue about the note Evan had found in the book.

He had also secretly hoped Williamson would be annoyed about Evan being her new neighbor.

It had gone better than he had planned. Especially when Emilie had showed up looking so deliciously flushed.

"Your arrogance will get the best of you one day, Rowlings."

"Before you leave," Evan said. "The reason I wanted to see you is that I need to know if my cousin gave you anything in the days previous to his departure."

"He didn't," Williamson answered with a scowl. "Why? Have you found anything? The chief told me the investigation was still in progress."

"It is, but I need you to think about the days before my cousin left. Did you notice anything strange? Did he receive any letters or meet with anyone?"

"No."

"Are you sure you're not missing anything? Think, this is important."

"Look, Rowlings," Williamson sneered. "I work for your cousin, not for you."

"Actually, you work for me now."

"What are you talking about?"

Williamson looked as if Evan had punched him in the stomach.

"Now that my cousin has disappeared, and I've been forced to come back, I'll be returning to my original duties."

"Why am I only hearing about this now?"

"Because now I need you to answer my questions." Evan raised his brows.

"I usually go through the correspondence first," Williamson grounded through clenched teeth. "And there wasn't anything unusual."

"You've been working for us for a while now," Evan started, watching him closely. "Ever since my cousin took pity on you."

"Be careful with what you say, Rowlings," Williamson warned, his fits rounded at his sides. "I have great respect for your cousin, but don't expect me to extend the same to you."

"My cousin went against the rules. By taking you in, he put

your life in danger," Evan pointed out. "A manager for the assets of the Organization. You work for it, but you can't be a part of it. That's what he said."

There was sweat at the edge of Williamson's forehead, and the color had disappeared from his previous flush.

"Lord Hardingham saved my life and I owe him. If I hadn't met him during that trip abroad, I would have died." Williamson looked at him with aristocratic arrogance. "I know that honor is not something you understand."

Evan looked at Talbot and Reeves. They hadn't moved an inch from their spots and were observing him with tension. His eyes met Talbot's. They had heard the story before.

Williamson had fallen victim to a vicious Haunter, one that Evan's cousin had been in the process of hunting. After that, Williamson had offered his services as an impoverished lord whose family had been struggling for years due to his father's mismanagement of their fortune.

"I was grateful," Williamson continued with a faraway look in his eyes. "Even though I still can't understand what happened, I know that what I felt was real."

In Evan's opinion, his cousin hadn't dealt with the situation as he should have. That he had chosen to involve a nonhunter had always baffled him.

"There's a reason we've been doing things like this for so long. A reason the Organization has been kept a secret," Evan said. "It's not a matter of admittance. You should know that by now. The ones who become a part of it are born with the ability to see and detect the unnatural. Their skills and abilities are honed since an early age. Hunters are trained once they reached the age of twenty. Lives depend on it. Theirs and yours."

"I know that. You don't have to remind me every time we meet."

"My cousin always assured me that he trusted you." Williamson's face relaxed. "But I can't say the same."

His cousin had always assured him that Williamson wasn't

aware of more than he should. But Evan's time spent abroad had taught him to always be on guard and to stay suspicious of others.

"Lord Hardingham unexpectedly decided to go back to his family home in the country," Williamson said. "He said he would return in a few days, but he didn't tell me his reason for going, just that he had to go see the property."

"Anything else?" Evan asked.

"No, we mostly talked about the properties I'm overseeing. Anything else is not part of our usual conversations." After a moment, Williamson added, "Do you...do you think Lord Hardingham's gone?"

Evan snapped his attention back to him.

"I don't know. Do you?"

"I'm serious, Rowlings. No one is telling me what's happening. I've spent the last ten years working with him. I deserve to know."

"In that case, you better hope you told me everything," Evan said with a quiet voice. "Otherwise, I'll hold you accountable for it."

"You arrogant bastard." Williamson shook his head as he turned to leave. "You give me another reason to make sure Emilie stays away from you."

"I'll make sure to let her know."

Evan watched as Williamson rushed out the door with Talbot and Reeves following close behind.

Emilie and her aunt were his responsibility while Lord Arundel took care of the Haunters situation back at the Grand House.

He hoped that Lord Arundel would be able to contain the threat. If Evan had to leave the city, it would put Emilie in danger.

Evan couldn't risk leaving her under any circumstances, and the sooner Williamson got used to it, the safer it'd be for him.

Emilie was finishing her cup of tea when Evan walked into the room.

"Are you feeling better?" he asked her while taking a seat in front of her. "It'll be a miracle if you don't end up with a hangover for the rest of the day, since you so freely helped yourself to one of my strongest whiskies."

"I'm fine; I'm just tired. After what happened last night, I couldn't sleep."

"Em..." Evan trailed off, reaching across the desk toward her hands.

She moved them to her lap.

Emilie didn't want to ask what had taken him so long, not when it probably had something to do with Lord Williamson and his outburst that he loved her.

Embarrassment prevented her from looking him in the eyes. She felt vulnerable; as if a part of her had been exposed.

"I'm not done asking questions," Emilie spoke, suddenly standing up. "But I think I've had enough for now and I should probably go back to my aunt."

"I'll walk you," he said, moving around the desk. "I think the rain has finally stopped."

Evan put his coat around her shoulders. She was startled by his gesture, but she accepted it and pulled it closer to her body.

The house was quiet when they exited the study. Emilie couldn't see the men anymore, and she couldn't help but look toward the spot where Lord Williamson had stood.

They went out through the backyard in silence. Droplets of water fell into their faces as the gloomy sky began to clear. Before she walked past the gate, Emilie did something on impulse that took her by surprise.

She turned and embraced Evan.

"Could you be my friend for a minute?" Emilie asked as she rubbed her cheek against the fabric of his shirt.

She wasn't sure why she was hugging him. Maybe the alcohol was lowering her guard.

Being close to him was bringing back all kinds of feelings and memories of their time together. Emilie missed the days before everything had changed.

He hugged her back without saying a word.

After a moment, she moved away from his arms and removed the coat from her shoulders.

"Thank you," Emilie said, handing it to him while avoiding his eyes.

"You're welcome, darling," Evan replied, taking the coat. As their hands touched, he reached for her face with the other. "Em..."

"Goodbye, Duke," Emilie interrupted him. She turned and crossed the fence toward her house.

Emilie didn't look back; she couldn't. It might be safer for everyone around her if she went as far away as she could and was glad she had started to plan her trip.

Hours later, after Emilie had taken a hot bath and asked Margaret how the packing of their luggage was going, she had felt the sudden need to find comfort on looking at the things from her past.

The chest in front of her bed was full of things Emilie hadn't used since her arrival—there hadn't been any need for them in the city—and soon, they had been forgotten in exchange for the dresses her aunt had insisted she wore.

The only thing Emilie had kept on wearing was the necklace with the small ruby stone that she'd had for as long as she could remember. Emilie was sure it had been a gift from Evan when they were children, but she had gotten so used to wearing it that she no longer associated it with him. She would occasionally wear it and only take it off whenever she had to dress for a party or dinner.

As Emilie stared at the old pants and shirts that she used to wear on her hunting excursions back at the Grand House, a realization dawned on her.

Two, in fact.

The first one was that she had remembered where she'd seen one of those books on Evan's desk.

The second one made her so mad that she wanted to take out the wrapped rifles at the bottom of the chest and go knock on her new neighbor's front door.

Emilie had caught Evan on his lie.

CHAPTER 39

The sun wasn't out yet, but Emilie could hear the sound of birds outside. She could already tell it was going to be another rainy day. Dark clouds extended as far as she could see from the window of her room.

Emilie had gone to bed angry at the new discovery of Evan's deception, and it had caused her to have a rough night full of disturbing dreams.

She had dreamed of the past, of when she was a little girl and had gone to a forest with Evan. They had been hiding from someone, but the stranger had found them. Emilie had seen Evan's parents running toward them in the distance, before everything turned black.

The next thing she remembered, Emilie was with her parents and they were telling her something important. Something that felt so right and natural that Emilie couldn't believe she had forgotten.

When she had woken up, Emilie couldn't remember what they had told her, and again, guilt had invaded her as it usually did whenever Emilie had the dream.

Was she the culprit behind his parents' deaths? Was Emilie the reason Evan had grown up without them? Her scar hurt every time she had that dream and she often wondered if it was because the dream was a memory of when she had gotten the scar.

Emilie quickly changed her clothes while thinking about all the events that had happened in the past week.

She had no idea how Lord Williamson had found out that Evan had moved in next to her, and worried that perhaps the wrong person had seen Evan leaving her house and that the gossip had already begun to spread.

Also, how had Evan known so many details about her relationship with Lord Williamson after being gone for so long? It was something Emilie hadn't put too much thought into until the previous night, when she started thinking about all of the possible things he could be lying about.

The list of what she didn't know was getting too long for her liking, and it was all somehow connected to Evan.

Emilie moved next to the open chest in front of her bed and bent over it.

She began to turn over the clothes until she reached the bottom, where her favorite weapons rested wrapped in fine silk. Aunt Augustine would faint if she saw Emilie with the weapons, but they were a reminder that tied her to her past.

She took out one of her small guns and placed it inside one of her purses. It might be a good idea to carry one with her until the danger in the area settled down.

Emilie then set out to find the book that might solve the first of the mysteries. She had seen similar books among her parent's belongings back at the Grand House, but this one in particular looked like the one on Evan's study.

The book she remembered was among the things she had brought when she moved to the city. It was old and had a weird engraving with a lock on the front.

Emilie was unsure about how it'd ended up with her clothes, but she had discovered it at the bottom of her mother's chest when she had moved to the city. Since Emilie hadn't been able to open the book, she hadn't bothered with it.

That chest was now stored at the back of her dressing room; the book had to be in there. She hadn't had any use for it.

The pale blue chest with bronze locks was easy to find. She opened it, but it was filled with blankets. Emilie dug around the corners to the bottom, but all she could feel was soft fabric.

Emilie rang for Margaret, and in a few minutes, the maid was at the door.

"Margaret, do you know what happened to the book that was inside my mother's old luggage?"

"A book? The chest was empty when Lady Augustine asked me to store the linens."

"Thank you, Margaret. That'll be all."

Emilie didn't know what to think.

Had her aunt taken the book? She didn't understand what would have been the purpose. Emilie wouldn't have bothered with it if it weren't for Evan's reaction.

Now, with the possibility of her aunt taking it, she felt even more intrigued.

Evan and her aunt seemed to be making the effort of keeping books out of her way. She had to find out the reason why.

Since his return, everything seemed to be falling out of place; some things more than others.

After waking up from the dream, Emilie had kept tossing on her bed and asking herself if she had actually had a conversation with Os before coming to the conclusion that she had.

She didn't know if it was a good or a bad thing, but it was time to start putting things in order.

Emilie would search every place where her aunt could have possibly stashed the book. The only place she wouldn't need to look was the library, since Emilie knew every book on those shelves.

She wanted to find out what the mystery was about.

Emilie headed down the stairs, careful to avoid anyone on

her way, and crossed the hall toward the study; she would quickly look for the book there.

Walking directly toward the shelves in the back of the room, she scanned for books, but there weren't that many, and none of them were the one she was looking for.

Emilie moved toward the desk, opening drawers without success. She looked through the books and papers on top of it, wanting to be thorough before leaving the room.

Unfortunately, what Emilie found there gave her no other option but to question her existence up until that moment.

CHAPTER 40

Evan had to accept Emilie had been clever, but the way Williamson had behaved the previous day had given him some insight.

She had told him that Williamson had been asking questions about her lover and how he had insisted on knowing his identity. Evan also remembered Emilie's reaction when she'd seen Williamson and how she had rushed over when he had accused Evan of taking advantage of her.

He smiled with satisfaction at his new discovery.

Like he had suspected, Emilie didn't have a lover. The only lover she had, according to Williamson, was Evan, and that conclusion suited him just fine.

He'd been on edge since he had read the note the creature had sent her two nights ago. This turn of events had improved his mood, and it had soothed the hunter inside of him.

His discovery had stayed with him while Evan gave instructions to his men and while he visited the posts to inspect the wall surrounding the city.

It gave him time to wonder why Williamson had chosen Anne Marie over Emilie when he'd had the opportunity to marry the perfect woman.

Of course, the idiot was regretting it now.

Evan was well acquainted with regret for different reasons and had vowed never to be an idiot again.

He clenched his fists. The feeling of her body inside his arms, of her face pressing lightly against his chest, was a constant reminder he couldn't let go of.

Evan had missed it.

He had been surprised when Emilie had hugged him. And, now, a part of him long forgotten was calling out to him, asking him to remember.

Evan knew Emilie had probably acted that way because of the whisky, but her words were the ones giving him pause.

He wasn't her friend anymore, and Evan could never be that again.

His return wouldn't have happened if it weren't for the Haunter and the news of his cousin.

Evan would have gone on living the rest of his life while fighting the need to see her, to touch her, just as he had been doing all of those years.

Through his men, Evan would have ensured that Emilie was safe and that she would never be found. He'd have made sure that she could live the life her parents had wanted for her.

A loud noise nearby interrupted his thoughts, and he immediately rushed through the door of the study.

There was a commotion at the end of the hall, and Evan ran in that direction. Once there, he saw his butler coming from the backyard.

"Your Grace, we're under attack," the always stoic butler said without a tremble in his voice.

CHAPTER 41

Emilie found an unfinished letter in Aunt Augustine's handwriting addressed to her uncle, dated the previous day. She wouldn't have given it a second thought if it weren't for her aunt's resistance to talk about his letter to her.

The first part consisted of all the usual greetings. It was in the second paragraph where things got confusing; Emilie had to rest against the chair as the words sunk in.

I'm worried about Emilie. If it wasn't for Evan, I don't know if the Haunter would have gotten her. Do you think it's the same as the one that attacked her when she was a child? I don't know what I would have done if he hadn't returned, especially with you unable to come to us.

I'm extremely grateful that Evan's back. I trust he will do everything in his power to keep Emilie safe. But I'm worried that she won't accept what we tell her, and that one day, our chance to explain ourselves to her will be gone.

I can only hope that Evan stays by her side and that soon we will call him our nephew.

I hope that Emilie never finds out about the Haunters. There's still a chance for my poor sister's wish to be fulfilled.

I truly hope that everyone is safe and that the Haunters are not invading the Grand House's territory. Please, be careful and don't worry about us. With Evan next to us, nothing will harm us.

Her aunt hadn't signed it yet and would probably return to finish it.

Everyone kept saying she was in danger, and after her encounter with the shadow, it was becoming clear that she might be.

Emilie could only assume, according to the letter, that what she had met was a Haunter.

She'd thought she had finally made progress and gotten Evan to tell her what was happening—that her involvement had been clarified and that the secrets had been revealed—only to realize that there was more; that Evan had been hiding something else, as if finding out the truth about Os hadn't been enough.

Evan kept lying to her.

Why would he write to her uncle that she was in danger if Emilie hadn't even received the threatening note until after they had sent the letters to Uncle Winston?

Now, Aunt Augustine was writing to her uncle about these Haunters. By *attack*... had she been referring to the dream Emilie kept on having of hiding in the forest with Evan? Was that what had been following them when they were children? Was the dream a memory after all?

There were too many questions that Emilie didn't have an answer to.

Shivers went down her back, and the pain on her scar became stronger and almost unbearable. Almost as strong as when she had encountered the shadow.

Fear crept down her body and settled on her stomach.

Even her aunt was aware that Emilie was in some sort of danger. She recalled her aunt's reaction when Evan had told them about the attack near their house, and how she had agreed to receive his help without hesitation.

Emilie also wondered what was happening back at the Grand House. Evan had avoided telling her what he knew, and now

Aunt Augustine was worried about Uncle Winston being in danger.

It was clear everyone was hiding something from her.

What annoyed her the most was that it all seemed to come back to Evan. He had lied every time, even though there had been plenty of opportunities to be honest with her.

Emilie had a right to know. Her life seemed to be the one in danger, after all.

She had hated when Evan had disappeared without explaining himself, leaving her behind with a broken heart. But now, Evan seemed to think that he had the right to reappear after ten years, take control of her life, and keep her in the dark about everything.

He claimed he had made promises to her parents, but Evan had also made promises to her, and he had broken those.

He must believe she was stupid.

Reading her aunt's letter increased her determination to find the book. Even if it wasn't anything useful, Emilie wouldn't stop until she had it.

It had become a matter of principle.

She wouldn't confront her aunt about the letter yet. But she would ask her about the book and observe her reaction.

Emilie looked through the rest of the papers on the desk in search of her uncle's letter, but when she couldn't find it anywhere, Emilie put her aunt's unfinished letter back in its place.

She had just left the study when a loud noise startled her to a stop. It had sounded like thunder. Emilie stood in the hall for a few seconds, trying to soothe the pressure in her chest.

Entering the foyer, Emilie saw Evan's men running toward the backyard. Not wanting to stay behind, alarmed by the urgency they were displaying, she followed them.

Margaret and her brother, Julian, stood in the hall near the backyard.

They whispered and pointed toward the back, behind the

trees and rose bushes, but Emilie couldn't see what they were pointing at.

"What happened?" Emilie asked when she approached them.

"My lady, we don't know, but it appears that something crashed against the wall," Margaret said nervously.

"The wall? But there isn't a street behind it, only an alley. Could a carriage have lost control?"

The siblings looked at each other.

"I saw what happened from the upstairs window." Margaret hesitated, exchanging glances with her brother. "There wasn't any carriage. I...I think it just exploded."

"I'm sure there's an explanation for it," Emilie reassured her with a smile while touching the maid's hand lightly. "I'll find out if there was an accident."

Emilie knew Margaret didn't tend to be superstitious and that the young maid was rather pragmatic. Pushing away her fear, Emilie clutched her purse holding the small gun, and moved away from the siblings to scan the area.

The sky was still full of dark clouds, but the ground was dry and there weren't any signs of rain.

She could see that Mr. Talbot was already standing near the back wall of her house with Mr. Alcott and another man she had never seen before. The dust from the crash obscured the scene, but she could also see that her butler stood nearby.

Emilie rubbed the pain on her chest. It wasn't a strong as it had been a few minutes ago.

She was about to walk toward Mr. Larson when Evan approached him with his butler following behind.

They exchanged a few words before Evan disappeared into the dust, leaving the older men behind.

Emilie approached them, and as she got closer, she saw that a big portion of the back wall had fallen. Almost all of it.

She stopped in awe and took in the magnitude of the chaos the collapse had created.

The cawing of the crows called her attention. They rested in the small fence between the two houses and behaved as if they were also curious about the scene.

Movement caught her attention once again. Emilie hadn't noticed that the big wolf was also there, walking among the men as he sniffed the scattered piles of bricks.

She walked toward the butlers and stood next to them.

"I've never seen these many crows before," Emilie commented pointing at the small fence before turning to point at the bricks in the ground. "It's going to take a few days to clear that mess."

"My-my lady," Mr. Larson stuttered.

"Why is there a hole in the wall?" she asked, feeling surprisingly calm.

Her eyes wouldn't stop tracking the wolf. If something was truly after her, every one of them could be in danger just by being in the same place as her.

"We don't know yet, my lady," her butler said. Mr. Larson looked nervous. "The men are still investigating."

"His Grace is personally taking care of it, my lady. He'll let you know as soon as he finds out what happened," Evan's butler added.

Emilie looked at both men. They looked tense. She nodded in understanding and turned to walk toward Evan and his men.

"My lady, it might not be safe to go near them."

"Don't worry, Mr. Larson," Emilie said, looking at them over her shoulder and trying to control the fear that had settled on her stomach. Even though the pain in her chest still bothered her, she tried to ignore it. "Os will let me know if it's not safe."

She saw the butlers frowning before she turned to walk away.

Emilie was beginning to wonder if anyone else could see the big black wolf in her backyard. With everyone being so calm at having him there, she wasn't sure they could.

CHAPTER 42

At the sound of steps, Evan looked up and cursed.

He was furious. His distraction had caused him to not feel the creature on time. It had fled as soon as the wall had fallen, not giving them enough time to stop it.

Os had felt its presence right before the explosion occurred, but it had been too late.

"Emilie," he said with a frown. "You shouldn't be here."

Evan walked toward her in an attempt to prevent her from getting any closer to the nonexistent wall. The energy coming from the hole was enough indication that it had been created by the unnatural.

It was clear to him that the Haunter was mocking them.

"How did this happen?"

"We don't know yet," Evan replied, looking over his shoulder. "We're still investigating. When was the last time you had the wall inspected?"

The Haunter had gotten this close to the property without being detected by anyone or stopped by the safeguards in the area. Evan had just reinforced them earlier that night, and they had already been compromised.

There could only be one possible explanation; something he

had hoped wouldn't be the case. But his instincts were never wrong.

He couldn't wait anymore.

"I'll walk you back. The wall is still unstable. It'd be best for everyone to stay inside."

Emilie ignored him and kept marching toward the piles of bricks on the ground, leaving him no choice but to fall into step with her.

"Listen to me, Em," he said, hearing the impatience in his voice. "You shouldn't be here."

But Emilie kept stubbornly silent and instead continued walking in the direction of the hole, pushing his limit with every step she took. She turned to him with a serious face.

"Don't lie to me, Evan. Margaret saw what happened. She said it looked as if the wall had exploded."

"That doesn't make any sense," he deflected, stopping himself from stuttering.

"Nothing concerning you makes any sense," Emilie accused with narrowed eyes.

She stopped at the end of the backyard where the wall had stood, and Evan grabbed her arm before she could go into the street.

"You better stay inside. There's nothing for you to do here. Go back."

"Don't tell me what to do," Emilie said, freeing her arm. "This is my house, after all. If anything, I'm the one in charge of finding out what happened to the wall and getting it fixed."

"Don't worry," Evan grounded through clenched teeth. "Talbot knows someone who can fix it."

They stood in front of each other, inches apart. Evan could feel everyone's eyes on them as Emilie and him glared at each other.

"We'll pay for it," Emilie finally said as she turned to walk away from him. "Have the bill sent to us."

He was surprised and relieved that she had given up. Evan

almost just stood there watching her leave before he began walking after her.

"How do you feel?" he asked. "You must be having a hard time after that night."

"I'm fine. I'm going back inside. You don't have to follow me."

"I'll walk you back."

"Your men need you," Emilie said, but he kept walking next to her. "Besides, you need to keep me safe, don't you? And that doesn't look like it's going to keep anyone safe."

She pointed out to the street where Evan could see curious people passing by and glancing in their direction.

"I'll have it fixed right away."

Emilie nodded. She suddenly stopped when they were about to reach the house and leaned toward him.

"Perhaps," Emilie began, her hand brushing lightly against the dust in his chest. "You should also think of an excuse about how the wall fell. I'll ask Mr. Larson to have some sausages ready for Os."

She turned and walked away without a second glance, but Evan watched her go with narrowed eyes and a racing heart.

CHAPTER 43

"*It's obvious*," a voice in his head said as Evan stared at Emilie entering the house.

"Please, enlighten me," Evan drawled, turning back to the wall.

Os sat in front of him.

"*You're obsessed with her. I can see it all over you. I've never seen you so alive before.*"

"Anything else?" Evan asked with a clenched jaw.

"*Yes.*" Os wandered toward the softest-looking patch of grass and lay down on it. "*She's not interested.*"

"Yeah, well, at least I don't scare her like you do," Evan grumbled, turning away.

"*You need to keep an eye on her. She's changing. Haven't you noticed? Something in her is different. Whatever was holding her back is getting loose.*"

"What do you mean?" Evan said with a frown as he observed the destroyed wall in front of them. He hoped it could be built back up in a couple of days.

"*I also think she likes me. She's always giving me sausages,*" Os said, and Evan could hear a yawn. "*I saved her, after all.*"

"You vain little..." Evan started, turning back to the wolf.

He had no other option but to swallow his words. The spirit was already gone.

"I hate when you do that," he muttered, hoping that no one had noticed the exchange.

Now, Evan was sure Os kept disappearing just to annoy him.

CHAPTER 44

Emilie met her aunt at the stairs. She looked nervous, and her clothes were in disarray.

"What happened?" Aunt Augustine asked. "What was that infernal noise that woke me up?"

"The backyard wall fell down."

"Oh, dear Lord!"

"Don't worry, the duke is already taking care of it. He said he's going to have it fixed for us soon."

"Oh, I'm so relieved! I don't know what we would have done if the duke wasn't here."

"You keep saying that, but why couldn't Uncle Winston send any of his men?"

Emilie thought she could catch her aunt off guard, but instead, Aunt Augustine looked calmer than Emilie had expected.

"They're all busy at the moment, dear. I'll go outside to take a closer look."

Emilie let her go without another word. Making sure no one was around, she walked toward her aunt's room.

She never thought she would have to resort to this, but

Emilie didn't have any other option. It was the only other place where she thought the book could be.

With quick steps, Emilie went inside her aunt's room and directly toward the vanity, where she looked through the drawers without success. Moving to the closet, she sorted through the things in there, but the book wasn't in any of those places.

Emilie was about to give up when she noticed a box at the bottom of the closet.

She opened the lid and found a few random objects inside, and under everything, something that felt like a book.

Emilie pulled it out, but it wasn't the book she remembered. It was a small journal, and it, too, had a lock. With a sigh, she started to put it back, but then noticed something else. Reaching for it, Emilie uncovered it from under the pile and discovered the book she had been looking for.

Her excitement died when she realized the book still had a lock. It wasn't a regular lock either; it was inlaid in the cover and had an irregular shape. The center of the lock was deep and it had a small space on either sides of it. It looked like it was big enough to fit a gem and something else. Like a gem on a ring.

The ring that Evan always wore and that was similar to her father's ring—the one now in possession of her uncle—came to mind.

If only she could borrow it from Evan to put her theory to the test, Emilie could try unlocking the book. Did Evan ever take it off? She had never seen him without it.

Placing the tome aside, she returned the box to its place before marching to her room with her new possession.

Emilie locked the door behind her and sat down at the vanity, observing the book in front of her.

It was old and potentially fragile, with leather bindings. It also had some strange carvings on the leather on each side, but there wasn't any indication of what sort of book it was.

She ran the tips of her fingers around the insides of the lock, caressing the unfamiliar shape that Emilie now was sure was the same shape as the ring Evan wore.

There was something different about the book, and it sent shivers down her spine as she stared at it.

Emilie rose from her seat, leaving the book on the vanity, and walked toward the window.

There was a limited view of the street from where she stood, and she could mostly only see the side of Evan's house.

As she stared out of the window, a chilly breeze came through. Her chest had been aching and the pain seemed to have gotten more intense, but Emilie welcomed the relaxing scenery. The weather was changing, and winter would be there soon.

She observed the people walking down the street. Emilie could hear birds chirping nearby, adding a relaxing quality to the whole scene.

Life had turned out to be nothing like she had expected. She had never considered that one day she would become a spinster. And now, as if her situation hadn't been tragic enough, Emilie had become a spinster in danger.

Thinking about her situation seemed to have made the pain on her chest even worse. She pushed against the windowsill to go back to the book, but something outside caught her attention.

Before, with all the people walking past, a man standing across from her window a few hundred feet away from her house had caught her attention for a moment.

Now, that same man was looking directly in her direction, startling her. Emilie hadn't thought she could be seen from where she stood.

The man wore a hat, and she didn't have a clear vision of his face, but there was something unnervingly familiar about the figure.

Her breath caught as Emilie stared at him, transfixed as the man slowly raised his head, allowing her an unobstructed view of his face.

The stranger smiled and tapped his hat before turning and walking away.

It took her a few seconds to overcome her shock enough to step away from the window. She stood in the middle of the room, asking herself if what she had seen was real.

Book long forgotten, Emilie left her room in a rush, running down the stairs.

Her aunt was returning from the backyard when Emilie reached the last step.

"Where's the duke?"

"Slow down, my dear. You shouldn't be running. He's outside, but I think he's returning to his house to send for the man who will fix the wall."

Emilie ran out as fast as she could. She scanned the yard and saw Evan approaching his house. She ran toward the small dividing fence as she called after him.

"Evan!" At the sound of her voice, everyone looked back at her. Emilie felt relieved that she wouldn't have to chase after him.

"Em, what's the matter?" he asked as she tried to slow down her breaths. There was a worried expression on his face.

"I just saw your cousin," Emilie panted, trying to swallow the lump that had formed in her throat.

It might be better to cancel her travel plans for the moment.

CHAPTER 45

"Where did you see him?" Evan asked.

"Through my window, he was standing across the street," Emilie said. He could see she was trying to catch her breath. "I couldn't see his face clearly, but he looked in my direction and smiled."

Everyone was searching for him, and there he was, looking up at people's windows as if nothing was the matter.

"Are you sure it was him?"

"Yes, I recognized Lord Hardingham right away," Emilie told him, clutching her purse against her chest. "It hasn't been that long since the last time I saw him; a few weeks at most."

"How did he look?"

"The same; although, his appearance...he looked different. His clothes weren't his usual style, and he didn't look dirty, but the smile he gave me was odd. Lord Hardingham recognized me, I think. I don't know why he walked away when you're looking for him."

Evan tried to contain his expression as best as he could. He didn't want to scare her or show her that something was wrong.

He tried to relax his hands at his sides, but he knew he was failing when Emilie looked at him with a worried expression. Evan signaled Talbot, who immediately walked in their direction.

"It *was* your cousin, right?" Emilie asked with a frown, looking back at the men standing near the wall.

The men were glancing in their direction, and Evan knew they were waiting for his signal.

"You're the one who saw him. Are you sure it was him?"

He saw her hesitation.

"I know it was him," Emilie confirmed with a firm voice.

"Did you see in which direction he went?"

"He walked toward the corner, but I couldn't see much from my window after that."

Talbot nodded at Evan and signaled Alcott to go with him. The two men stalked off in the direction of the street.

"Are they going to look for him?"

"They're going to search the area. Thank you for letting me know; at least now we know he's alive, if it was him."

"Lord Hardingham must know you've been looking for him, especially since he came all the way here to find you. I should have told him not to leave, but I was too startled when I saw him."

"No!" Evan exclaimed, and she looked at him with surprise. "I don't want you to go near him if you see him again. Instead, come to me right away like you did today."

"Why not? And I thought I had made it clear to you to stop giving me orders."

"I'm sorry. I didn't mean it as an order; I'm just concerned."

Evan noticed she kept rubbing the same spot on her chest as her expression softened. Her temper seemed to be rising more easily these days than before.

"We don't know what is going on with him," Evan explained, trying to keep his voice restrained and serene. "Like you said, it's weird that he didn't come to us instead of leaving."

"Are you saying he might be dangerous? But he's your cousin!"

"We'll find out. I have to go now, but please, stay inside until the wall is fixed." Evan hoped Emilie wouldn't argue. He was anxious to go after his men.

"Let me know if you find him."

Evan nodded and immediately crossed the small fence. His butler, Mr. Gidley, was already in the hall giving orders to one of the maids.

He knew the only man outside at that moment had been Reeves, the young agent. If the Haunter had been nearby, Reeves had probably encountered it.

"Did anything happen to Reeves?" Evan asked, walking faster down the hall.

"He was attacked," the butler replied. "Fortunately Mr. Reeves is still alive, but he's struggling. Mr. Talbot brought him inside before they left. We put him in the room next to the foyer."

Evan walked into the room. There were already two other maids inside; one of them put cold compresses on the man's forehead while the other tried to hold him down.

When Reeves saw Evan, he attempted to sit. Evan moved next to him with a couple of strides.

"Your Grace, I'm sorry," Reeves said in a rough whisper. "I tried to stop him."

The young man's eyes were unfocused, and he looked like he had a fever. The bastard liked going after the young ones.

"We'll talk later. You need to rest now." Evan turned to the maids. "Leave the room."

The butler waited for the maids to step outside before closing the door after them. Once they were gone, Evan reached for the ring in his left hand and connected the ruby stone to the one on the young man's finger.

It would take a long time to heal him, but he was relieved that there was still something Evan could do to save him.

The life energy the Haunter had taken from the young agent

was beginning to affect him. Reeves looked like he had lost twenty pounds in just a few minutes.

The energy Evan was channeling began to bring color back to the agent's face, until the man slowly fell asleep. It'd be better for him to recuperate while he was unconscious. Evan knew Reeves would feel weak for a couple of weeks until his energy fully returned, but at least he would live.

He stepped back to let him sleep. The questions could wait.

Evan walked outside the room and toward the foyer with the butler following after him.

"Wait here, Mr. Gidley."

The butler nodded, and Evan marched through the front door before he let his anger out.

He'd hoped his cousin's fate would have been different, but Evan had been a fool for hoping otherwise. All it had taken was for Emilie to see him to fully destroy his foolish hope.

It explained some things, but not all of them. Evan knew it had to be the reason the Haunter was so hard to track.

Even at that moment, he could barely detect any traces.

"Os, where the hell are you?" Evan muttered to himself as he stomped down the front steps.

"*Who do you think saved him?*" a voice grunted in his head, startling him.

Evan hid his surprise and turned to Os, who stood next to him.

"You need to stop acting by yourself," Evan said. "And start telling me what's happening."

"*We have an agreement, but don't push it,*" Os snarled and showed his fangs. "*You know I don't have to save any of your people. Don't expect me to do it again. I've missed my sausages. Get me some.*"

Evan was starting to get a headache.

"Stop making me look like a crazy person," Evan said as he noticed a man walking past the gate and glancing in his direction. "Did you go after him? Did you find him?"

This hadn't been the same as the first attack that had led to the death of his agent. At the time, Evan had felt the creature right away. The Haunter must not have been using his cousin back then.

"*I don't need to go after him,*" Os said with a lazy yawn. "*You know he'll be back. After all, what he wants is still here.*"

"You call it *he*. Who is he?" Evan asked. He looked around and noticed he was alone. "Why do I bother?"

Evan was itching to go after his cousin, but he couldn't leave the house yet; not until his men returned. Not with a wall destroyed and an agent down.

He paced across the yard until Talbot and Alcott returned. Their faces showed grim expressions.

"We couldn't track him," Talbot spoke. "There was a faint trace, but it didn't take us far. It dispersed after half a mile."

Evan cursed under his breath.

"The bastard is using him to hide from us. Where did you find Reeves?"

"Os was with him. Reeves was lying with half of his body outside the gate," Talbot answered. "If the Haunter was standing across the street, Reeves must have thought it was your cousin. It didn't even have to get near him."

"We need to let the other agents know," Evan said, trying to keep his voice steady. "I'll do the rounds today. I don't want anyone getting caught by surprise."

"Do you want me to go with you?"

"No," Evan said firmly. "There's enough going on in here, and I'd rather be the one running into the bastard. Make sure your contact fixes the wall today. We already know what to expect. I'll put extra safeguards, but I'm not sure they will affect it."

"I'll prepare more charms."

"Make sure Reeves wears his amulet," Evan instructed. "He's going to need all the extra help he can get to heal."

The two agents nodded and briefly looked at each other. Evan knew the men were stepping into unknown territory.

Evan, on the other hand, was ready to take the city apart for as long as it took him. Nothing would stop him from hunting down the bastard.

"Now," Emilie said from the top of the stairs, surprising everyone. "You should come up with an excuse for what I've just heard."

CHAPTER 46

Emilie hadn't meant to spy on Evan and his men.

The appearance of his cousin and the way Evan had reacted had made her uneasy.

She had thought he would be happy with his return, but Evan hadn't seemed surprised or happy when Emilie had told him the news. After all the effort he had put into looking for him, Evan hadn't even appeared relieved to know his cousin was still alive.

Emilie had also felt conflicted. There had been something different about the way Lord Hardingham had looked and acted. It hadn't felt the same.

His behavior had been overly pompous, almost mocking, and the way he had greeted her had been nothing like the last interaction they'd had a couple of weeks before.

Ever since Evan had left, his cousin had behaved coldly toward her—polite, but always keeping her at a distance.

Emilie had never understood why his behavior had changed so much toward her, but that morning had been different. It was odd that he had been so excited to see her, and the uneasiness had stayed with her.

Instead of following Evan to his house, she had walked down the service hall in her house to see if she could find out something of what was going on, and had ended up spying on them, finding out more than Emilie had been looking for.

"What are you doing outside?" Evan asked with an expressionless face.

"I came to find you," she replied, quickly thinking of an excuse. This time she didn't have any good reason besides wanting to know the truth. "Aunt Augustine wants to know if you'd like to come for dinner tonight, but aren't you going to explain what I just heard?"

"There's nothing to explain. Why were you spying on us?"

"I overheard you by accident. And what happened to Mr. Reeves? Where is he?"

"I don't have time for this. You need to return inside. I have to go."

Emilie began to get angry at his dismissive behavior. The pulsing pain in her chest kindled her anger.

"I know you lied to me. I asked you for an honest answer, and you lied to me."

Evan frowned and stalked toward her.

"What are you talking about?"

"Yesterday, in your study," Emilie began, closing the distance between them until she stood in front of him. The small brick wall defining the line of the property prevented her from getting any closer. "You said you told my uncle that I was in danger when you sent him the letters, but how did you know? I hadn't even received the note when you sent them, and then, what I saw the other night..."

Evan cursed. The men behind him stayed quiet.

"I'll come later this afternoon," he said. "We'll talk then."

"At what time shall we expect you?"

"I'll try to be back by sunset. Now, go back inside and stop wandering. Talbot, go with her and make sure she doesn't leave the house anymore."

The man nodded and quickly moved next to her.

The indignation Emilie felt at Evan's arrogance was indescribable. She was furious that she had let herself be concerned and worried about how his cousin's sudden appearance could have affected him.

Evan had even dared to order someone to watch her, as if Emilie would be stupid enough to leave and risk encountering the shadow again. She had been the one facing it, not him.

Mustering all the dignity she could, she rose to her full height. Emilie knew she emanated authority whenever she did that.

"There's no need," she said with a straight back and a voice full of coldness. "I expect to see you later, and this time, I also expect the truth."

Emilie turned and walked away before his man could follow her. Now more than ever, it was clear that the duke would never tell her the whole truth.

CHAPTER 47

Emilie went back inside her house. Her whole body was shaking, and her legs felt weak. They would give out if she didn't sit down soon.

She made her way to their small library, needing the feeling of familiarity and normalcy it brought her. Her aunt was coming down the hall accompanied by Margaret, their only maid, when Emilie reached the door.

"Emilie, I was wondering what took you so long."

She had hoped she would be able to get inside before her aunt saw her.

Aunt Augustine turned to the maid and asked her to bring them tea. Emilie walked inside, resigned to her luck. She had hoped for a moment of peace, since she needed time to think about what was happening.

"Why were you looking for the duke?" Aunt Augustine asked as she entered the room.

"It was nothing," Emilie said, approaching her favorite chair and hoping her aunt wouldn't take too long to leave. "He'll be coming this evening."

"Oh, good!" Aunt Augustine exclaimed, fanning herself. "At least we'll get something good out of the backyard wall falling down. We're so lucky to have the duke as our neighbor. He's such a dear. He personally told me that someone will be coming today to fix the wall and not to worry about anything since his men will be taking care of it."

"We can't just let him decide everything. He just moved in next to us; people must have already started talking."

"Oh, let them talk! I'm sure they wished the duke was paying so much attention to them. He's extremely handsome, and he's newly arrived from his travels. Of course, everyone wants him for their daughters. Have you given any thought about renewing your engagement with him?"

"We were never engaged."

"Oh, you shouldn't be wasting any time! If you don't secure his affection, someone else will. Don't wait until it's too late. You know you're going to regret it if you lose him again."

Her love life was surprisingly the least of her concerns, even though some would argue that without marriage, there was no life for a woman in her position.

Emilie allowed herself to wonder if any of the men she had rejected in the past were glad to see her alone. If they rejoiced at her failed hopes, and if perhaps any of them would try to approach her again.

It didn't matter. There was now something more urgent.

The more Emilie realized that everyone was hiding something from her, the less satisfied she felt with the idea of going on a trip.

She had thought it would give her the independence that she so deeply desired, but now that Emilie was learning that her life was more tied to hidden truths than she could have possibly imagined, her situation was somehow becoming more interesting to her than traveling; especially when the truth became more of a mystery with each passing day.

"Aunt, I've been meaning to ask you," Emilie began, trying to appear unconcerned. "Have you seen a book that was inside of a chest I brought from the Grand House?"

Her aunt looked at her with a perplexed look.

"A book?"

"It had a lock on the front," Emilie said, watching her closely. "The chest was in my room."

"I can't recall. Was it in one of the trunks we used for storage?"

"Yes, there are linens in it now."

"Isn't the book in the library?"

"No, I left it in the chest, but now it's gone. I wanted to know what happened to it."

"Oh, I'm not sure, dear."

At that moment, a knock on the door interrupted them. The maid came inside with the tea, followed by Mr. Larson.

"My lady, the men that will be fixing the wall have arrived. Mr. Talbot is taking them to the backyard."

"What a relief! Did he say how long it would take? It's unsettling to have that hole in the wall for everyone to see. Especially with all the ruffians in the area these days."

"Yes, my lady. Mr. Talbot said it should be done by this afternoon."

"So fast! Thank you, Mr. Larson. Please make sure they get refreshments as they work. Didn't I tell you?" Aunt Augustine turned to Emilie with a pleased sigh. "A man of action is a powerful man. You better get engaged to the duke soon."

CHAPTER 48

Emilie couldn't stop thinking about what Evan had been saying when she'd walked in on them.

He'd been talking about agents, but was he referring to the authorities? It was clear that Evan wanted to go after his cousin, but she couldn't understand the rest of what he had said.

Emilie had also taken some time that afternoon to inspect the book more closely.

After their conversation, she had hoped her aunt wouldn't go looking for it and realize Emilie had taken it. She wanted to keep it hidden for now.

Besides the unusual carvings in the cover, Emilie hadn't found a way to open it, and it was closed too tightly to get a peek at what was inside.

She had given up when she had run out of options.

Emilie changed into her evening gown when it was almost time to meet Evan. She wanted to see with her own eyes if Mr. Reeves was keeping guard outside like he'd been doing these past few days. What Emilie had overhead about him had made her worry.

Making her way down the stairs, she headed toward the front

door. The house was quiet, but when Emilie opened the door, she noticed the street outside was busy.

She looked around and couldn't see anyone, but as soon as she stepped outside, Mr. Talbot came forward.

"Is there anything you need, my lady?" he asked, walking up the stairs.

"Oh!" Emilie exclaimed, surprised. "I just wanted to know if the duke has returned."

"Not yet, Lady Arundel. Do you have a message for him?"

"No, I'll wait for him, but thank you. Where is everyone else?" she inquired, looking around as if expecting them to come out of nowhere. "I wanted to thank you for taking care of the backyard wall. It would have taken us longer to get it fixed if it wasn't for you."

Emilie smiled, her eyes focused on him. She noticed him hesitating for a moment.

"We were only doing our job."

"I'll ask our cook to prepare something special for you tonight. Is there anything in particular you would like?"

She was determined to make him tell her what was happening.

"There's no need, my lady. We get all our meals prepared by the duke's cook; we wouldn't want to impose."

"Oh, but I insist. It's the least we can do for all the help you have given us. All of you. I'll also ask Mr. Alcott and Mr. Reeves what they would like to have," Emilie said, looking around. "Is Mr. Reeves here? I haven't seen him all day. I'm sure he would love our cook's chocolate cake."

"He's not here at the moment."

"Oh, where is he?"

"He's not feeling well today."

Her suspicion increased, but Emilie didn't have time to ask anything more because at that moment, a voice called her name.

Mr. Talbot immediately moved in front of her, blocking her view. Emilie leaned past him and almost groaned.

Anne Marie was standing on the other side of the iron gates. Emilie couldn't believe she had dared to return.

Emilie moved next to Mr. Talbot; she didn't need protection from her. If anything, Anne Marie should be glad the closed gates stood between them.

"Yes?" Emilie said, not willing to move another inch for her.

"Aren't you going to let me in?" Anne Marie asked with raised brows.

"What do you want?"

"I heard that Evan moved in next to you."

Something inside of Emilie protested at Anne Marie using his name so freely.

"The duke can live wherever he wants."

"Oh, dear, there's no need to be so stiff when talking about old friends. Well, I guess some of us are allowed more liberties than others. I've come to look for the duke, and no offense, Lady Arundel, but he's more entertaining than you are." Emilie wished she could wipe the smile off her face. "Have you seen Lord Williamson lately? He didn't take it too well when I called off our engagement. I kept telling him we both had to move on and that with time, everyone would forget. I just couldn't accept being his wife."

"That's not what he's been telling me," Emilie said, taking a step toward her and leaving Mr. Talbot behind. "He seems to have regretted his decision to marry you from the moment the engagement was announced."

"It doesn't matter anymore. What's important is that you can have him. I prefer to be with someone more worldly; someone with whom I share a history. And well, now that the duke's back, you can imagine my happiness." Anne Marie suddenly looked at Emilie with a surprised expression on her face. "Oh my! Didn't you know? Of course you didn't. You've always been slow with these matters. We used to meet in secret all the time! I'm surprised you never caught on, but I should have known; you were always distracted with silly things like riding and covering yourself with dirt."

Her mouth twisted, and there was silence for a few seconds. Then, Emilie burst into laughter, an abrupt sound filled with mirth.

Anne Marie looked shocked, but Emilie couldn't stop; her laughter caused tears to come out of her eyes, and soon, Anne Marie turned from shocked to offended.

"Dear Lord," Emilie gasped, cleaning her tears and turning to Mr. Talbot. "I need to go back inside, since the duke will be here soon. I'll ask our cook to prepare a feast for you tonight."

"Yes, my lady."

Emilie returned inside and closed the door behind her, resting her back against it.

Her shoulders slumped in defeat, and in a moment, she had to force her eyes to push back the tears.

Emilie hadn't wanted Anne Marie to know how much her words had hurt her. She didn't know why she felt like crying, so many years later.

Her aunt's words came to mind, and Emilie couldn't help thinking that, somehow, Anne Marie had been involved with Evan's hasty departure.

It was obvious Anne Marie wanted him. Emilie couldn't believe how she hadn't seen it before, all those years ago.

Moving away from the door, she straightened her gown, feeling silly for indulging in thoughts of the past. Especially when there were more important things happening in the present.

She had to concentrate. She had things to do and information to gather.

Emilie hadn't walked far from the door when a rapid knock stopped her.

CHAPTER 49

Evan had been debating with himself about how much he should reveal to Emilie. He knew there was the risk she wouldn't believe what he was going to tell her, but Evan had wanted to protect her, to let her live in a world where she'd never have to step into the darkness.

He was almost there when he saw Anne Marie standing in front of Emilie's house.

"What are you doing here?" Evan asked as he dismounted. One of the footmen would be there soon to take his horse back to the stables.

Anne Marie turned to him with a smile that made him flinch. She quickly bounced toward him.

"Hello, Evan, I was waiting for you," she said, reaching for his sleeve, but he moved out of her reach. "We couldn't have a proper conversation the last time we met. I can't wait to hear all about your stay abroad."

"I'm afraid that'll have to wait. I'm busy."

"But what can be more important than getting reacquainted with each other?" Anne Marie grabbed him by the arm and leaned closer to him.

Evan broke off her hold and strode past her. He didn't have

time for Anne Marie's games. He'd had enough of them years ago.

"Plenty of things. I don't think I'll ever have time for it."

"Are you sure you don't want to hear what I have to say?"

Evan walked past the iron gate that Talbot was holding open for him.

"Maybe next time," he said, before climbing the short stairs.

CHAPTER 50

Emilie turned back to the door, thinking it had to be Mr. Talbot, maybe with a request for their cook. She didn't think she had been standing there for long, but when Emilie opened the door, Evan looked at her with impatience in his eyes.

"I wasn't expecting you yet. Come in."

Evan didn't move; instead, she felt his eyes searching her face thoroughly.

"Fine. Stay there if you want."

Emilie turned and walked away. She didn't like this Evan—unpredictable and unwilling to cooperate with her.

He must think she was naive, that's why he lied to her and didn't tell her the truth of what was happening. Emilie knew Evan had more secrets than she could ever imagine, but she wouldn't let him intimidate her into silence.

Emilie would pry the truth out of him if she had to.

The door closed behind her, and footsteps followed her down the hall. Anxiety settled in her stomach as she entered the drawing room. Emilie thought of the book that she had hidden under her mattress. It was likely Evan knew what it was, but she wouldn't ask him and let him know she had it.

She could keep secrets, too.

Emilie was already sitting by the time Evan entered the room. His posture was relaxed with his hands in the pockets of his pants, but that wasn't what she saw in his eyes. Her back stiffened against the chair.

"Why were you crying?" He asked.

"Crying? When was I crying?"

"I saw Anne Marie outside. What did she want?"

"Did you? I'm sure you two had plenty to talk about, but I'd rather you tell me why you keep on lying to me."

"What are you talking about?" Evan asked, striding toward her. "I don't talk to her about you, and I don't lie to you. There are just some things I won't be able to explain."

"Try."

"You will have to trust my judgment. Your parents did."

"It's been a long time since I stopped trusting you. You'll have to do more to convince me than to mention my parents."

"When have I ever betrayed your trust?"

His eyes sparkled with fury and his arms encaged her on her chair, but Emilie didn't move. She couldn't believe he was asking her that question. It was more than clear that it would be useless to discuss the past with him.

"Explain to me what I heard this morning," she said instead with a wave of her hand. "Why were you talking about amulets and charms? And what about Mr. Reeves? What happened to him?"

"Will your aunt be joining us?"

"Why? Should I call for her?"

"No. You can't repeat what I'm about to tell you to anyone."

"Well, what is it?"

"Promise me first that you won't say a word to anyone."

Emilie frowned at his insistence.

"I'm not one to gossip," she said, feeling slightly offended.

"Em, it's important."

"Fine. I give you my word, Your Grace."

Evan looked away from her and stared at the fireplace instead, as if he needed to gather strength for what he was going to tell her. The sound of burning wood was the only thing that filled the silence.

Her eyes stayed on his face, watching his expression closely and waiting for him to talk.

"For the longest time," he started, almost in a whisper. "A group of men has existed in secret, whose only purpose has been to protect humanity."

"What? Protect humanity from what?"

"From the unnatural."

"You mean..." Emilie hesitated. "You mean there's more like that shadow I met? Since when have you known this? Am I the only one who doesn't know about it?"

"Listen to what I have to say first. It's better for everyone involved if people don't know that the Haunters exist. It makes our job easier since there's nothing they can do about them. This is why we've always hidden it from you."

CHAPTER 51

Evan looked at her closely, making sure she heard every word.

"Over time, a few of us were born with the ability to detect these Haunters. This ability was passed down from generation to generation, and each time one of us is born, we are taught how we're different from others. When we're old enough, we swear to hunt the Haunters for as long as we live."

Evan paused and waited for her reaction. A long silence followed his short speech.

"Do you expect me to believe this? You thought I would fall for this?"

Evan sighed, feeling frustrated.

"You might decide not to believe me, but you can't accuse me of not telling you the truth."

"How is this related to me?"

"A hunter was on guard the night of the ball. The agent died stopping the Haunter from getting close to our carriage when we arrived at your house."

"What?" Emilie asked. He noticed her face changing color and her hand pressing against her chest.

"The Organization has always protected you. That night, the Haunter was coming for you."

"Are you saying it's my fault he died?"

"No, don't diminish his sacrifice. Because of him, you're still alive."

Emilie gasped. He saw her hand moving to the purse next to her and grasping it tightly.

"But who was he trying to stop? Is it true then? Am I also the reason your parents died when we were younger? I keep having these dreams about it...I've never asked you, but I know my aunt is afraid of something coming back," she said with a quivering voice, looking straight at him as she pushed her hand against her chest. Her body shook as much as her voice did. "If I could see the shadow, does it mean that my parents could see these Haunters too?"

Evan nodded, his eyes fixed on her face.

He didn't know what to say. Her revelation made him wonder how long she'd been having these dreams. Had that night been haunting the two of them even after all these years? Evan immediately moved toward Emilie, kneeling in front of her and bringing her body close to his.

Evan rested her head against his chest, trying to show her that he would help her through everything and be there for her.

The sound of hurried footsteps alerted him, and he immediately stood up, knowing that something was wrong.

"Duke, you have to come with me," Talbot called, bursting into the room. The man didn't wait for Evan's answer before rushing out again.

"Em, wait here. Don't leave the room."

Evan was ready for a fight as soon as he left the house. Talbot pointed toward the closed iron gate, where someone was leaning against it. The man was grasping the bars tightly, as if his life depended on it. When he saw Evan, the man spoke in an eager, strained voice.

"Hello, cousin."

CHAPTER 52

Evan and Talbot marched into his house while carrying his cousin, who could barely stand.

"This way, Your Grace," his butler indicated. "I have a room ready down the hall."

Evan could see that Robert was barely conscious, the movement proving too much effort for him.

"Almost there," Evan said, trying to reassure him.

The butler led them down the hall, past the room where Reeves still lay unconscious, until he finally opened a door and immediately went to a bed in the back.

Talbot and he rushed inside, and by the time they laid his cousin on the mattress, Robert was unconscious.

"How did Lord Hardingham do it?" Talbot asked, stepping away from the bed.

Evan saw Argyle enter the room.

"I don't know," Evan replied, looking back at his cousin. "But it must have taken a lot out of him. He couldn't have been far. We'll have to wait until he wakes up to hear what he has to say, but for now, I have to make sure he stays alive."

"Whatever you need," Talbot said, and the butler and the other agent nodded.

Evan turned to his cousin and leaned forward to inspect his body. He didn't look as dirty as Evan had expected.

Robert's clothes were clean, and even his face had been recently shaved.

The ring was missing from his left hand, though, and Evan wondered if his cousin would have it on him. Patting his pockets, he felt a small bump on the front pocket of his jacket, and once Evan dug through it, he found the ruby ring.

When he inspected it more closely, Evan could see something was wrong. Instead of the colorful, bright ruby, a big, dark stain had appeared in the middle of the stone.

He immediately put it side to side with his own ring, and the bold color of his stone was a clear indicator that his cousin's had lost all of its shine.

It was as if the stone was dying.

"Hold him," Evan said.

Talbot and Argyle immediately moved around the bed— Talbot to the head, holding down his cousin's shoulders, while the other agent went for the legs. Even Mr. Gidley moved to the foot.

He stayed in the middle, close to Robert's chest. Evan placed his cousin's ring in his own pocket for safekeeping. He would have to take care of the ring as well.

"Ready?" Evan asked, his eyes focused solely on his cousin.

"Yes."

He leaned over Robert and let go of the control he had over his senses.

They immediately became sharp and sensitive to their surroundings. Evan could see and feel everything more clearly.

His cousin reeked of darkness, of desperation and fear. It was almost too late. Evan couldn't imagine what it had cost Robert to break free from the Haunter's control.

Evan lifted his arms and put his hands over his cousin's chest, right in the middle, then pressed.

Robert screamed in pain and tried to free himself from Evan's grasp, but Evan didn't let go of his hold.

The red stone on his ring became intense and bright, pushing it to its limit.

"Duke, don't!" Talbot said.

But it was too late.

CHAPTER 53

It was already dark by the time Robert woke up. Evan had stayed by his side watching over him, not listening to any of his men's urgings to go rest until they'd had no other option but to stop insisting and leave them alone in the room.

When Robert opened his eyes, his first reaction was to struggle against the sheets while trying to get out of the bed.

"Robert, it's me," Evan said, moving closer to the light coming from the window.

Once Robert saw him, his face transformed in utter relief. He stopped struggling and immediately relaxed against the bed. By the time Evan lit a candle and moved to stand beside him, his cousin was already struggling to lift himself into a sitting position.

"Robert, what happened to you?" Evan asked, helping him rest his back against the pillow.

There was silence for a moment, during which Evan thought he might not be ready to talk yet, but after a few seconds, Robert raised his eyes.

Evan saw darkness staring back at him.

"What have you done?" Robert asked, his voice coming out in a rough whisper.

"I had no choice."

"You should have let it consume me. I was ready for it, but now, you..."

"You know I couldn't do that." Evan's voice was firm, but a sudden pain in his chest made him stop.

Silence stretched, heavy and tense. The crackling of the fire became prominent in his ears. Evan dragged a chair next to the bed and sat down, waiting.

"I was on my way back to the city when it showed up. I had received a letter about a week before I left," Robert began.

"Who sent it?"

"It was a warning; a message from the Legion, sent by my contact. There had been reports of rare activity close to our territory."

"I know that. It's been going on for a while. But if the Legion contacted you, why didn't you let me know?"

"I did," Robert said, looking at Evan with clear eyes. "I sent you a letter before I left... but from your reaction, I can see you never received it."

"Talbot showed up to inform me you had disappeared, but I was already on my way back when he did." Evan stood up to pace the room. "I didn't find the letter the Legion sent you, either. What was the warning about? I'm surprised they knew what was happening and that they told you. I'd been tracking the Haunter for weeks before I lost it, but I was told it was coming in this direction. The Legion doesn't usually bother informing us about that kind of thing."

"I was surprised, too, but you know they don't give explanations. All the letter said was that the attacks were advancing in our direction, and it'd probably reach us in a couple of weeks." Robert rested the back of his head against the headboard, closing his eyes. Evan could see that speaking was tiring him. "The way they described it reminded me of a story. A superstitious legend that I read years ago in one of the old books. But I couldn't find the story in any of the ones I had with me. I thought it would be back at the family house. I didn't remember the details of the story, but I remembered enough to know that we were facing something serious. Too serious to discard it as a coincidence. I had to go back."

"Why didn't you take anyone with you?" Evan asked. "Why did you go by yourself?"

"If the Haunter was indeed heading in this direction, I couldn't risk leaving the city unprotected. I was counting on you receiving my letter. I had to take the risk. If it was what I thought it was, I couldn't waste any time."

Evan saw that Robert was exhausted, but he needed to know.

"I found a note while looking through your books. I recognized your handwriting. It looked like a message, but the note was torn, and half the message was missing. It said, 'You must return or...' I knew the message had to be for me. No one else could have had access to those books."

"'You must return'?" Robert frowned. "The only note I left you was in my study and it wasn't anything like that. I had explained my thoughts in the previous letter I had sent you. I didn't want to risk this information getting leaked, but I needed to make sure you knew, in case I wasn't back before you arrived. In case anything happened to me...but if you didn't get the letter, and the note *I* left you was taken...do you still have the torn note? Let me see it."

"I don't have it with me, it's in my study. I'll show it to you later, but I assure you, it was your handwriting. Tell me what your note said."

"'I'll go look for the book,'" Robert quoted. "'The book with the legend of the prophecy and the soul-sucking Haunter.' It's not back at the estate; I don't know what happened to it."

"I know which story you're talking about. Once I saw the bodies the Haunter leaves behind, I also thought of the same story. My dad used to tell it to me."

"I never thought it would be true. It was hard to know if the translation was correct, since the legend is so old. It felt more like a children's story than anything else. But, now, I know better."

A thick silence fell in the room. Evan could feel the weight of the darkness surrounding him. He lit another candle and set it on the floor next to him.

"How did it get you?" Evan asked.

"I was on the road on my way back when I felt them. They were waiting for me."

"*Them*? Is it more than one?"

"It's a group of Haunters," Robert explained in a somber voice. "They follow a leader; a soul leech. That's the one that used me."

Evan kept quiet for a few seconds, thinking about what his cousin had told him, and what it implied.

"Were you also there when the attacks on Arundel's territory happened?"

"No, the Haunter had me in the city. It went through the safeguards because of me. It must have been planning this for a long time."

Robert grabbed his head between his hands, as if trying to push back pain.

"Robert?"

"I was in this dark room. I couldn't see anything, and I couldn't move. I thought the safeguards would stop them from getting into the city, but I was wrong."

Robert looked up at him with something Evan recognized as horror. Evan felt his body go completely still. He waited for Robert to explain himself.

"I don't know what happened to my ring," Robert whispered, looking down at his bare hand. "Every time I came to myself, I wouldn't have it on me, and I couldn't signal any of you."

"We can continue later. You need more sleep."

"No, I need to tell you everything before it's too late." His wide eyes made Evan stay still. "Sometimes, I could hear it. I think it was using other bodies as well. There are Haunters waiting outside of the city, waiting for the safeguards to go down. I think it was using my abilities to damage them in some way."

"That would explain some things."

"It was always in my mind, mocking me. The few times I found myself conscious, I knew I only had two options: to push it out or to stop myself. That way, it couldn't use me anymore."

"Robert..."

"But something happened," he continued, and Evan thought he saw a spark in his eyes. "It's been so long, but in my darkest moment, I couldn't help but think of her."

"Her?"

"Yes. Lilly."

"You mean...you mean Emilie's...?"

"That's her."

"I...I never knew," Evan said, his hand holding the side of his neck.

"She has always been the one," Robert admitted, shaking his head. "I haven't seen her in years, but for a brief moment, it felt as if she was there with me. As if the thought of her helped me push it out and regain control of my body."

"She might have heard about you. She might have also been looking for you."

"I don't deserve her help. Not after what I did. I don't even know where she is. I've lost her."

"But she found you," Evan said as he began to pace the room. "Emilie...Emilie must know where she is. She probably still keeps in touch with her. Don't worry; I'll find out."

Robert kept quiet while Evan continued to pace the room. The flames in the fireplace began to extinguish.

"The Haunter was here earlier today," Evan broke the silence. "It was Emilie who saw it. We went after it, but we couldn't trace it. The bastard was using you to hide."

"Sometimes, when it was distracted, I could get a glimpse of what was happening. Before I pushed it out, there was a moment when I became aware. We were standing in front of your house." Robert sighed. "But the Haunter was distracted. At first, I wasn't sure what it was looking at, but then I saw Lady Arundel looking out." Evan clenched his fists, digging his nails against his skin. "She hadn't seen it yet, but I could hear its thoughts. Then Reeves approached us, and a second later, he was lying on the ground. The Haunter used me to destroy the wall, but there's something else preventing it from coming inside this place, even while using my body."

Evan frowned. There were so many things they didn't fully understand, and many questions to which they didn't know the answers.

"It didn't notice you were conscious?"

"No, and I managed to stay aware," Robert said, a faraway look on his face. "I would drift in and out, but I wanted to know what it was doing, what it was planning. The Haunter met with people. It was paying them for something, but I don't know where it got the money from. It inspected the safeguards surrounding the city and seemed pleased, but I don't know what it was looking for. It walked around the edge of the city for hours before I realized it was spying on the posts of the agents. That's when I decided I had to end it. That's when I felt her."

Robert took a few minutes to catch his breath, and Evan served him a glass of water from the pitcher on the bedside table.

"With Lilly's help, I fought to take back control of my body," Robert said. "The creature was in pain. I was in pain. But I started feeling in control, and I got us as close to the safeguards as I could. My plan was to banish it to the other side, but I'm not sure I succeeded. I don't know what happened to it. It took me a while to make my way back here, but I know it's still out there. It could be anywhere."

Evan's mind began racing with possibilities.

"There's something else. It wants her. The Haunter believes

it's going to have her soon. It's all it thinks about, and it won't stop until it does."

"Like *hell* it's coming near her."

"All that it's been doing has been with the purpose of getting her. It wants to take the city, but it wants her first. Care to explain why?"

Evan couldn't hide it anymore. It was time to confess what he knew.

CHAPTER 54

Emilie stood by the window in her room, watching as the sunset covered everything with a golden glow while the lamps began to fire up in the distance.

Had her parents belonged to the group Evan told her about? Had they died because of it? In all her life, she hadn't seen or noticed anything out of the ordinary, not until the night when she had met the shadow.

Emilie thought about Evan's parents and their death when he was a boy; it had been sudden and unexpected, not unlike her parents'.

The thought sent shivers down her spine. That seemed to be the fate of anyone who belonged to that mysterious group. Emilie refused to think about Evan and his fate.

She moved away from the window. A nice, warm cup of tea would help soothe her for the night. Emilie had told Aunt Augustine that Evan's cousin had appeared unexpectedly. Her aunt had been utterly shocked and had retired early.

Emilie didn't understand why her aunt was so affected by it; they had never been that close to Evan's cousin.

"Lady Arundel," Mr. Larson said when he saw her come

down the stairs. "I was about to send you word. You have a visitor."

"Oh, who is it?" Emilie asked, regretting leaving her room.

She hadn't heard from Evan since his cousin's appearance earlier that evening, and she didn't feel like seeing him again. Emilie was still trying to accept everything that he had told her.

"Lord Williamson. Shall I tell him you're indisposed?"

Emilie sighed. She thought he had given up after his outburst at Evan's house.

"Please show Lord Williamson to the drawing room," she instructed, reluctantly walking toward it.

As Emilie walked down the hall, she peeked through one of the windows.

The darkness made it difficult to see, but Emilie thought she could see Mr. Alcott heading toward the gate, most likely to allow entrance to her visitor.

At least Mr. Alcott had bothered to ask first. Who knew what Evan had told them to do. Probably to deny all visitors.

Emilie went inside and chose her usual spot, which would allow her to sit as far away from him as she could, all the way to the back of the room, next to the fireplace.

A few minutes later, she heard steps coming from the hall.

"Emilie, I'm so glad you agreed to meet me," Williamson said, throwing open the door.

He immediately strode toward her, but Emilie raised her hand to stop him.

"I'm tired of you showing up whenever you want. This will be the last time I agree to meet you. Tell me what you want."

Emilie looked directly into his eyes, and she could see the desperation in them as he stood in front of her.

"Emilie, please. I wanted to tell you the reason for my engagement to Anne Marie."

"I don't want to know anymore. I don't want to hear any explanations about it; it was your choice, after all."

"But you need to know what happened. Anne Marie came to see me the day of the ball."

"She did?"

"She wanted to know if I was going to marry you. Asked me if I was going to announce our engagement that night."

"What? How could Anne Marie have known that?"

Emilie wondered how far Anne Marie's deception went and how well connected she had to be in order to know something so intimate about them. Something that was supposed to be a secret.

"She said it wasn't a good idea to marry you, and asked me if I had heard the rumor," Lord Williamson said, averting his eyes from her. "The rumor about what you had done in the past."

"What do you mean?"

"She told me that you had been compromised years ago. That you had already promised yourself to someone else, and that you had been fooling me. When I saw you with the duke that night, when I found out that you two had known each other for a long time, I knew it had to be him."

"Don't try to justify yourself," Emilie chided, frustration and anger shooting through her voice. "It doesn't make any difference who you thought it was. When you saw us together, you had already announced your engagement to Anne Marie. You had already betrayed me!"

Emilie burned with the fury and adrenaline that rushed through her body. Her vision narrowed and focused on him standing across from her. She despised seeing him.

What Anne Marie had done was despicable; trying to ruin her reputation when both of them knew the truth. Emilie couldn't keep still anymore.

She jumped to her feet.

"It disgusts me to think I was going to marry you. I can't believe how witless and obtuse you are. Thank goodness for Anne Marie taking you away from me!" Emilie said unable to control herself any longer. Her etiquette lessons erased from her mind. "Tell me, have you finally realized that she lied to you?"

"Yes," he replied, gazing desperately at her. "That's why I have come to beg you to forgive me. To give me another chance. Please, let's put this behind us and become my wife."

"You dare to bring this up again?" Her voice displayed all the disbelief she felt. "How did you know Anne Marie lied to you? All this time, you believed that I had a lover, but what made you change your mind?"

"I found out the truth; that there was no way the duke wanted you in that way. Not when it was Anne Marie he wanted."

Emilie was speechless. She couldn't believe what she was hearing.

Her pride rebelled against his words, and she felt a strength inside of her that Emilie hadn't felt in a long time. Had he always been this condescending? Why hadn't she ever noticed it before?

"You're pathetic," she sneered, slowly stalking toward him. "Anne Marie hasn't done anything but lie to you. She just wanted you to break the engagement, and like a fool, you went and did it."

Emilie exhaled. A sudden peace surrounded her as she looked at him with a certainty she hadn't felt in a long time.

"Evan doesn't want her. He wants me."

Lord Williamson scowled.

"I want you to be my wife. He doesn't have any intentions of marrying you."

"Lord Williamson," Emilie said, an icy feeling sliding down her body. "I'll never become your wife."

"Then, are you saying you'd be willing to accept the duke as your lover?" Lord Williamson asked her abruptly, a big scowl on his face.

Emilie knew she had made it clear in the past that she would never be satisfied with just being Lord Williamson's lover, and that she had been waiting to marry him for the longest time.

She looked at him with the corner of her lips slightly raised.

"But darling, I already have."

Seeing his reaction was as satisfying as if Emilie had slapped him.

He stared at her, unable to say a word, before leaving in a rush, slamming the door behind him.

Her satisfaction began to diminish when Emilie realized that she might have to accept Evan's offer after all.

CHAPTER 55

Evan had just checked up on Reeves and his cousin and had settled for the night on the sofa in his study a couple of hours before dawn, when his ring began to receive signals. Within seconds, they came one after another making his ring shine with an intense red.

The agents threw open the door of his study as they ran inside, but Evan was already on his feet, grabbing his coat.

Evan patted Robert's ring in his pocket. He would have to take care of it later.

"Talbot, you and Argyle stay here," Evan ordered, putting his coat on. "Alcott, you come with me."

"Do you think they've found it?" Talbot asked. His face looked as tense as Evan knew his own to be. "In your condition…"

Evan looked at him, and Talbot lowered his head and kept quiet.

"I've never seen my ring shine this much," Alcott said as he looked down at the bright stone.

"I want you to keep a close eye on Reeves and my cousin. They'll probably be sleeping all morning," Evan instructed, looking at Argyle's injured leg as he reached beneath his desk. He pulled out a big chest and put it on top.

"I won't move from their side," Argyle promised.

"Keep the gates locked and don't let anyone out until I come back." Evan gave Talbot a pointed look before opening the chest. It was full of peculiar and unusual items, crystals, and rocks, along with some odd, metal weapons. "I've had these for years. Arm yourselves and make sure not to lose them. We have a long history together. Alcott, if you don't need them, give them to the others. I know the trainees could use them."

The agents filled their pockets without a word. Their jackets were thick, and Evan knew it would be impossible to notice the bulk under them.

"Whatever happens, I want you to be ready," Evan said.

"What are you planning?" Talbot asked.

"I'll go to Jones's since he's the closest from here. They might have seen the Haunter. I'll be back after that. The sun will be out soon, so it'll need to hide before that."

Evan walked out of the study, the men following after him, and met with his butler in the hallway.

"Your horses are ready, Your Grace," the butler informed, falling into step behind them.

"Remember what I told you," Evan told the men as they descended the front steps. "If you feel it close, don't try to do anything stupid. Warn us first. It likes to go after the young ones, so keep an eye on them at all times."

The early morning was at its darkest, and the street was quiet. His words felt loud in his ears.

When they reached the closed gate Evan turned to Talbot.

"Have you seen Os?"

"Not since early this morning."

"Os?" Evan called, and his voice boomed through the early morning darkness. Os was being too quiet, especially with everything that had happened that day. The following silence was answer enough. "Where did he disappear to? If there are any problems, let me know immediately."

Evan paused for a second and looked up at the nearest window of the house next door. He would see her as soon as he returned.

"I'll be back when the situation is under control," he said with a last glance at her window.

With the sun yet to rise, the street was unusually quiet when Evan and Alcott walked into it.

"The street is eerily silent. This better not be a bad omen," Alcott noted, looking around them as they mounted their horses.

Evan heard Talbot locking the gate behind them and hoped that it wouldn't be.

CHAPTER 56

When Emilie woke up, she found that a dress was placed on the side of the bed. Margaret must have left it there without waking her up.

After Lord Williamson's visit, Emilie had decided to stay in her room. She had needed space to put her thoughts in order; especially when her conversation with Evan was still racing through her head.

Emilie felt emotionally exhausted.

She had spent the night trying to open the book still hidden under her mattress, but the lock had been unmovable.

Not feeling like putting much effort on getting dressed, she didn't bother with putting on any of her usual jewelry, not even the simple necklace she liked wearing, and instead, picked up her hair on a loose bun and grabbed her purse with the small gun in it, the one thing she hadn't stop carrying with her for the past few days, before heading downstairs.

The house seemed unusually quiet for the hour, but she was hungry. Emilie walked to the parlor, but the room was empty; wanting to find either the young maid or her brother, she walked from one room to the other, but there was no one in sight.

Worried that something terrible had happened, Emilie

thought of looking in the backyard, the only place she hadn't checked, but a sudden knock stopped her as she passed the front door.

She opened the door, hoping it would be one of Evan's men, but instead, a man slightly older than her stood on the other side.

The man looked relieved to see her and started talking in a rush.

"My lady, I ran over a man with my carriage. He's unconscious, and no one I've asked knows who he is. Can you tell me if he works here?"

Emilie hesitated. She looked around but didn't see any of Evan's men. She worried one of them might have been the one in the accident.

"He's losing a lot of blood. He needs help."

The man touched his hat, turned, and ran down the steps. Emilie looked back inside.

"Is anyone there?" she yelled.

The house stayed silent; not the young maid in sight nor any answers to her call. Emilie felt unsure but tried to reassure herself while squeezing her small purse.

She heard the chirping birds as she stepped outside, leaving the door open behind her. Crows stood on the gate, basking in the sun.

It was a nice, sunny day.

Emilie saw the man turned left when he reached the gate, and wondered how he had gotten inside when none of Evan's men were around to let him in.

She followed him, and as soon as Emilie walked past the gate, the man covered her mouth and dragged her to a carriage waiting in the street.

Emilie kicked and scratched and tried to open her purse to take out her small gun, but in the struggle, she dropped it and left it behind.

She tried to bite him and call out for help, but the street was quiet, and her only witnesses were the crows that flapped and fussed at the commotion.

Her efforts were muffled by the strength of the man's hand. The smell of sweat and dirt impregnated her nose, and Emilie dug her nails into his face and arms until she could feel blood seeping from the marks she'd made, but the man was stronger than her.

A cloth covered her nose and mouth, and Emilie struggled against the stench as her eyes slowly lost focus.

The stranger gagged her and threw her against the back seat.

Pain went down her back and her head throbbed as she hit the edge of the seat. Panic exploded inside of her.

The sound of cawing crows faded into the background as she became unconscious.

Oh, how she hated crows.

CHAPTER 57

"Lady Arundel was kidnapped," Talbot said with a desperate look on his face.

Evan and Alcott had just returned, and Talbot had run to them before they even had a chance to dismount their horses.

"When?"

"It just happened! Where the hell were you? A man grabbed her and shoved her into a carriage. I tried to follow it, but I lost them," Williamson said coming forward, almost pushing Talbot aside. "I knew you couldn't keep her safe!"

Evan narrowed his eyes.

"And what were you doing here?"

Williamson's voice immediately took a defensive tone.

"I came to see her," Williamson replied. "You're all just wasting time! I know in which direction the carriage went, but the longer you delay it, the more it's going to take to find her."

Evan ignored him and focused on Talbot.

"What happened?"

From the corner of his eye, Evan saw Alcott looking nervously between Talbot and him, but Talbot listed what had caused him to leave the front of Emilie's house, and how Reeves,

Robert, and even Emilie's aunt had appeared to have a reaction to the Haunter.

Now they knew with what purpose.

"I was guarding the house when your cousin, Lord Hardingham, started to scream. Soon after that, Reeves started reacting as well. While Argyle and I were trying to control the situation, one of our maid's saw Lady Augustine suddenly fainting in the backyard. Lady Arundel's staff were all helping us move Lady Augustine to the spare room on the first floor of your house, close to the backyard. When I sent for Lady Arundel to inform her of what had happened, her maid couldn't find her in the house. The gate must have been left open when the footman went to find the doctor for Lady Augustine, and that must have been when Lord Williamson saw Lady Arundel getting taken."

Evan was exhausted.

Alcott and he had been running from one post to another since they had left.

The safeguards that Evan and the agents had created around the fissures in the city wall had become an extension of the fissures themselves. The infection was spreading faster than it had been in the past, as if the fissures were synchronized to expand at the same time.

Evan and his men had spent the morning creating new safeguards around the ones they already had, hoping that it would delay the expansion and buy them some time.

Now, Evan knew the bastard had fooled him.

The Haunter had taken his distraction as an opportunity to get Emilie, but how had he done it?

"I can't detect any traces," Evan said after a moment, looking between the agents for confirmation.

"Me neither," Talbot spoke. "It must have been just a man."

Evan dismounted his horse and stood next to Talbot on the sidewalk.

"What are you doing?!" Williamson yelled. "The only reason I came back was to make sure you knew what had happened."

"You came back because you're a coward," Evan growled. There wasn't much distance between them, and he had to restrain himself from touching him.

"How dare you!" Williamson said with a red face.

Evan felt both Talbot and Alcott moving behind him—ready to intervene if necessary, he was sure.

He stared at Williamson for a second before pushing him to the side and stalking toward his house.

"You need me!" Williamson shouted. "How do you expect to know where they've gone?"

Evan heard a carriage stopping in the street.

"Lady Augustine is inside!" Talbot spoke, signaling to whoever was inside to follow. Probably the doctor and the footman.

Evan's throat became tighter with every second that passed. He couldn't allow the realization that he had failed her to paralyze him. Evan had to find her.

"Is Robert awake?"

"He wasn't the last time I saw him," Talbot replied.

"Then, we'll have to wake him up."

CHAPTER 58

Emilie woke up, disoriented, in a dark, humid place. Whatever was in the rag the man had pressed against her face had made her lost her senses.

Immediate pain urged her to press her hands against her chest, but her arms lay unresponsive at her sides.

She didn't know how long she had been unconscious, but her eyelids felt heavy, and her sight was unfocused.

Emilie had to fight with herself to come out of her daze, and when she could finally open her eyes fully, she saw nothing but darkness. It might have been her imagination, but Emilie could see shadows moving in front of her.

The buzzing in her ears also made her think that she could hear whispering voices saying words that she couldn't comprehend.

Emilie tried to move her legs and arms, but she still couldn't even lift her fingers.

Coldness crept up her back and settled between her shoulder blades. Her back was leaning against hard rock. She opened her mouth to call for help, but the strong smell of humidity and putrefaction caused her to moan in disgust.

Emilie had never seen her kidnapper before, no one had seen

her getting abducted, and they probably wouldn't know where to look for her, either. She would have to pay the price for letting her guard down and being unable to take out her gun on time.

The possibility of dying was high.

A sudden noise startled her out of her thoughts. The noise repeated, followed by a loud, merry laugh. Emilie froze with dread. Someone stood next to her.

"I'm sorry I'm a little late," a voice said.

The hairs on her arms rose at the melodic sound. Emilie pushed herself against the wall as far as she could with her limited movement.

"Don't be afraid, my love," the voice whispered in her ear.

She moved away, looking frantically around her. Emilie squinted, attempting to pierce through the darkness while trying to ignore the pain in her chest. But no one was there.

Fear finally crawled into her gut, and her stomach clenched.

"I demand you let me go," Emilie said, forcing herself to speak.

The numbness in her arms was fading.

"So fast?"

"Who are you?"

"Oh, dear. We have met before; don't you remember me? We saw each other a few days ago in front of your house."

Her chest clenched at the realization. Emilie remembered the shadow, and the pain that still haunted her after that night.

"Our meeting was cut short last time by that annoying spir-it," the voice continued. "But I don't blame you, my dear. Tell me, did you at least enjoy my letters? You didn't tell me if you did."

Emilie tensed, her heart sunk, and her desperation bubbled to the surface. She swallowed, trying to push the fear out of her voice.

"Why am I here?" she asked.

She realized the reason Emilie couldn't see the voice was

because there was nothing to see. If it was anything like the last encounter, the darkness and the shadow were the same thing.

"It's rude to not answer my questions, dear. But I'll let it go this time. I know the shock must be too difficult to handle for a lady like yourself."

Emilie pressed her lips together. She could finally move her arms. Her hands became wet when she touched the floor, but her legs weren't strong enough to stand.

"You're right," she said. "I don't know what's happening, and I don't know the reason why I'm here."

"Don't you worry, my dear. Why aren't you looking at me? Can't you see me?" the voice asked with concern. "I can see you; you're even more beautiful than I remember. I promise you, everything will be over soon. I hope the man didn't hurt you on your way here. If he did, he'll pay with his life."

"I think you might be confusing me with somebody else," Emilie said, trying to move her toes.

She heard an offended gasp.

"You don't seem pleased to be with me, but there are no mistakes, my dear. I've been looking for you. If it wasn't for that arrogant hunter, we would have been together sooner," the voice replied, and Emilie could feel its hatred pinning her to the floor. "Are you in pain, my dear? Let me know if you are; that will be our warning that we need to finish this and leave."

Emilie remembered what Evan had told her about the Haunters and the work he did. She also remembered what had happened to the back wall in her garden, and how she had seen Evan's cousin out in the street that day.

"How is it possible?" Emilie asked aloud, unable to stop herself. "It was Lord Hardingham who I saw in the street, but it wasn't him, was he?"

"You're finally understanding!" the shadow exclaimed. "I needed a body to borrow and meeting him made everything so much easier. What better body to use than that of a hunter, and one in control of the city at that? He was so easy to defeat. I'm surprised no one had done it before. Of course, no one is as good as I am. This place is full of ineptitude, but everything will be over soon. There are no limits with you by my side."

Emilie didn't fully understand, but she also didn't care.

For whatever reason, the shadow wanted her, and that was enough for Emilie to know she needed to leave.

The feeling in her legs was returning. She wasn't sure about the layout of the room, but Emilie would follow the wall and see where it took her.

She tried her best to keep her voice polite and non-confrontational.

"Forgive me," Emilie began as she slowly pushed herself to the side. "But since we haven't been formally introduced, I don't know how to call you."

"No, you must forgive me," the voice replied with as much pompousness as if they had been in the middle of a ball. "With all the excitement, I forgot my manners. I feel as if we have known each other for the longest time. There has never been a queen as beautiful as you, my love. Lord Lazaro, at your service."

Emilie had slowly been pushing herself against the wall into a semi-standing position, trying her best to be discreet, but she froze on the spot at the mention of being his queen.

"Does it surprise you, my dear?" the voice chuckled. "I can give you what you've always wanted. Everything will be yours. All you have to do is stay by my side and do a little something for me."

"My lord," Emilie greeted, feeling silly and not knowing what to say.

She considered the idea that she might be talking to an imaginary voice, but her surroundings and the wet stains on her skirt told her she wasn't imagining anything.

"I don't believe I have heard about you before," Emilie continued, pushing against the wall with conviction.

A merry laugh.

"It doesn't surprise me. No one ever gets a chance to talk about me."

"And why is that?" she asked with the intention of keeping him talking, but Emilie was sure she already knew why.

"Because they are dead soon after meeting me," the shadow answered with a laugh. "Your sense of humor is delightful. The hunters have always failed to defeat me. They're nothing but annoying rats that need to be exterminated. Why do you think it took me so long to rescue you? The way they had you trapped. I'll make them suffer for it, but it'll be my pleasure to kill that arrogant hunter."

Emilie knew he was talking about Evan.

Funny. She had always known his arrogance would get him in trouble someday, but Emilie had never thought it would get him killed.

She preferred Evan alive, especially if there were any more of those Haunters out in the world.

"And what do you need from me?" Emilie asked.

"I see you are impatient, my love. Am I boring you already? I wanted to have a few more minutes to enjoy our conversation, but if you insist, let's start."

Emilie stopped moving and looked in the direction of the voice.

"I don't understand."

"Oh, you don't have to pretend with me. We'll love each other for eternity; there's no need to hide anything from me."

Her instincts told her she needed to be extremely careful.

"I'm still not sure what you mean, Lord Lazaro, dear," Emilie spoke. The urge to run was strong, but she kept it under control. Emilie could feel an opening in the wall not far from her. "Would you please explain it to me?"

"Of course, but you need to know you can trust me. Your secret is safe with me," the voice said gallantly. "I need you to give me your power."

Emilie was close to the opening when she stopped.

"What power?"

"You're so charming, my dear. How do you think we are talking right now?"

"I...I don't know," Emilie admitted, her anxiety escalating. "I don't know much about these things. No one has ever explained them to me."

"It's a disgrace! But don't worry, my dear. I'll teach you all there is to know," the voice promised. "Now, shall we begin? The sooner we start, the sooner everything will be over. This will be slightly uncomfortable, but just leave it all to me."

"What are you going to do?"

Her hand had reached the opening. There was a way out of the room. Emilie turned and ran through the gap, not waiting for his answer.

She almost tripped when her feet bumped against a hard surface, but relief filled her when she realized it was a staircase.

Emilie ran up the stairs as fast as she could.

"Don't tire yourself, dear. You can't leave."

Coldness spread from Emilie's chest to the rest of her body. She felt paralyzed, but Emilie struggled against it. She remembered what would happen if she didn't keep going.

Her body slammed against the stairs, and a sharp pain took her breath away. Emilie didn't want it to be over. She wanted to leave and go back home. Emilie had to see Evan again; there was too much she hadn't told him.

She pushed through the numbness and kept crawling up the stairs.

"Stop!" Lord Lazaro ordered. The pain increased, forcing her to dig her nails into her chest. But Emilie was angry, and she dragged herself up the stairs, one step at a time. "Let me help you; you know who you are. You don't belong with them; they can't treat you badly anymore. Together, I will lead my own to what we have always been denied."

A heavy-looking door stood at the end of the stairs. The sight of it fueled her to take the last step.

Emilie leveled herself up as she fumbled with the handle. Relief filled her when she found it unlocked. Pulling with all her strength, she opened the door wide enough to squeeze through it, walking into an empty room with dirty windows. She desperately looked around, searching for a way out, and when she located another door, Emilie ran toward it.

Dark shadows exploded from within her, shooting from her chest like twisted arms.

A loud scream rang in her ears, mixing with a sharper one.

The sounds were coming from her.

CHAPTER 59

A flock of crows burst through the windows—hundreds of them—but Emilie ignored them. She was too focused on wanting to get away from the pain and the odd shadows coming out of her chest. Her ears hurt with the intense cawing and loud shrieks of the crows surrounding her.

Emilie fought with her body to keep straight and to not fall onto the floor. She noticed she wasn't far from the exit. Immediately, the crows around her moved away from her as one, clearing the path to the door.

"How dare you intrude!"

She could hear the annoyance in the voice and she gave a little smile. The pain in her chest ceased, and the shadowed arms in her chest looked welcoming once they helped her stand.

She felt lighter and free.

Emilie blinked in surprise when she found herself standing and noticed the black birds acting as a barrier between her and the shadow in the staircase.

The dark shadows of arms in her chest were gone, and that was enough for her. Without wasting time, Emilie ran to the door.

"Don't go!" the voice shouted. "I can give you what you want!"

Emilie didn't look back and ran out into a dark street.

Tall buildings blocked the remaining sunlight, and Emilie realized she had been there all day.

She ran to the end of the street as fast as she could with her heavy skirt, stumbling a couple of times when she looked back to confirm that no one was following her.

A couple of men stood in a corner, looking at her without much interest, but besides them, there wasn't anyone else in sight. Emilie kept aimlessly running forward, wanting to put as much distance between her and the building as she could. She wouldn't stop until she was surrounded by a crowd of people in a busy street; wherever Emilie wouldn't be easily found by the shadow.

The noise of traffic called her attention. A carriage was heading toward her as she approached the intersection.

She tried to get the driver's attention, but he ignored her.

Emilie tried to stop every carriage she could see, but none of them did, driving past her without a second glance.

She looked down at her dress and at how filthy it looked. Her face must look dirty as well. No one would stop to help her in her current state. People probably thought she was crazy, and Emilie would never find a way home.

When a carriage stopped by her side, she felt extremely grateful, giving a sigh of relief.

The door opened.

"What are you doing here?" A familiar man smiled.

Emilie turned to run, but he grabbed her by the arm.

"No! Help!"

Everyone in the street ignored her.

She immediately scratched the man's face, aiming for his eyes.

"You bitch!" He slapped her across the face, stunning her for a moment.

The man used the time to pull her closer, pressing her arms against him, but Emilie redoubled her efforts, trying to hurt him as much as she could.

"Let her go!" someone yelled from the other side of the street.

Her resolve to free herself increased, and Emilie turned to bite the man's hand, who screamed when she sank her teeth deep into his flesh, momentarily releasing her, surprised by her attack.

"Emilie!"

Her attacker looked up, and Emilie took the chance to push him off balance.

She didn't wait and ran.

"Emilie, it's me!"

She thought she recognized the voice, but Emilie didn't stop to look back, only thinking about putting more distance between her and her kidnapper.

"You piece of scum!"

Finally risking a glance back, she saw Evan punching the man she'd been running from.

"Duke, wait!" Mr. Talbot was yelling, grabbing Evan by the arm before finally pulling him out of reach from the unconscious kidnapper.

Evan turned to look at her, and the expression on his face reminded Emilie that she must look awful, but seeing him made her feel like she had finally woken up from a bad dream.

It was his untidy suit and the hair all over his face, the compassion she saw in his eyes, that made her heart ache.

Emilie ran toward him, feeling like the distance between them was endless. All she wanted to do was touch him to make sure he was real.

Evan must have seen the urgency in her face, because in a couple of strides, he had her trapped against his chest with his arms in a strong clasp around her.

"Are you hurt?" Evan asked.

But Emilie wasn't looking at him. As she had allowed herself to be hugged, something in her arm she hadn't had time to notice before had distracted her.

"I think there's something wrong with me," she said.

Emilie lifted her left arm to show him.

Marks had appeared around the palm of her hand in intricate patterns that Emilie couldn't decipher, and they seemed to go all the way up her sleeve.

When she looked up at him, Emilie noticed that his face had turned paler than it had been.

CHAPTER 60

"Come with me," Evan said, putting his cloak around her shoulders.

He led her across the street where a carriage awaited, guarded by a couple of his men. Evan opened the door and helped her inside.

"Are you hurt anywhere?" he asked.

"No, I'm fine," Emilie replied, sitting across from him while rubbing the cheek where Evan had seen the man hit her.

He pressed his lips to suppress a curse while she rubbed the red spot that was beginning to swell on her face. Evan had to control the urge to get out of the carriage and hit the man again.

"Can you tell me what happened?" he asked, holding her hand.

"I'm not sure what happened," Emilie said, shaking her head. "No one was home when I woke up, and that man was at the door, saying that someone had gotten hurt."

Emilie looked out the window, and Evan frowned when her gaze became distant.

"I was in a dark room when I woke up. I couldn't see anything; I couldn't move but...I knew someone was in the room with me."

"Who was it?"

Emilie shifted in her seat.

"I...it told me its name was Lord Lazaro. It was the same shadow I saw outside my house. When I was escaping, it tried to take something from me, but then something else happened."

"What did it want from you?"

"I don't know, but afterward, there were birds coming into the room... crows... I think the crows at my house followed me... and these...things burst out of my chest."

Evan slid closer to her, his hand briefly squeezing hers.

"It's hard to believe, but I...you have to believe me," Emilie pleaded, holding onto his hands. She looked at him and Evan knew she was waiting for his reaction. "I was in so much pain; it felt like something had ripped inside of me. There were screams coming from my chest, and then the crows flew in, lots of them, and they helped me escape. They cornered the shadow, and I could run."

Emilie gazed down at the palm of her hand.

"You're going home now," Evan promised, caressing her swollen cheek. "We'll take care of it."

Emilie's first impulse was to grab him by the arm.

He saw the stress on her face, but he couldn't console her. The threat they faced was too big. Evan had to kill it.

Unable to stop himself, he leaned forward and kissed her on the cheek.

CHAPTER 61

The kiss startled Emilie. It made her momentarily forget the fear she felt as her cheeks warmed, and not because of the pain.

It only lasted for a brief moment, but she had felt a sudden spark when his lips had touched her cheek.

"Can you tell us where you were?" Evan asked, gently holding her face in his hands.

"I can show you," Emilie replied, trying to regain her focus.

The carriage door was yanked open, and Lord Williamson stood on the other side, breathing heavily and staring at them with wide eyes.

"Are you alright?" Lord Williamson asked. Emilie moved away from Evan. "You could have sent word that you had found her. Emilie needs to return home."

"My men will take her back," Evan said, not taking his eyes off her. "Are you sure you can show me? You can just tell me how to get there."

"Yes, it's not far from here."

"What's going on?" Lord Williamson demanded.

"We'll go there in the carriage," Evan continued, ignoring him. "Just tell me in which direction to go."

"Go down that street." Emilie pointed in the direction where she had left the shadow behind.

Evan poked out the door.

"Follow us!" he yelled to the twenty or so men Emilie had seen gathered outside, before turning to the driver to give him instructions and closing the door behind him once he had.

"What are you doing?" Lord Williamson asked through the closed door.

When the carriage began to move, Emilie saw Lord Williamson running to his horse, through the window.

Since they hadn't been far from the place it had been a quick ride. She kept quiet for most of it, speaking only occasionally to give him directions. Soon, they had stopped a block away from the building Emilie had escaped.

Evan wrapped his hand around hers and squeezed it gently.

"You should go back now," he said. "We'll take care of it."

Emilie let go of his hand, but she couldn't keep still. Her nerves urged her to stop him from leaving.

"What are you going to do?"

"Kill it."

"I don't think it's something that can be killed," Emilie said, pressing her hands against her chest. "This isn't a good idea."

But Emilie couldn't convince him. Evan opened the door and stepped out of the carriage.

"The most important thing right now is that you go home," he told her. "Stay inside, and you'll be safe."

"Emilie!" She heard Lord Williamson calling. He had stopped his horse next to the carriage and the men that had ridden with them, and was now running toward her. Evan immediately moved in front of the door to block him from getting any closer.

"You're not going inside."

Lord Williamson moved back.

"Emilie, please."

"Why are you here?" she asked with a frown from inside of the carriage. "This is not a good time."

"I just want to make sure you get home safely. I'll follow you until you get home."

Lord Williamson ran back to his horse without waiting for her reply.

"Take her to my house," Evan ordered to the riders around them. "Make sure the carriage goes back without stopping, and keep the gates locked once you get there."

Evan turned to her.

"Don't worry," he said, leaning forward to caress her cheek. "It will be over soon. Wait for me."

Emilie nodded, but her throat had tightened and she couldn't say a word.

Evan closed the door and stepped back, and the carriage started advancing.

She looked at him through the window. Her eyes lingered on him until Emilie had no other choice but to let him go.

CHAPTER 62

Once Emilie was gone, Evan crossed the street to where his men had brought the now conscious kidnapper.

Fear had been a constant pain in his chest until the moment his eyes had landed on Emilie.

They had wasted too much time.

If the crows had helped her, it could only mean they had brought her back, but Evan doubted they had managed to do any real harm to the Haunter, let alone kill it.

"He's over there," Talbot said, coming to his side, while pointing to the man on the ground.

Evan reached the man they had tied up and lowered himself to examine his face.

He recognized right away that the man in front of him was a human, which didn't explain what he was doing working for the Haunter.

"Who are you?" Evan asked him.

"It's none of your concern," the man spat through clenched teeth.

"It is when you take one of our own."

His clothes weren't the clothes of a vagabond. The man looked clean, and the way he stared at Evan told him he felt resentful at being mistreated.

Upon closer inspection, Evan noticed the man wore gold rings, and the nails in his hands were neat.

He was probably someone for hire.

The man's expression shifted with hesitation. Evan saw him scan the group of men behind him.

"Listen, I was only doing my job. A man paid me to bring the lady to him. I didn't ask questions. That's not the way it works. As long as I get paid, I do what I'm hired to do." He looked down at his tied hands. "I have no problem with the lady. Now, let me go. This isn't my problem. She escaped, but he won't get the money back. I'm sure he doesn't need it anyway."

Evan's interest increased, but he chose his words carefully.

"What did the man look like?"

The kidnapper lowered his hands when his request was ignored.

"I don't know what he looked like. I don't stare when someone hires me," the man said. "He wore fancy clothes like yours, and he paid me with gold coins."

Evan looked down at himself. He was wearing his hunting clothes, nothing that would have been considered fancy, but the mention of his clothes and the gold coins made him weary.

He shifted his eyes to the rings on the man's fingers.

"I see you've spent them already."

"I melted the coins," the man immediately said with a grin. "I turned them into rings like he told me to do."

"Why would he ask you to do that?" Evan asked. He saw the man looking at him with interest. "Were there any marks on the coins?"

"There were, but nothing I had ever seen before. They had some words, but I don't know what they meant. As long as the gold is good, that's all that matters."

"Looks like whoever hired you didn't want to be traced," Evan said before turning to one of the agents behind him. "See what else you can get out of him."

He mounted his horse and signaled Talbot and the remaining group to follow him to the building Emilie had showed him.

The agents spread behind him, slowly moving around the building, the only sound coming from the tapping of the horses' feet against the ground.

"Wait here," Evan ordered, dismounting his horse. "Create a safeguard while I go inside."

As soon as he approached the building, Evan knew the Haunter was gone.

A dark room was the first thing he encountered once inside. There were signs of a recent commotion, and Evan could see several footprints on the dusty floor, but they weren't the same size. A chair had been overturned, blocking the way to a door at the back of the room.

Pulling it open, he walked down the staircase, his feet splashing against puddles of water as he walked further into the room. His blood boiled at the thought of Emilie lying on the floor among that putrefaction.

There wasn't anything in the room.

Evan sprinted up the stairs and reached the top floor in a few seconds. Something shiny caught his attention from the corner of his eye, and when he moved closer to it, Evan uncovered a small, gold coin smeared with dirt.

He stroked his thumb against it and felt an inscription.

Bringing it closer to the light, he read the marks on the surface then tossed the coin into one of his pockets. His jaw clenched with anger.

"It's gone," Evan announced as he strode outside the building. "It can't be that long since it escaped, if the women were involved."

Why was the Haunter always slipping through his fingers?

Talbot came to stand by his side, waiting for instructions. Evan couldn't call off the search yet. The Haunter was still inside the city, but the chances of finding it became slimmer by the minute.

He knew he couldn't give room to his desperation and frustrations. Evan had to keep his head clear to beat the Haunter at its own game. Otherwise, he would be playing until it was too late to win.

"Let's get him once and for all," Evan said, mounting his horse. "In groups of three, let's circle the area. Be on the lookout for anyone suspicious. We don't want any surprises."

Before he could move, a deafening sound started bouncing all around, seemingly coming from everywhere.

People began running out to the streets in alarm with their hands over their ears. The sound seemed to emanate from the city itself.

"Are we under attack?" a man yelled to another as they exited a building. "What's that noise?"

"Go back inside!" one of the agents told them.

They weren't standing too far from the edge of the city. The wall around it must be under attack.

"Listen, the same plan stands!" Evan ordered. "Advance toward the wall. I have to make sure the city safeguard is still standing, but while I'm doing that, keep scanning the area for the Haunter."

Talbot stepped forward.

"I'm coming with you."

"No," Evan said. "Stay here and make sure everyone stays safe. If any of you spots it, summon the others; don't try to take it alone. If you can't find it, meet me at the southern post."

Evan lifted his ring so everyone could see it and covered it with his hand.

"This is an emergency. Send people back into their homes. If the city wall is breached, we're the only barrier that's left."

He removed his hand from the ring, and the ruby stone shone a bright red.

Evan hoped Emilie had already made it back to her house. It would be the safest place for her.

"Os, where are you?" Evan asked aloud as he rode into the dark.

CHAPTER 63

"We need to go back," Emilie repeated as she nervously paced through the foyer.

Two of Evan's men blocked the front door. She recognized Mr. Alcott, the older man, but not the one standing next to him. They were both preventing her from running out. She had tried doing that as soon as the sounds had begun.

"Calm down," Lord Williamson said. "You heard the duke; you have to stay inside. It's not safe."

"It's not safe for anyone!" Emilie said, turning to glare at him. The sight of his pristine light blue jacket annoyed her even more. "Why are you still here? You don't understand. But *you* do understand, don't you?" Emilie turned toward the two men blocking the door. They averted their eyes. No one wanted to cooperate with her; every one of them was set on waiting until Evan came back.

She also felt different. Her body didn't seem like her own, and Emilie was filled with anxiety.

It also didn't help her feel better that the marks on her arm had suddenly begun to ache. She had kept them hidden from view as much as she could. Since Emilie didn't know what they meant, she thought it better not to disclose them to everyone.

The news about her aunt hadn't helped her calm down, either.

They had brought Emilie to Evan's house, where her aunt still lay unconscious in one of the rooms.

Emilie had gone to see her as soon as they had arrived, relieved to see that Margaret was the one looking after her. The pale face and the bandage around her aunt's head had had Emilie shaking within seconds.

She couldn't stand the waiting. The ongoing sound had her on the verge of panicking, and all Emilie could think about was that the noise wasn't a good sign.

To her, it could only mean that the shadow had escaped.

Her senses were everywhere, and Emilie felt extremely hot and uncomfortable.

"Let's go to the drawing room. You need to eat something," Lord Williamson said. "Your aunt might wake up soon."

Since they'd arrived, Lord Williamson had been trying to lead her away, to take her mind away from Evan and what was happening outside. But the more he insisted, the more stubborn she became.

Emilie felt uncomfortable being in Evan's house without him.

"Lord Williamson is right, my lady," a voice spoke up, and she turned to see Mr. Larson coming to her with a tray. "You've been gone all day. Please, have something to eat first."

"I'll have a cup of tea then," Emilie relented reluctantly. "But I'll take it here, not in the drawing room."

"Here, dear." Lord Williamson pulled a chair and waited for her to sit down.

He tried to take her hand to assist her, but Emilie avoided it. Even though she could see the hurt in his eyes, Emilie refused to acknowledge it, simply sitting down in the chair he had pulled for her.

A sudden scream coming from one of the rooms in the back

startled them. Her cup shook against the saucer in her hand, and she almost dropped it.

It hadn't occurred to her until then to ask Evan's cousin about what was happening. It was possible that Emilie could get answers from him rather than anyone else in the room.

Evan's cousin might understand her need to know, even if he'd never liked her.

Emilie handed the half-full cup back to Mr. Larson.

"Where's Lord Hardingham? I need to speak to him."

She saw the guards exchanging looks.

"Well?" Emilie prompted, walking toward the room closest to them.

"My lady, Lord Hardingham is sleeping at the moment," her butler replied. "I'm afraid he can't be disturbed. It hasn't been long since he fell asleep."

Another loud scream echoed inside the house.

"Is that Lord Hardingham?" Emilie asked, following the sound down the hall.

She heard Mr. Larson following after her, and the hurried footsteps of one of the men, but neither dared to stop her. When they approached the room, the guard, Mr. Alcott, finally walked in front of Emilie and extended his arm to stop her.

"That's Lord Hardingham, isn't it?" she asked.

Her question didn't need an answer. Their furtive glances said it all.

"My lady, you can't go in. It's not decent. Besides, Lord Hardingham is not feeling well."

"You don't have orders to stop me from seeing him, do you?" Emilie asked the older guard. She needed to see Lord Hardingham for herself and speak with him. She wouldn't be satisfied until she did.

"No, my lady, but I must insist. Mr. Larson is right. This is not the best time—"

Emilie ignored their protests and barged inside.

"My lady, wait!"

The room was dark and slightly humid. Emilie had the sudden urge to look for a window to air the room, but she stopped herself.

Mr. Gidley, Evan's butler, was inside. He stood up when he saw her, and Emilie nodded in acknowledgement.

"Please, give us a moment," she requested.

The butler hesitated.

"I can't leave you alone, my lady," Mr. Gidley replied.

"Please."

"I can only leave you for a few minutes. I'm afraid I can't give you any more time."

"That'll be enough," Emilie said, relieved.

"I'll be right outside."

She watched as Mr. Gidley glanced over his shoulder toward the back of the room before he carefully closed the door after him.

There was a small bed pushed against the further wall, with the figure of a man lying on his side facing away from her.

"My lord?" Emilie called, but he seemed not to hear her. She tried with a louder voice. "It's Emilie, my lord. May I speak with you? It's urgent."

She saw him slowly turn on his back. He tried to lean on his elbows to get a better look at her, and Emilie rushed to his side.

"Please, you don't have to get up."

She moved one of the chairs resting against the wall closer to his bed.

"That infernal noise," Lord Hardingham complained as she sat next to him.

"I'm sorry to disturb you, my lord, but I'm worried about the duke. I saw...something. Something I can't explain...and I know the duke is in danger."

On an impulse, Emilie lifted her arm to his eyes so he could see the marks that had appeared on her.

He didn't look at them at first, but when he did, Lord Hardingham stared at them for a few seconds before resting his head back against the pillows and closing his eyes, leaving Emilie anxious to hear what he had to say about them.

But as seconds stretched into minutes and he remained quiet, her self-control started to slip.

The noise had become a constant drill in her head.

Emilie was desperate, and her pressed fists against her lap were the only thing stopping her from shaking his prostrated body.

Then, his pale eyes were on her when she least expected them.

They used to be so bright. It scared her having him stare at her like he couldn't recognize her.

"There's nothing you can do," Lord Hardingham spoke. "The only thing you can do now is wait. You have to stay inside the walls. Not one step out of them. If you do, you'll only become a liability and a risk to everyone."

That didn't sit well with her.

It made her feel useless and helpless, and it was a feeling Emilie was tired of having. She knew the shadow had wanted something from her.

It was probably the same thing that had saved her.

"What are these marks?" Emilie pushed. Evan hadn't bothered to explain them to her—if he even knew. "What do they mean?"

Another long pause, but this time, his eyes never left hers.

"I can't tell you everything right now. You'll have to wait for Evan to explain it to you when he comes back. But it's the lock. It's gone. Your parents did a good job of keeping it inside."

"Keeping what inside?" Emilie insisted while dread crawled up her back. "What are you talking about?"

Lord Hardingham looked at her with a curious expression before closing his eyes and resting his head back on the pillows.

"Your power," he said. "Your power is unlocked. Now, the Haunter can't afford to lose you."

CHAPTER 64

The agents on the southern post were already waiting for Evan when he arrived.

Evan could see from a distance a group of shadowed figures crashing against the big wall of energy that surrounded the city, and the impact of the creatures against it was the cause of the ongoing noise.

The hunters were doing their best to make sure that none of the attacks to the wall caused it any damage, reinforcing it when one spot on the web of safeguards was in danger of giving out.

So far, the two agents had been able to handle the attack.

"Jones, tell me what happened," Evan said.

"Your Grace, we felt a presence a few minutes ago," the man began. "We know there's one Haunter loose in the city, so we didn't notice the first presence coming from the other side of the wall."

"It hasn't even been ten minutes," the other man added. "And we're already surrounded by hundreds of them."

Evan froze for a second as he stared through the wall at the Haunters waiting on the other side of it. There were more creatures than he had ever seen together in his whole life; Evan couldn't even see where the crowd ended.

The shadows mixed with one another, but they were all intent on destroying the barrier in front of them. Evan had never experienced a coordinated attack from the creatures.

The reality of what he was facing, and the purpose the creature had had for his cousin's and the young agent's rings, stared at him in that moment.

The only protection the city had against the group of Haunters was the wall in front of them.

It had to stand the attack.

CHAPTER 65

It only took a few seconds.

One moment, Lord Hardingham was lying in bed; the next, he was shaking convulsively. Emilie jumped from her chair.

"Lord Hardingham! Help! Something's wrong!" Emilie screamed at the men outside.

She leaned over him with the intention of keeping him from falling out of the bed. Distracted by the men coming through the door, Emilie didn't notice Lord Hardingham launching himself at her.

He threw her to the ground and grabbed her by the neck. Emilie's reaction was slow because of her confusion at what was happening. Lord Hardingham's eyes were full of something she couldn't identify.

If it weren't for the butlers and Evan's men rushing toward them in that moment, Emilie wouldn't have stood a chance.

The older guard and Mr. Gidley pulled him off her and laid him on the bed, restraining him and stopping any attempt he made to reach her, while Mr. Larson helped her stand and led her away from the bed and out of the room.

Emilie glanced over her shoulder and saw Mr. Alcott putting his hands on Lord Hardingham's chest. The stone on the man's ring was shining, and it looked as if something was coming out of his hands.

"Are you hurt, my lady?" the butler asked, closing the door behind them.

"No, Mr. Larson, thank you," Emilie replied, feeling dazed as she dusted off her clothes. She noticed a small cut on her left wrist, right where the marks began, but she kept it hidden from him. "Has he been behaving like that since his return?"

"I think it just started recently. From what I've heard, he's been having these episodes all day. They don't know why, but Lord Hardingham doesn't seem to be able to control himself."

Emilie touched the marks on her arm.

"He didn't seem like himself. The way he looked at me, it was as if he couldn't recognize me."

She stood for a moment in the hallway, trying to make sense of what had happened.

Emilie felt a sense of urgency deep inside of her.

"I need to go back to the house."

"Is there something you need me to bring you?"

"No, I'm going to change my clothes. But first, I want to check on my aunt." Emilie wished her aunt would wake up soon. She had so many questions about her parents, about things she had never even considered before. "You knew my dad since he was young, didn't you?"

Mr. Larson looked taken aback, but he quickly composed himself.

"I did."

"I wonder how much you know."

Emilie looked at him closely, watchful of his reaction. The butler's face didn't give anything away. She let him lead the way to a small room in the back of the house, close to the backyard.

Two of Evan's maids sat on chairs by the door.

"Has something unusual happened?" Mr. Larson asked, and they shook their heads.

Emilie opened the door and stepped inside while Mr. Larson waited outside for her. Margaret, her maid, was sitting by the bed. She stood once she saw them, making room for her.

"Has she woken up at all?" Emilie asked her.

"Not yet, my lady."

She turned to her aunt and leaned forward to move a strand of loose hair from her face. Aunt Augustine looked so small in comparison to her usual liveliness. It made her heart ache.

"Please, take good care of her," Emilie said, taking the maid's hand and squeezing it lightly.

"Emilie," a faint voice whispered. She would have missed it if not for the light tug she felt on her dress.

Emilie quickly bent down next to the bed and grabbed her aunt's hand, pressing it tightly against her chest.

Her aunt's hand was cold, and Emilie could feel the moisture collected inside her palm. She rubbed it, trying to bring the warmth back, but it didn't seem to be enough.

"Aunt, how are you feeling?"

Aunt Augustine tried to swallow, but Emilie could see the dryness in her mouth was making it difficult. She reached for a cup of water and helped her take a sip.

"What is that wretched noise?" Aunt Augustine asked. "Where are we?"

Aunt Augustine touched her forehead, right where the bandage was. Her eyes widened in alarm.

"We're in the duke's house. You fainted and hit your head earlier today. Do you remember?"

"I fainted? I don't even remember leaving the house! What time is it? How long have I been here?"

"It's already midnight. Don't worry about the noise; it's nothing," Emilie said. She looked back at Margaret. "Could you give me a minute with her?" She waited for Margaret to leave, then turned her attention back to her aunt. "I need to ask you a question. It's important that you tell me what you know."

Aunt Augustine looked at her with round eyes.

"What's wrong?"

Emilie saw the fear in her eyes, and it was all the confirmation she needed.

"I saw the letter for Uncle Winston. I know there's something you've been hiding from me."

Aunt Augustine stared at her as if she didn't understand, but the paleness in her face and the nervous fumbling of her fingers gave her away.

Emilie waited, noticing as her aunt's eyes moved to the marks in her hand. She looked at Emilie with alarm. Emilie figured her clothes were probably not helping to soothe her aunt's alarm.

"What happened to you?" Aunt Augustine asked with a hoarse voice. "Where have you been?"

"Please. Do you know what my parents used to do? Do you know what they did before they died? You need to tell me the truth; you can't hide it from me anymore. It's important you don't."

Emilie opened the palm of her hand, pulling the sleeve of her dress up to show her the rest of the marks until she could see the resignation on Aunt Augustine's face.

She felt afraid.

"I dreaded the day when I would have to talk to you about this," Aunt Augustine started, her eyes moving away from hers. "I hoped I would never have to. I hoped you would never find out."

Emilie waited.

"I didn't want you to experience what your mother did. After that young man died outside our house, I knew it would all start again. I knew they had found you. Your poor mother..." Aunt Augustine trailed off with tears rolling down her cheek.

"What happened to her?"

"She tried to protect you. Your mother knew the only way to do it was to keep your powers locked inside of you. Maybe that way the Haunters would stop chasing you, looking for a way to use you. Your parents almost lost you once when you were younger."

"What? What do you mean *Haunters*?" Emilie asked, and the discomfort in her arm grew. "What happened to me? Why didn't I know about this?"

"Only a few people know the truth," Aunt Augustine said, staring at her.

Emilie felt a pang in her chest, and not precisely from the usual pain in her scar.

Evan.

Evan knew.

Was this the promise he'd made to her parents? That he wouldn't tell her about the Haunters and about what had happened to her in the past? That her parents had kept her away from it all, never telling her the truth of who she really was?

Emilie felt frustrated at being so ignorant when everyone seemed to know about her. The mention of her mother had been enough to regret having asked her aunt for the truth in the first place.

Emilie knew she couldn't expose a whole life of hidden truths in just a few minutes, but she had to try.

A bright light struck the sky, and the whole room shone for a second.

Aunt Augustine squeezed her hand, but to Emilie, it was a reminder that the clock was ticking, and that Evan was still out there.

"I found the book in your room," Emilie said. "I need you to tell me what it is, and if there's any way of opening it. We can't waste any time. Evan is out there with that thing."

"You mean...you mean you have seen them?" Aunt Augustine asked, touching her own throat.

"Yes. I made a stupid mistake today, and it happened. When I escaped, Evan found me."

"God, I knew he would take care of you. That if one of those things came to find you once more, the duke would stop them again."

Emilie looked at her in alarm with a sinking feeling in her stomach.

"What do you mean *again?*"

"You must have known," Aunt Augustine said, her voice quiet. "The duke has always taken care of you."

"But he was gone. I never saw Evan; not even once," Emilie replied, her heart aching at the mention of it.

The sound of rain became louder.

Emilie walked to the window, but she could barely see anything. A heavy mist had fallen, blocking the view of the backyard.

It made her stomach clench with anguish.

"Do you know what the book is for?" Emilie asked, turning back to her aunt.

"I don't know. Your mother gave it to me years ago, before she died. She asked me to keep it for you until you needed it and told me you would know what to do with it when the moment came. I had hoped I would never have to give it to you. I don't know how it ended up in your luggage," Aunt Augustine admitted. "Maybe it's for the best that you don't know how to open it. Maybe your mother was wrong."

"I don't think she was," Emilie said, frustrated. "I think my parents knew this was inevitable."

Aunt Augustine kept quiet, and without another word, Emilie walked out of the room and asked Margaret to go back inside.

It was time to look into the book again.

"My lady," Mr. Larson called after her. "Please allow me to send Margaret for your things."

"There's no need. I'll change in my room."

Emilie noticed that Evan's men were back in the hall. Lord Hardingham must have calmed down. She recognized Mr. Alcott, the older man, but not the one who seemed to have an injury in his leg.

Their expressions caught her attention. They looked nervous, as if they were trying to keep still. It could only mean that something bad was happening.

A red glimmer caught her attention.

Emilie had noticed that all the guards wore a similar ring and thought she might be able to use one of those to open the book hidden in her bedroom, and now that she paid closer attention, Emilie could see the stone was shining a very bright shade of red.

Something in her memory pulled at her.

"What are those rings you're wearing?" She asked.

The injured man tried to hide his hand, but the gesture alone betrayed the importance those rings had for them. Both men still kept stubbornly silent.

With a last glance at the rings, Emilie turned and walked away.

The ring looked like the one her father used to have.

Mr. Larson stayed behind, but she could hear one of the men following her. Apparently, they had decided they wouldn't let her out of their sight. Emilie entered the quiet house, and the footman quickly came to her.

"Is there anything you need, my lady?"

"No, thank you, Julian. I'm just here to change."

Once inside her room, Emilie marched straight to her bed and dug under the mattress.

She grabbed the book from under the blankets and held it in her hands for a few seconds. There wouldn't have been anything unusual about it if it wasn't for the strange lettering on the cover and the lock on the front.

Other than that, it looked no different from any of the books in their library.

The symbols in the cover suddenly shined as the light hit

them, catching her attention. It was one of them in particular that she found extremely peculiar.

It reminded her of something else.

Emilie flipped the book upside down, trying to find any meaning to it. The sense of familiarity became stronger, but she still couldn't remember where she had seen it.

Frustrated with herself and with everything that had happened that day, Emilie threw the book on the bed and walked toward the wardrobe.

She pulled up her dress, and as she grabbed the sleeve to slide it off, she noticed something that made her heart jump.

The similarity between the marks on her arm and the marks on the book was astonishing.

The symbol that had caught her attention in the book was the one that stood out the most on her arm.

Emilie looked back and forth between the two to make sure she wasn't imagining the connection, but there wasn't any doubt.

She fully took off her dress and her slip to see how far the marks extended, and to her surprise, they went up her arm and across her chest, to the place where she could feel her heart beating rapidly.

Emilie traced the marks with her finger. They were mostly lines crossing each other in no specific order.

How had her parents known that she would have those marks one day? Had they made them happen somehow? Emilie quickly put on another dress and went back to the book.

Perhaps she needed to press different spots at the same time to unlock it. She had already tried different things every night before bed, and the lock had always stayed the same, but Emilie was desperate. If she couldn't open it, she didn't know what else she could do to help Evan.

Emilie pressed the book tightly to her chest. The feeling of despair was overwhelming. The thought of facing the shadow once again terrified her, but the thought of Evan facing it terrified her even more.

If having the book didn't help, she would have to try something else.

Emilie heard an unexpected click, and she felt the lock on the book shift against her chest. Surprised, she looked down, curious to see what had happened.

To her astonishment, the lock lay to the side, leaving the book open.

The marks on her arm and the symbols in the cover shone with the same golden light.

She flipped through the book with excitement, but to her dismay, it had nothing but blank pages.

The book dropped from her hands, landing open on the floor.

Emilie felt so disappointed, she couldn't stop the tears from falling onto the empty pages.

She walked out of the room after cleaning her face, leaving the book lying on the ground.

"I'm done," she told the older guard waiting for her by the stairs.

They walked back to Evan's house. Nothing had changed. Everyone still waited in the hall next to Lord Hardingham's room while Mr. Larson quickly moved to her side holding a tray.

"My lady, please sit. I insist that you eat."

Evan's men looked more stressed than when she had left. Emilie peeked at their rings again. They still had that bright red shine.

"I want you to go; the duke needs you," Emilie ordered. She looked around the hall. "Where's Lord Williamson?"

Suddenly, there was silence. The loud noise coming from outside finally stopped, and the men looked at each other, surprised by the change.

Before Emilie had a chance to say anything else, a sudden explosion shook the building, shocking them all.

Her stomach clenched, and a burst of dizziness almost made her lie on the ground as she knelt on the floor.

Emilie felt as if the marks on her arm and chest were on fire.

As if she were burning from the inside out.

The men rushed to her side, but the pain was all she could focus on.

A repetitive sound sneaked through her cloud of pain, calling for her attention.

Someone was knocking on the front door.

CHAPTER 66

A sudden explosion and a wave of energy almost knocked Evan and the other hunters down. A spot in the wall vibrated as waves of energy moved through the safeguards in both directions. Evan could see a group of shadows gathering in front of it, fighting each other to get closer to the wall, and waiting for the moment to attack.

The two hunters ran with him toward it, with no other option but to try to reinforce the site. But it was too late. The safeguard shimmered, and the spot that had been hit opened, creating a hole in the wall.

"Create a safeguard, quick! I'll stop them from advancing any further," Evan yelled to the men, running to meet the creatures that were eagerly coming through the fissure.

He planted his feet on the ground, ready to face them, and hoped to delay them as much as he could.

Evan knew his men couldn't be far behind. The agents would probably come this way after the explosion.

He had no time for fear. His most important job was to not let the Haunters penetrate the city through the wall. It would only take a few minutes before the men arrived. That's all he needed. A few minutes.

Evan's body automatically took control of the situation and his instincts kicked into place.

He invoked the ancient power he rarely accessed without a second thought. As the energy ran through his feet and arms, Evan pointed it in the direction of the darkness.

A wave of plasma crashed against the Haunters on the other side of the wall, dispersing them.

"They're still crossing!" Jones shouted.

It didn't matter how much Evan tried to disperse them, an endless stream of shadows and darkness kept making its way through the hole.

"They keep breaking the safeguard," Jones yelled. "There are too many of them. We don't have enough time to put up a shield!"

"Forget it!" the other shouted. "Come on, let's kill them!"

The men started fighting next to him. Evan believed they could keep them from crossing. To think otherwise would be their doom.

"Just keep pushing them off!" Evan called out, not taking his eyes away from the Haunters.

He knew it would take more than the three of them to create the energy necessary to rebuild the damaged section of the wall. It had taken generations to bring it to what it was.

Evan hoped the other posts weren't having the same issue. As long as the damage stayed small, it would be something they could control.

"As soon as the others get here," he yelled over his shoulder. "Build a safeguard together!"

Evan turned and ran toward the hole.

"Your Grace, wait!"

He heard the calls, but Evan didn't turn back.

His entire focus was on stopping as many creatures as he could.

Unexpected help began killing the Haunters that had made it through. Talbot and the rest of the hunters had finally arrived.

Evan pushed through the shadows until he knew that none of the men could see him anymore; until he was completely surrounded by darkness.

Evan had crossed to the other side.

CHAPTER 67

Emilie tried to stand on her feet, assisted by Mr. Larson and one of the men, while the other went to the front door. The knocking was loud and urgent.

"My lady," Mr. Larson said, and she could see the worry in his eyes.

The pain had stopped almost as soon as it had started, and it'd left her feeling weak and disoriented.

"I'm fine, Mr. Larson," she reassured.

Emilie forced herself to stand straight, eager to make it to the door, but her legs were weak. She stumbled and had to force herself to slow down.

"Please, be careful," Mr. Larson urged, holding her elbow and waiting until she could stand straight.

For a split second, Emilie foolishly thought it'd be Evan at the door, before realizing it couldn't be. It had to be the agent keeping guard outside.

When the guard opened the door, he looked back at her with surprise on his face.

"Who is it?" Emilie asked as she got closer to the door.

"May I come in?" Anne Marie spoke, stepping forward.

Emilie could see the tension on her face and was shocked to

see her that late at night. Then again, it hadn't been an ordinary day.

She gave the man a short nod, and he moved away, allowing Anne Marie entrance.

"You shouldn't be here," Emilie said impatiently.

She felt as if there were nothing but obstacles that night.

"I'm here because you need my help," Anne Marie replied, stopping in front of her.

"Why would I need your help?" Emilie narrowed her eyes in suspicion. "I have no time to deal with you tonight."

"Believe me, I'd rather be anywhere else, but you'd be wise to listen to me."

"What is it?"

"Where's Lord Williamson?" Anne Marie asked instead.

That surprised Emilie. She had wondered the same thing. Emilie looked back at Mr. Larson, but he shook his head.

"Lord Williamson left a while ago," the injured guard that opened the door said. "He said he needed to go back to his office, but that he would be back soon."

Anne Marie shook her head.

"He's not coming back," she declared.

"What do you mean?" Emilie asked, her stomach clenching with anxiety.

"He came to see me. He said something that made me think he's not returning. It seems to me he's leaving the city."

"What? What did he tell you?"

"That there wouldn't be any escape, and that the city is going to fall soon. He said he didn't want to be here when it happened." At Emilie's shocked face, she added, "Oh, don't bother. I know more than you do."

"The nerve of that man!" Mr. Larson exclaimed, startling her.

Emilie felt anger burn through her veins, adding to the discomfort she felt in her arm. She couldn't tell the difference anymore. Evan's men looked tense at Anne Marie's revelation.

"Why are you here then?" Emilie inquired her with narrowed eyes. "Shouldn't you be trying to leave the city as well?"

"If what he said is true, I know there's no point in leaving. I'd rather stay here than bother with muddy roads; especially at this time of year. Besides, I want to be here when Evan returns."

"Evan?" Emilie asked her with disbelief and anger. "I don't have time for this. If that's all you came for, you should go."

"No. Besides bringing you the news that Lord Williamson is a coward, I have something that you need." Anne Marie dug into one of her pockets and took out a small, transparent sphere, holding it against the light. Light reflected easily through it. "Father Ross, my guardian, gave it to me. Apparently, it was your mother's. She told him to save it in case you ever needed it. He gave it to me before I came to the city so I could give it to you, but nothing horrible had happened, so I didn't think there was any need for rushing. It looks worthless to me, but if Lord Williamson's right and the city is falling to pieces, it might be a good time to use it. Especially if Evan is involved."

Anne Marie handed her the crystal, and Emilie took it with a dazed look on her face.

She had gotten different pieces from a puzzle, but Emilie had no idea how they all connected. For every mystery she untangled, three more got knotted into the web.

"What is this?" Emilie asked. "Why would my mother give Father Ross something like this?"

"They worked together; didn't you know?" Anne Marie said, looking impatient. "It's surprising how much you don't know. You make it extremely hard to feel sorry for you. I suggest you find out what you're supposed to do with that."

"It doesn't make any sense." Emilie looked at Mr. Larson, who averted his eyes. "I have no idea how this could be of any help. I don't know why there has to be so much secrecy."

"Yes, well, I'm shocked," Anne Marie drawled, rolling her eyes. "You're weak. Everything has always been handed to you. You always get help, even from me."

"That's just how it looks to you," Emilie said, staring at the sphere in her hand while thinking.

Lord Williamson leaving without saying anything to her…it was very possible, but why?

She also didn't know what to do with Anne Marie. The only thing Emilie knew was that she needed to act quickly.

The discomfort in her arm was getting worse, and she didn't want Anne Marie to see her marks.

Looking down at the palm of her hand, Emilie noticed the marks had turned a golden color. She put her hand in her pocket, trying to hide it from sight.

"My lady," the guard next to her, Mr. Alcott, said. "I think I know what it is."

"You do?"

"What did I tell you?" Anne Marie said with a sneer.

The two guards gathered and looked at it for a second.

"Yes," Mr. Alcott said, gazing at Anne Marie. "It's an energy reflector. I have only seen it in books."

"It's an old tool," the other continued. "They're rare. I thought they had all been destroyed."

"Do you know how to use it?" Emilie asked. "Could this help the duke?"

"I know it can only be used by someone extremely power-ful," Mr. Alcott said. "The capacity of the sphere is great, but people have died because they didn't have enough power to control it."

Emilie was silent for a second, considering the man's words.

"If it's something that powerful, we need to bring it to him," she decided with a firm voice. "It might help the duke."

"He just said Evan could die!" Anne Marie exclaimed.

"But my mother left it for a reason."

Emilie started to pace back and forth in the foyer. She knew the men were worried; they looked like they needed to answer a call only they could hear, but Emilie knew they wouldn't defy Evan's instructions.

"We'll bring it to him, but you have to stay here, my lady," Mr. Alcott finally said, looking at Anne Marie closely.

Emilie opened her mouth to protest, but then she nodded.

"You should go then," she urged, putting the sphere in his hand. "There's no time to waste."

The men looked at her with suspicion, but Emilie tried to reassure them with a smile.

"Mr. Gidley will take care of Lord Hardingham and Reeves. They won't wake up for a while," Mr. Alcott told Emilie's butler before turning to his companion. "Make sure everyone stays inside. It'll only be you in the property, so be careful."

It was all Emilie needed to hear.

She waited while the older man opened the door and signaled to the one outside before stepping out and closing the door behind him. The guard who was left inside moved in front of it.

"You should take this chance to eat," Mr. Larson said. "I'll bring a tray to the drawing room."

Emilie nodded and turned to Anne Marie.

"Please, walk with me."

Anne Marie looked surprised, but Emilie ignored her and turned to the man in front of the door.

"Mr.... I'm sorry, I haven't asked your name before."

"I'm Argyle, my lady."

"Mr. Argyle, would you be so kind as to ask Mr. Gidley if a maid can prepare a room for me?" she requested. "I'd like to rest."

"Oh, of course, my lady," the man agreed, but Emilie could see him hesitate.

She walked down the hall toward the drawing room with Anne Marie following close behind. Emilie waited for the sound of his retreating footsteps before turning to Anne Marie.

"Is your carriage still waiting outside?"

Anne Marie sighed.

"Yes."

Emilie quickly returned to the foyer and carefully opened the front door to make sure no one would stop them from leaving. Once she confirmed it was clear, Emilie hurried to the gate, with Anne Marie following after her.

"They're gone," Anne Marie noted. "How will you know where they went?"

"You don't have to come," Emilie replied, opening the gate and stepping outside. She saw the carriage waiting on the street. "I know in which direction they're going."

Emilie looked up at the sky. Something was wrong. It was already past midnight, but the horizon looked like it was on fire.

"What can you do?" Anne Marie asked her with an exasperated tone. "You'll only be in the way."

"You don't understand," Emilie said, opening the door of the carriage. "You haven't seen what I've seen. I'd rather be there than regret not having done anything at all."

Emilie gave instructions to the coachman and climbed into the carriage. Anne Marie followed her.

"You're just going to make things worse," Anne Marie said, shaking her head.

As soon as the carriage started moving, they saw the lone guard running through the front door.

"Stop!" he yelled, desperately waving at the coachman.

It was too late. The horses were faster than him.

The last thing Emilie saw was the man struggling on his way to the stable.

CHAPTER 68

Darkness and mist surrounded him. Evan couldn't see where he was, but he could sense the Haunters.

He wasn't sure if he had crossed to their dimension or if he was still in between.

"Duke!" a distant voice called.

Was it a trick? Or was one of his men trying to break through as well? Evan couldn't see the wall anymore; blackness was all his eyes met.

A faint laugh reached him. He could barely hear it, but it was there.

"Well, well, what a pleasure," a voice intoned. "We finally meet. It's been fun having you chasing me, but you didn't actually think it would be over so soon, did you?"

Evan tried to gauge where to look at, but the voice came from everywhere, like an echo.

"Can you believe we've never been introduced? What a shame!" it continued. "But you don't have to be intimidated by my greatness. Lord Lazaro, at your service. I've heard a lot about you, Duke of Rowlings. I've heard the stories about the conceited hunter everyone fears. I was wondering if you were only a myth."

"Well, now you know I'm not," Evan said, concentrating on finding where the creature was hiding in the darkness.

"I was excited to meet you, but I was disappointed by your lack of interest. I'm afraid the excitement is over."

Evan carefully advanced through the darkness in a wide circle.

"I haven't heard much about you," he commented. "I guess you're just not that famous."

"I was right. You are too arrogant for someone so weak. You forget that the city is already mine. You need to stop resisting it; it'll make your last moments more enjoyable."

Footsteps pounded behind him, and silhouettes appeared through the mist.

"Isn't this fun?" the voice cheered. "They won't have to keep looking for me. They've found me."

Evan tensed.

"Duke!" Talbot's voice came from the direction of the running steps.

"What a beautiful reunion!" the creature cackled. "Which feeling makes people act in stupid ways? I've always wondered, every time I taste it. Well, it doesn't matter; I'll still enjoy it. Thank you, Duke, for bringing them to me."

"Talbot, wait!" Evan shouted, but the running didn't stop.

The silhouettes of the hunters kept coming in his direction after also going through the hole in the wall.

Talbot wasn't far from Evan when the man bent over with an anguished howl, causing Talbot to fall to the ground.

"No!" Evan shouted. "You bastard!"

The men who had followed Talbot stopped and gathered around him.

Evan ran toward them, but before he could reach them, one by one, the men fell to their knees, grabbing their heads and screaming in agony.

He was the only one left standing.

Evan positioned himself in front of them and focused on

creating a safeguard to protect them while trying to block the sound of theirs screams.

Once the shield was standing, the screams stopped, and the men fell unconscious to the ground. Evan ignored the Haunter's sneers and focused on finding it.

He sent a big wave of energy around them. The energy expanded in all directions, taking with it the creatures that were still waiting by the wall.

The sound of laughter told him it hadn't been enough. That burst of energy had taken most of his.

"There's no need to get mad," the creature taunted. "I just wanted to get a taste of their feelings. You don't have to be so dramatic."

"Why don't you show yourself, then? You must be hideous if you're afraid of showing your face. Oh, wait, I forgot you don't have a body."

Evan noticed an edge to the Haunter's laughter.

"I can look however I want. Have you forgotten? I can even look like you. Do you think she will like that?"

Evan felt an involuntary growl escape from his chest.

The Haunter laughed.

Evan needed to bring it out of its hiding spot.

Steps behind him called his attention. Through the glom, he saw a line of men moving toward him. Fifty or sixty hunters marched forward, pushing through the mist, sending waves of energy in every direction, and killing Haunters as they advanced. Their lines never breaking.

From where he stood, Evan could see in the distance how the gap on the wall had gotten bigger, as if the energy barrier was slowly fading away, allowing more creatures to enter the city.

"Rowlings!"

Evan recognized the voice of the man calling him. It was Lord Arundel.

He'd hoped that Lord Arundel would be able to contain the Haunters back in the Grand House territory, and was glad that his promise to send his men to help Evan with the creature had included Lord Arundel himself. He must have been concerned about his niece and had brought his men just in time.

The sight of him filled Evan with relief. It'd all be over soon.

The air shifted around him, becoming heavy and making it hard to breathe. The Haunter's annoyance was palpable.

It had to be close.

"Looks like things aren't going your way, after all," Evan said.

He gripped his chest while trying to summon more energy after depleting himself—first with Robert, and then with his useless attempt to kill the creature.

Evan wasn't sure he could do it again, but he had to try while Lord Arundel was containing the creatures that had crossed the vanishing wall.

He moved away from the shield he had created around the unconscious men, leaving them on the ground.

It happened faster than Evan could understand. Lord Arundel and his men had been advancing toward him when they also fell to the ground, as if they had fainted on the spot.

"It's your fault they're dying," the creature taunted.

Evan became desperate. He had run out of options, and he wouldn't be able to keep going for much longer.

"Once I kill you," Evan told the darkness around him, feigning casualness. "I'm going back to her. I heard Emilie refused your proposal, and I don't blame her. How could she be interested in something that doesn't even have a body?" He made a pitying sound with his tongue. "And to lose her once you had her? Embarrassing."

Silence.

"Do you know what she did as soon as she got away from you?" Evan paused. "She ran straight into my arms, and it felt good. But you'll never know how that feels."

Evan saw shadows moving to his right.

"Don't waste your energy," the creature said. "I know you're dying. The prophecy will be fulfilled, and she will be mine."

Evan had finally found the spot where the Haunter was hiding.

"Your Grace!" a voice called out in that moment.

He saw a couple of men running toward him through the chaos.

Alcott was there. "Catch!"

Extending his hand, Evan caught what the agent had thrown at him. It was a sphere. Recognition dawned on him, and he clutched it in his hands.

He only had one try.

Evan threw up the sphere with all of his strength as darkness rushed toward him.

The sphere shone with a bright golden light when he filled it with the last remnants of his energy. As the sphere fell, Evan grabbed it and threw it in the direction of the moving shadow.

A bright explosion illuminated the area, vanishing the surrounding darkness.

He heard the men that had brought him the sphere suck in their breaths when they stopped behind him.

Evan's heart beat rapidly, his hope increasing as the light began to fade.

"You did it!" one of the agents exclaimed. "The Reflector worked!"

"I'm glad we came! Your Grace, are you alright?"

Evan stayed quiet. He kept staring into the distance, in the direction where the darkness had been.

"It's gone, Your Grace. You killed it with the Reflector."

"It wasn't enough," Evan growled, clenching his fists.

"What?" The men looked in the same direction.

The light had faded, and the darkness had gathered into the shape of a man.

"Get out of here!" Evan ordered, fighting at the same time to keep himself standing.

"That was the weakest attempt I've ever seen," the creature sneered.

"Quick!" Alcott behind him, screamed. "Put them up!"

They immediately began setting up safeguards in a circle around them.

"You look so defeated. I almost feel sorry for you," the Haunter said. "Your fame doesn't account for much after all, does it? Did you think that Reflector would do anything to me? I was looking forward to your impressive reputation, but all you had was that old thing. I'm disappointed."

The shadowed man strolled slowly toward them.

"But now that I've had my fun..." The shadow lifted its arms, pointing them behind them. Evan noticed a red sparkle inside the shadow and realized it must be the stone of the young agent's ring. "It's time to stop playing games."

Behind him, Evan saw the work of hundreds of years crashing down in less than a second. The energy that generations of hunters had used to create the city wall vanished in an instant, aided by one of the stones that had created it.

All around, thousands of Haunters raced toward the city with nothing to get in their way.

CHAPTER 69

"Wait!" Emilie heard Anne Marie calling when she jumped out of the carriage.

She had seen the light of an explosion in the distance and immediately knew Evan would be there.

Her heart was beating erratically, and her chest and arm were raw with pain, but she ignored them as Emilie ran toward the explosion.

As she got closer, the unmoving bodies lying on the ground increased her panic. To Emilie, they all seemed to be unconscious, and she couldn't detect any wounds or blood on any of them.

The shapes of men in the distance kept her going.

Her heart skipped a beat when she recognized Evan among them; he was standing between the two men she had sent with the sphere.

Fear joined her panic when she got closer and saw that the shadowed figure was also present.

Emilie could see that Evan was struggling to stand as, no matter what the men did, the shadow kept moving forward.

She stumbled at a sudden explosion. Fire set off everywhere

she looked, extending around the edge of the city as far as she could see.

"Evan!"

The world began to move in slow motion when Emilie saw the shadow closing in on him. No one seemed to see it, and her chest clenched in pain at the sight. She tried to scream, to warn him, but it was as if her throat was trying to repress her voice.

Emilie wished she could run faster, could reach Evan before the shadow did. She was so close that Emilie almost felt like she could touch him.

But the figure was faster than either of them, and all Emilie could do was watch as the shadow quickly slid through Evan, leaving him standing with an expression of pain in his face.

It looked as if nothing had happened, but somehow, Emilie would have preferred to see blood or any other evidence that he had been hurt.

The expression on his face told her he would die. The shadow had hurt him in a way Emilie couldn't comprehend.

Her voice finally broke free from her throat, and it was like something else had broken free inside of her, ripping at the scar in her chest.

Thousands of needles burst from her body like arrows, piercing through the air all around her, and especially, toward where the shadow and Evan were, causing the former to immediately move away from him as his body crashed against the ground.

A big gasp helped her relieve the aching pain in her chest.

CHAPTER 70

She shook her hair free of the knot pulling at the back of her head and inspected the scene before her. After being under the fog for so long, it felt good to get rid of the self-imposed restrictions that hadn't allow her to be her true self.

She hadn't felt so free in a long time.

Looking around, she saw Evan lying on the ground with his men at his side. She raised a brow at their attempts to keep the Haunter away. They thought their efforts would keep them safe, but that hope was in vain.

"Welcome, my love. I've been waiting for you," the Haunter spoke.

She scoffed while rolling her eyes as she turned in the direction of the voice.

"You made a mistake," she said with contempt as she crossed her arms and leaned her chin on the back of her index finger. "You should have never looked for me."

"Join me!" the Haunter exclaimed. "Together, we'll create a new world. Everything can be ours if you join me. We can be the ones deciding how we want to live. If we don't do it now, it'll be too late."

"Join you? I'm already tired of talking to you."

"Lady Arundel, I know you're in there. I'll give you what you want," the shadow said, changing tactics. "Don't listen to her. Remember our plans. Fight her! You have to regain control, or the plan won't work!"

"She's not here to help you," she replied, smiling. "How dare a lowly being like you think you have a chance at having glory."

"*Wait!* If we don't do it now, we'll miss our chance! *They're* coming!"

"Don't worry about that. It's too bad you wasted your efforts, but have solace in knowing that you were never meant to be the one."

"But listen! You don't know what's happening!"

"I don't need to know. I have everything I need right there." She pointed to the body lying close to the shadow. "And I don't like it when you hurt what's mine."

The marks on her arm detached from her body and surrounded the creature in a tight grip, anchoring it to the spot.

"It's been a long journey for you, hasn't it?" she crooned, walking around the chained darkness. "Goodbye, darling. We'll never meet again."

"No! *He's coming!*"

She squeezed the shadow until the golden symbols carved into the darkness, causing the shadow and darkness to dissipate until a shrieking echo was all that was left in its place.

"Now, gentlemen, allow me."

She walked between the two agents kneeling next to Evan, who hovered their hands on top of him in an attempt to keep him alive, but she knew their efforts would be futile if they couldn't restore his energy on time. It'd require more power than the one they could provide.

The men moved away when she stood next to them, leaving more space for her. She bent over Evan as he lay unconscious on the ground and observed him carefully, inspecting the damage that had brought his life to the edge.

"Look at you; you're almost dead." She grabbed his face,

turning it from side to side. "What a handsome man you've become. It'd be a waste for me if you died, wouldn't it?"

She moved her hands over his body, scanning the remnants of his life energy. A spot of light passed from her hands into his body.

The color returned to his face, and his lungs filled with air. Slowly, he began to move.

"Your Grace!"

"There," she said, standing up. "He'll be fine."

She moved away and looked at all the scattered bodies on the ground. Emilie had finally freed her, and it had all been for doing an annoying chore.

CHAPTER 71

Evan opened his eyes and looked around him, trying to understand what was happening.

"Your Grace, you're alive!"

"What happened?"

"The lady!" The men pointed at Emilie, and he remembered the look on her face as he fell unconscious.

"Emilie!"

Evan stood on his feet with the agents' help and began trudging toward her. The pain slowed him down, but he kept moving with a clenched fist against his chest.

"Emilie!"

She stopped and glanced over her shoulder.

"Hello, Evan, darling. It's been a long time, hasn't it? Did you miss me?"

She turned and kept walking past the waking bodies, further away from him.

"Wait!" he yelled, stumbling on his feet.

Evan had to hold the men's arms to regain his balance, but his desperation was too big to slow him down.

Emilie stopped, and after a second, she fell to the ground.

"Em!"

He tried running toward her, but he could barely move. A couple of agents waking near her got to her faster. They checked her pulse and laid her on her back. Once Evan arrived at her side, he fell to his knees, picking her head from the ground and placing it on his lap.

Evan saw the shining, golden marks on her arms and the paleness of her face, but at least she was still alive.

"Emilie, please."

He ignored the sounds of the hunters waking around them, his focus staying on Emilie. He had to save her.

Lifting his arms, Evan let his hands hover over her chest.

"Duke, don't," someone said, grabbing him. "You can't do it. Let me."

Talbot kneeled next to him, making no attempt to remove her from his side. Evan still pulled her the slightest bit closer to him.

"My dear girl!" Lord Arundel exclaimed, running to them and kneeling on his other side.

Evan, feeling ashamed to have failed him, turned his head away from the older man.

The sound of clicking heels coming in their direction caught his attention.

"Well," Anne Marie said, pushing through the men and stopping at their side. "I have to say, that was quite the show."

Thoughts of Evan came to her when Emilie opened her eyes, and she immediately panicked. She wasn't sure where she was or what had happened.

Focusing on her surroundings, she realized she was in her own bed.

Her head pounded painfully, but Emilie needed to know what had happened to Evan. She couldn't waste any time.

"Dear, wait."

A hand reached out to keep her in bed. It was Aunt Augustine.

"Aunt, what happened? Where is he?"

"Calm down, the duke's fine. I'm so relieved you're finally awake."

"I don't know what happened. The last thing I remember is that he...I thought he was dead."

Emilie could feel her throat closing up, overwhelmed with emotion.

"The duke has stayed by your side since the moment he brought you back. I had to insist he needed to go rest. He's been here non-stop, and he hadn't even left to freshen up. I told him you'd be waking up soon and if you saw him like that you probably wouldn't like it. You've been unconscious for two days, my dear. I was so scared."

"Two days? I need to see him. I need to talk to him."

"Don't worry, dear. Margaret will make sure Mr. Larson informs the duke you're awake," Aunt Augustine said, patting her hand and turning back to signal the maid, who immediately ran out of the room. Emilie hadn't noticed the young maid sitting behind her aunt. "The duke just left. He won't stay away for long. I had a hard time convincing him to leave even for a moment. Now, how are you feeling? Are you hungry? You should eat something. You must be starving."

"I...I'm fine," Emilie replied. Her body ached, but something about it felt different. "Are you sure Evan will come?"

"Yes, dear, of course."

"I think I'll eat something, then," Emilie complied, resting her back on the pillow. "But first, I'd like to get dressed. How are you feeling? Did you remember what happened to you?"

"No, but I'm sure it was nothing. I probably just tripped." Emilie frowned. Her aunt wasn't the clumsy type. "All that matters is that you're safe. My heart almost stopped when the duke carried you here."

"Have you heard about how Lord Hardingham and Mr. Reeves are doing?"

"The young man is already up and about. From what Mr. Larson has heard, Lord Hardingham hasn't improved."

"I wish there was something I could do," Emilie sighed.

"There's nothing we can do. I heard that Lord Williamson left. I still can't believe he did that. But now, shall I call for a tray? I think we should stay here until you feel better."

"No, I want to get dressed. Evan will be here soon, and I'd rather meet him downstairs."

Aunt Augustine brought her some of her clothes and helped her change. Once they were done, Emilie realized she felt more energetic than usual, even though her body ached. Oddly enough, the pain in her chest had diminished, though she could still feel something on the same spot of the scar.

Emilie and her aunt went to sit in the drawing room, and shortly after, the footman brought them a tray with food and some tea.

When Mr. Larson came into the room a while later, Emilie had already finished eating, and they were in the process of drinking the tea and waiting for Evan to return.

"Lady Augustine, there are some women looking for you."

"Oh? Who are they?"

"I think it'd be better if you came to the door," he said.

Something in his expression made Aunt Augustine stand up without any further questioning.

"Wait here, dear, and rest. It's probably some of the women I met at the charity commission last week."

Mr. Larson followed her, closing the door behind him.

Emilie got up, curious to see what was happening. She had just walked into the hall when she heard her aunt's angry voice carrying over to where Emilie stood.

"You're not welcome here!" Aunt Augustine scolded.

Emilie had never heard her so angry. She slowed down and stayed out of sight, unsure of whether she should interfere or not.

"You knew all along," a woman spoke in a high-pitched voice. "You shouldn't have kept it a secret. Your sister should have known better."

Emilie's stomach clenched at the mention of her mother.

"Don't you dare talk about her! And you! How dare you come here? After all my sister did for you!"

"Don't blame her. She did nothing wrong. You can't stop this, Augustine. You can't do anything about this," the woman said. "Come out, child."

Emilie froze. She had stayed out of sight; there was no way the woman could have known she was hiding.

"I know you're there."

"What are you talking about?" Aunt Augustine interjected. "I don't have time for this. Leave and never come back."

Something in the woman's voice was hard to resist, and before Emilie knew it, she had stepped out into the foyer.

"Lilly!" Emilie called out once she moved out of her hiding spot. She hadn't seen the housekeeper in a long time. "What are you doing here?"

There was an older woman standing next to her, looking straight at Emilie with shining eyes.

"Hello, Emilie," Lilly greeted with a smile. "I'm here for a visit. Do you think we could talk?"

"Is anything the matter?" Emilie asked, looking back at her aunt.

"No, dear," Aunt Augustine replied. "Please go back to the drawing room. They were just leaving."

"How kind of you to acknowledge our existence, Augustine," the woman said.

"Leave!"

Emilie didn't move, shocked by her aunt's behavior.

"It's you whom we wanted to see," the woman spoke directly to Emilie. "My name is Mrs. Clarence. I've known your aunt for a long time. I used to know your mother, too. Your aunt has been trying to cut all connection with us for years."

"Enough," Aunt Augustine interrupted. "You have no right to talk to her."

"Oh, but you're wrong. It's out of your control, Augustine. There's nothing you can do anymore."

"Aunt, please," Emilie said, annoyed at the woman for upsetting her aunt. She turned to her with narrowed eyes. "What do you want?"

"It's not about what I want," the woman replied, taking a step forward. "It's about what you'll want from us after we explain ourselves. I'm here because of what happened to you. I'm sure you have plenty of questions, but so do we."

Emilie controlled her expression, not allowing her surprise to betray her.

"Your mother went to great lengths to hide them, and your aunt certainly had no intention of informing us of what your mother had done."

"Hiding who?"

"Not who; what. Your powers. Your ability to absorb the Haunter's powers. There's plenty of evil that would like to use you right now. You need to be careful and learn how to control them," Mrs. Clarence said, and Emilie felt the coldness in her voice. "I'm sure you couldn't remember who you were before, but now you know, don't you? You need to come with us."

"She's not going anywhere with you!" Aunt Augustine exclaimed with rage in her voice.

"Come with you where?"

"To where you belong," the woman declared. "Where your mother and your aunt belonged. We take care of each other. We've been fighting evil for centuries, but no one ever hears from us until they have no other choice. And now that you remember who you are, you need to learn about yourself."

"There's no need for that," Aunt Augustine said, stepping in front of Emilie. "You've seen her. Now leave."

"It's your right," Mrs. Clarence continued as if she hadn't been interrupted. "Your mother stole that right from you. If it weren't for her interference, you would have learned to control yourself a long time ago."

Whether she agreed or not, Emilie still didn't like the comment against her mother.

"Well, I'm sorry to disappoint you," Emilie began, moving closer to her aunt and looking directly at the older woman. "But I have no intention of leaving."

"Emilie, please," Lilly entreated, but Emilie didn't move her eyes away from Mrs. Clarence. "I know it's scary, but you have to learn."

"We could teach you," Mrs. Clarence said. "You wouldn't be

alone; you would have our help and protection against what's coming."

"It's your birthright," Lilly added, coming forward and grabbing her hand. "You could finally understand who you are."

Emilie stayed silent, and she saw the women's faces shifting with resignation.

She wanted to ask what they meant and what evil they were talking about, but Emilie resisted the urge, not wanting to show any weakness in her resolve.

Mrs. Clarence took a card out of her handbag and gave it to her.

"You can contact me with this if you change your mind," she said, grabbing Emilie's left hand and looking down at the marks on her palm before putting the card on top of it. "But remember, girl, dark times are coming, and you're going to need our help sooner that you think."

Mrs. Clarence and Lilly turned and walked out the door and down the front steps, leaving Emilie and Aunt Augustine without another word.

"Don't you listen to her!" Aunt Augustine snapped. "She's trouble, that's what she is!"

But Emilie was looking at the paper the woman had given her.

The card was blank.

CHAPTER 73

"The duke's here," Aunt Augustine announced, still trying to reign in her rage.

Emilie immediately looked up from the card, wanting to find him and confirm Evan was well. Her body filled with anxiety when her eyes reached him, and her stomach became uneasy with nerves as she scanned him from where she stood.

He met with Mrs. Clarence and Lilly at the gate.

"Hello, Your Grace," Emilie could hear Lilly say.

"Ms. Lilly," Evan said, and Emilie could see him hesitating for a moment, but he didn't look surprised to see her.

She couldn't hear the rest of their conversation, but Emilie saw them exchanging cards, and she wondered if he had received one just like hers.

Evan held the gate open for them and waited until they were out of sight before closing it.

"Evan!" Emilie called as he climbed the steps.

She had to stop herself from the sudden urge to run to him and hug him. Her tension had lifted at the sight of him. Finally, she could have him close to her.

"Come on in." Aunt Augustine waved him inside, closing the

door behind him. "Emilie, escort him to the drawing room. Won't you stay for lunch, dear? After all that's happened, you deserve it."

Aunt Augustine left in a rush without waiting for his answer, leaving them both standing next to the entrance.

Emilie and Evan looked at each other, with Emilie unable to say anything. She had to keep controlling her urge to hold on to him to make sure he was real. The image of the shadow striking him kept playing in her mind.

"I'm glad you woke up," Evan spoke first. "I don't know how much longer I could have stood not seeing you awake."

Emilie paid closer attention to his face, and for the first time since she had set eyes on him, she noticed the dark circles under his eyes. His face looked gaunt and like he hadn't slept at all.

She wondered if that would have been her if Evan hadn't survived the recent events.

The pain in her chest became more acute at the thought of losing him.

"Who was that woman with Miss Lilly?" Evan asked with a raised brow.

"Mrs. Clarence," Emilie answered, turning to the hall after shaking the mental picture of him dying. She grabbed her hands and kept them in front of her as they walked. "Apparently, she's an old acquaintance of my aunt and my mother."

"Your aunt looked upset. Was she angry at them?"

"Yes," Emilie said, giving him the card. "She clearly owes me another explanation."

Emilie saw him carefully inspecting the card.

"That woman gave you this?"

"To contact her. She wanted me to go with her. That's why my aunt was angry. But the card is empty. I don't know; it was too odd. The woman said that I belonged with them; that my mother had kept me a secret, and that's why I couldn't learn anything about my powers." Emilie raised her left hand, looking at the marks in her palm. "She said they could teach me; that I'll understand who I am if I go with them."

"And what did you say?"

"I told her I'll stay here," Emilie answered, looking up at him. "She said dark times are coming, but what can be worse than what we just went through?"

Evan put the card back in her hand, lingering for longer than he had to, and Emilie didn't want to move her hand away.

"I don't know what I'm supposed to do with a blank card," she said, trying to ignore the tingling sensation in the palm of her hand.

"Let me know if you ever decide to contact her. I know how to use it."

And to think she had been considering leaving on a trip just a few days ago. Everything had changed for her since then, and now, Emilie knew she didn't want to leave.

Not now that she had learned so many things about Evan's world. Her world, too, apparently. Emilie couldn't leave him.

Not now.

The first time he had left, at least he had still been alive.

This time, he had almost left her for good, without the option of ever seeing him again.

Emilie thought he had died, but there he was, standing next to her.

There were still many things Emilie didn't know about their relationship and what it meant. About his reason for leaving her in the first place. But this time, she would try to make the effort to sit down and listen, even if it had been too hard for her to do that in the past.

After all, his actions could never lie to her, and she needed to trust herself to be able to decide if his reasons for leaving were something she could accept.

Evan strode ahead to open the door.

Her eyes couldn't stop following his every move, but then again, she had also noticed how Evan kept walking closer to her.

Emilie thought she had caught him trying to hold her a couple of times.

Even now, his eyes kept inspecting her face and body.

"How are you feeling?" Evan asked. "You should be lying in bed instead of running around. You need to rest."

"I'm better now."

He kept holding the door for her, and Emilie thought he would stop her when she walked past him.

"Your uncle was here. Has your aunt told you?"

"What?" Emilie asked, looking around. Evan chuckled.

"He's not here anymore. Lord Arundel had to return to the Grand House, but while he was, he stayed at your side the whole time."

"What was he doing here? I haven't seen him in so long. I'm sad I missed him"

"He and his men were inspecting the road from the Grand House toward the city. They found Haunters gathering and coming toward it. Lord Arundel knew something had to be wrong. Thank goodness he came when he did."

Emilie took a deep breath. She knew the moment to revisit what had happened had arrived. She sat on her favorite chair and Evan sat on the chair next to her.

"I...I don't know where to start," Emilie said, gazing at him. "The last thing I remember is..."

Her voice shook, and she had to look away from him.

"I saw the shadow slid through your chest. I thought that'd kill you," Emilie finished, fear filling her body once again.

"You saved me," Evan told her. "That's what happened. If it weren't for you, the city would have fallen, and we would all be dead."

"But how? How did I do that? And my hand—the marks feel tender."

Emilie caressed the lines. She had been careful to cover them as much as she could while getting dressed so that her aunt wouldn't see them.

"The feeling will probably last for a while," Evan said, sitting across from her. "I want you to understand something for now. Things will be different. I'm sorry I couldn't protect you, and I'm sorry I failed your parents. Your life won't be the same now that the prophecy has been confirmed."

"What prophecy?"

"The prophecy about a woman born with the power of two worlds. I want you to understand that now, more than ever, we will be here for you. That I'll be here for you."

Emilie thought about his declaration. He would be there for her.

"What makes you think it's me?" Emilie asked, standing up. "Why didn't you tell me about this before?"

"You've always been under our protection. I'll help you learn if you want me to. I'm sorry I couldn't do more for you before, darling. After they locked your powers and your memories, I promised your parents I wouldn't get you involved and that I would keep all of this away from you."

She looked at him, but Evan hid his face from her, and Emilie remembered the dream that kept waking her up in the middle of the night. Except it wasn't a dream.

It was a memory.

Emilie was sure of it now.

Pain clutched her chest when she realized it had been her fault his parents had died, and even then, he still wanted to protect her.

Words failed her, and all Emilie could do was stare at him for what felt like forever. Neither of them said a word, which made her heart ache even more.

"Why did you leave without my answer?" She asked, surprising herself.

It had been the constant question that had plagued her ever since he had left.

Evan looked at her with surprise on his face, and she saw him hesitate for a moment.

"I knew you didn't want to marry me."

"What?" Emilie asked. Of all the possible answers she had thought were possible, she had never expected that. "Why did you think that?"

"I overheard a conversation with Anne Marie. I heard her saying you had told her you didn't want to marry me."

"I never told her that!" Emilie exclaimed, trying to hold back the tears. "I was so excited. I couldn't imagine anything better than marrying my best friend, but you left before I could give you my answer, and you broke my heart."

Emilie kept looking straight at his face, watching his reaction closely. She needed to know if his reasons were true, or if maybe he was lying to her to not hurt her feelings. But the expression on his face was one of shock. The paleness of his face confirmed it as she moved her eyes away from him.

"You never wrote; you never came back," she continued. "I thought you regretted asking me to marry you. I thought you were running away from me."

Evan cursed, and the feet of the chair he sat on dragged across the floor as he stood up and began pacing in front of her.

"I should have known," Evan said. "She was always trying things with me. I should have waited to speak with you, but I was so happy I had asked you to marry me that it surprised me to hear you didn't want to. My useless pride was hurt, and like a fool, I fell right into it. I was an idiot," he finished, kneeling in front of her and holding her hands. "I'm sorry I hurt you, Em. Please, forgive me."

Emilie studied him, paying close attention to his eyes.

She could see he was being sincere. A weight lifted from her chest when she realized he had wanted to marry her.

They could have been together all this time. She grabbed his arms and helped him stand.

"I forgive you," Emilie said, touching his cheek. Evan immediately leaned on her hand. "I'm sorry you thought I was going to reject you. It seems we missed our timing."

"Please," he whispered, putting his hand on top of hers while he stared into her eyes. "Could you give me another chance?"

Emilie gazed at him, at his black hair and big, blue eyes; the most handsome man she had ever met.

She still couldn't believe he was there, in front of her, and that she could touch him.

The sorrow that had settled in her chest for the past week vanished. Emilie felt so grateful that Evan had come back to her, and that he was still alive.

On impulse, she grabbed his face with both hands and kissed him.

Emilie couldn't let him go anymore.

She hugged him and held tightly on to him, burying her face in the crook of his neck as she tried to hold back her tears.

"I missed you," she murmured. "I've missed you for the longest time."

"Oh, darling," Evan said, squeezing her between his arms. "I missed you, too."

After a moment of silence in which Emilie tried to hold on to the feeling of his arms around her, she finally lifted her head from his shoulder. There was a glimmer in his eyes when she looked into them.

"Do you really believe that Anne Marie wanted to keep us apart?"

"Well, she had wanted me to meet her later that day, but I was so disappointed that I just wanted to leave, and I never went to see her."

"Oh! That would explain her scandal."

"What scandal?" Evan asked.

"Are you done yet?" a voice interrupted.

Emilie jumped in surprise as Evan's arms tightened protectively around her.

Anne Marie stood in the doorway, holding the door open with her hip and glaring at them with disdain.

CHAPTER 74

"What are you doing here?" Emilie asked.

Anne Marie ignored her, looking directly at Evan. "Now that you're done talking about the old times, I want a word with you."

"Why would I want to talk to you?" he asked, feeling his annoyance rising.

"In case you don't know, I was the one who gave her that sphere, and the one who gave her a ride there," Anne Marie said, moving toward him. "If it weren't for me, the whole city would be gone."

"And what do you want?" he asked.

"I want to join you. I want to join the Organization."

Evan looked at her with narrowed eyes while Emilie gasped in surprise.

"How do you know about it?" he prodded, feeling suspicious of her. Evan had never thought Anne Marie could be involved in *that* part of their world.

"Oh, please, I've known all about it for the longest time. I want to belong to it, too."

"That's not how it works," he said. "We don't recruit."

"Lord Williamson was in on it, and he was useless, in my

opinion. I can do a better job than him." Anne Marie tilted her head with a smile. "I was going to marry him so I could join, but since you came back, I had to consider my options once again. I hope there are no hard feelings about the past."

"You can't," Evan declared, not wanting her to interfere with the truce he had reached with Emilie. "You don't have the ability. You're either born with it or you're not; it's not something I get to decide. Lives depend on it, including your own."

"What about her then?" Anne Marie accused, pointing at Emilie. "She's clumsy and useless, just like Lord Williamson. Does she belong to it now?"

A pang in his stomach reminded him of his failure to protect her.

"Well, she has always belonged."

Anne Marie looked at him with narrowed eyes.

"You can't get rid of me so easily," she said before turning and marching out of the room.

The uneasiness in his stomach increased at her warning.

CHAPTER 75

Evan stood in his study. They had begun the work of rebuilding the wall around the city, an exhausting job that would take months, probably even years, before it was completed. It was a good thing that up until now, none of his men had detected any remaining Haunters.

A knock on the door interrupted him, and Mr. Gidley entered the room.

"Gidley, what's the matter?"

"There's a man at the door, Your Grace," the butler informed. He held a silver tray with a note on it. "He asked me to deliver this."

"Thank you, Gidley," Evan said, taking the note in a rush. He recognized the seal. Evan opened the card and read the name inside. "Please bring him in."

"Of course, Your Grace."

After the butler left, Evan paced the room with the card in his hand. He had been expecting a letter from his contact, not a visit.

"Rowlings."

A tall man with blond hair entered the room.

"Brookstone." Evan crossed the room to shake the man's hand.

"I'm sorry I missed all the action."

"I'm glad you missed it. I didn't expect you to make the trip here."

"I'm afraid the situation is more serious than you were probably expecting." The man shook his head. "The attacks in this territory left things clear enough for me, and I'm afraid it's not good news."

"What did you find out?"

"It's the Legion," Brookstone said with a grave tone in his voice. "They've turned against us."

"What? Since when? The Legion has been hunting Haunters for centuries. The thought would have never even crossed my mind."

"The letter you sent me made me suspicious. Ever since you left to follow the trace of the creature into the mountains, a lot of unusual activity has occurred. The Legion has always gone after any trace of unnatural activity, but lately, they've been dismissing simple incidents. When I brought up your case to them, to my shock, they told me not to worry. I began to wonder if what you wrote in your letter was connected in any way. I don't think we can rely on them anymore."

"Well, that explains why they haven't shown up at all," Evan noted, running his hand through his hair. "We were close to losing the city for good. It was a miracle that we survived the attack and that we could protect the city."

"Did you get rid of the Haunter?"

"I think we did," Evan replied, not wanting to mention Emilie and her involvement in the battle. "But it behaved in a way I had never encountered before. It led me astray the whole time I was after it in the mountains, and then, after it came to the city. It was as if it was trying to distract us on purpose. And now, with what you're telling me regarding the Legion, and from what a couple of my hunters witnessed during the battle, it leads me to conclude that the Haunter must have been working with the Legion until it decided to betray them. The creature seemed to have been gathering Haunters to form a group of its own."

"But that's impossible."

"It gathered enough creatures to put the city in danger."

"But how could he destroy the wall? The energy necessary only comes through us."

"The creature killed one of our younger agents when it came into the city, and it stole the ring the boy was wearing. It must have used it to channel enough energy to modify and weaken the wall during this time," Evan replied, not wanting the information about his cousin's involvement to be known outside of the city just yet.

"Well, I'm just here to warn you that the Legion has lost control of itself. It seems it's been ongoing for some months now."

"I knew something must have been wrong when the creature suddenly left the mountains. The Old Spirit has been warning me about upcoming danger ever since. I appreciate you coming over to inform me of this," Evan said, trying to fit the information he had just received with the retelling he had received from the agents who had witnessed what Emilie had done. At least, who they thought had been Emilie. "You're welcome to stay. I know it must not be safe for you to return anymore."

"Thank you. I'm afraid I'll have to take your offer," Brookstone admitted. "I'm still waiting to hear back from my sources. It shouldn't be long until we know if going back would be a trip through hell."

"Now that the Legion has turned, let's hope we can at least stay long enough to stop these bastards."

CHAPTER 76

Emilie glanced around the room.

It hadn't been that long since the last ball she had attended, but things couldn't be more different.

She smiled at the memory of how stressed she had been that night, just a month ago, when nothing had seemed to be going her way, and at how anxiously she had been waiting for the announcement of her engagement to Lord Williamson.

If Emilie could go back in time and tell herself to forget about him, she would. But then, she had probably been too set on marrying him to make any difference.

Emilie looked down at her red gown, this time with no wine stains on it, and smiled.

The music and the dancing couples around her relaxed her.

She and Margaret had taken great care in making sure the marks on her arm and chest were hidden under her dress and gloves, and Emilie was confident her outfit was doing a good job at it.

Aunt Augustine moved next to her.

"He's almost here," Aunt Augustine said, looking around the room. "All eyes will be on us, I'm sure of it. It's the first time we're making a public appearance with him, and, oh, all of my friends will be so jealous. They've asked me three times tonight if an engagement is imminent. Of course, I told them it was."

"Aunt," Emilie scolded her with a smile. "You know we're not engaged."

"Oh, dear, you and I both know you almost are. The duke's clearly been courting you. I'm just glad things are better now. As soon as that girl left, everything seems to have improved. I just knew it. Any time she's involved, trouble is not far behind. Do you remember that time she caused a big commotion? I still can't believe they found her in the stables with a man. The only reason anyone tolerated her was because of her connection to the cleric, but now that Lord Williamson left her behind like that...she had the right idea when she decided to leave."

Emilie knew nothing good would come out of arguing with her aunt about not being unkind, and perhaps, Aunt Augustine was right.

After the chaos, these past couple of weeks had been an improvement.

Evan hadn't left her side, making sure they could get reacquainted with each other. He appeared more relaxed than he had been since his return, and he had spent a lot of time visiting her and courting her.

He still insisted on having a guard on her property, and every day he'd asked her for an update on the marks on her arm.

Evan had also insisted they needed to start training her now that her abilities had awoken.

"He's here!" Aunt Augustine exclaimed excitedly.

Emilie looked in the direction her aunt was pointing, but it wasn't necessary to point at all. The Duke of Rowlings could command anyone's attention once he stepped into a room.

A crowd was already gathering around him, making his journey toward them longer than it should have been. Evan kept glancing at her with a look that said, "Get me out of here," but Emilie waited until he finally made it to her side on his own.

Once he did, the whispers immediately started.

"Is everything alright?" Emilie asked with a smile.

"I'm sorry, I'm late," he apologized, looking at her with a twinkle in his eyes. Ever since their kiss, he had made it clear with his actions that he wanted her.

"Don't worry, my dear duke," Aunt Augustine said. "You made the wait worth it."

"Were you saving your first dance for me?"

"No," Emilie said. "But you can have the next one."

Evan took her gloved hand and guided her to the dance floor where couples whirled around them.

"I might have to go on a trip," he said.

Emilie could feel his breath on her cheek.

"Where to?"

"Back," he replied. "It's only going to be a short trip, but Os is urging me to return to the mountains. I don't want to leave you alone, and this could be a good chance to work on your abilities away from all of these eyes."

The excitement in her stomach told her she couldn't wait for him to ask her to go with him.

Emilie didn't want to be on the sidelines anymore.

Most of society thought of her as extravagant and too old to raise brows at her sudden departure.

She opened her mouth, but whatever she was about to say was lost in the noise of a sudden commotion.

Screams and shouts began to fill the ballroom.

"What's happening?" Emilie asked, looking behind him and trying to find the source of the panic.

"Wait here," Evan said, blocking her path. "Go back to Aunt Augustine."

Evan ran toward the main door, where the majority of people were gathering, but Emilie didn't wait.

She ran after him, following the direction of the screams. It led them all the way through the front door and out into the street, where a crowd of people had gathered in the middle of the road.

They were looking and pointing at something on the ground.

She stopped next to Evan, and as they stared at the figure, Emilie thought she could recognize the light blue jacket Lord Williamson had been wearing, although, it was almost completely ruined by the spots of blood.

Emilie found herself reaching for Evan's hand.

"I told you you didn't have time," she heard Os's voice as the wolf appeared next to them. Evan didn't seem surprised by his sudden appearance. "They're here."

"Who is?" Evan asked.

"The Legion and Wolstencroft are here. The reason for the end. You have to return to the mountains. To the source of it all."

Evan kept quiet, but after a moment of silence, he turned to her.

"Do you want to come with me? We'd have to leave right away."

"Yes," Emilie answered, swallowing. She didn't want to stay behind once again only to long for his presence, especially when dangerous situation kept coming his way. "I'm going with you."

THE STORY CONTINUES

WHAT HAPPENS NEXT

You have just finished Book One.
Emilie knows what she is now.
Evan knows what is coming.
And the Legion has just made its move.

Book Two of the Hunters of Haunters series is next.

Be the first to know when it arrives:
www.miriamgomez.com

PLEASE LEAVE A REVIEW

If you enjoyed this book, please consider leaving a review on
Amazon, Goodreads, or wherever you purchased it.

Reviews help other readers find the series and mean everything
to an indie author.

Thank you.

READ THE HUNTERS
OF HAUNTERS SERIES

THE HUNTERS OF HAUNTERS SERIES

Book One: Lady Arundel and the Hunter of Haunters

A dark gothic romantasy of slow-burning tension, second-chance
romance, and a love shaped by absence, restraint, and second chances.

Book Two: Coming Soon

Get the series at

www.miriamgomez.com

ACKNOWLEDGMENTS

This book wouldn't be possible without the love and support
I've received from my husband.
Dreams do come true, and it's often they become real when you
have true love by your side.
That was my case.

Thank you also to my friends and family for their unconditional
support and to all the wonderful people I've met on this journey.
You have become an important part of my book world.
You know who you are.

And to you, my wonderful reader friend. Without you, this world
couldn't exist.
Thank you for being here.

ABOUT THE AUTHOR

Miriam Gomez writes romantasy with a gothic heart, where slow-burning tension, hidden supernatural worlds, and the kind of love that survives absence and silence meet in richly atmospheric settings.

She loves bringing luxurious elements into everything she writes, from the foods her characters savor to the locations they move through, and she has a particular weakness for mystery, suspense, and romance arcs that take their time.

Lady Arundel and the Hunter of Haunters is the first book in the Hunters of Haunters series.

www.miriamgomez.com